Baptist Confidential

Winner of the 2005 Bluestem Poetry Award

for Sally — from one cracked Carolina belle to another

Baptist Confidential
THOMAS DUKES † POEMS

*love & hugs,
Je Dukes
Summer 2007*

*for Britni,
with great
liking and
respect
JL Dukes
September 8, 2014*

Bluestem Press, Department of English
Emporia State University, Emporia, Kansas

Requests for permission to reproduce material
from this work should be sent to:
Bluestem Press
Department of English, Box 4019
Emporia State University
Emporia, Kansas 66801-5087

Project Directors: Kevin Rabas and Amy Sage Webb
Cover and text design: Kellye Sanford
Cover image: Getty Images
Printed in Canada

Library of Congress Cataloging-in-Publication Data

Dukes, Thomas.
Baptist confidential / by Thomas Dukes.
p. cm.
ISBN 1-878325-34-5 (cloth: alk. paper)— ISBN 1-878325-35-3 (pbk.:
alk. paper)
I. Title.

PS3604.U44B37 2006
813.6—dc22
2005028691

to Diana, Rich, and the memory of Sam Ella and John T.

Contents

Acknowledgments   ix

One

Wild Turkeys at Brokensword Creek   3
Before Houses   5
Havana Afternoon   6
Driving Fast through Texas, 1973   8
Pecan Grove in White Pond, South Carolina   10
Some of You Folks Got to Say Amen   12
After Winter   14
Astronomy   16
For Ruth   17
Waiting in Key West   18
Winterlust   19
Honky Tonk Jesus   21
Chicago   23
Three Lesbians Enter a Bookstore, Singing   24
Snow in Ohio   25
Communion   26

Two

Sunday, Mentor Headlands Beach   31
Whale Song   33
Riot in New Delhi   34
Poem for Women Betrayed by the Music of James Taylor   35
Open Lane in the Cuyahoga Falls Natatorium   37
The Evangelist's Daughter   38
Baptist Confidential   40
Expert Witness   43
Once   44
Summer Seduction   46
El Paso Elegy   47

Persephone in South Akron   48

My First Real Date Happened When I Was Sixteen   51

Three

There'll Be Peace in the Cuyahoga Valley   55

The Challenge   56

Writing Daddy   58

Desire   60

High Water Warning   62

The Horses Next Door   63

Blessed Assurance   64

Taking His Name to the Lord   65

Mama Would Be Seventy-Five on Halloween   69

Key Deer   70

Childless   71

Minerva, Ohio   73

Mennonite Funeral in Southwest Ohio   74

Midnight   76

Florida Reliquary   77

Baptism   78

Acknowledgments

These poems previously appeared in the following publications:

"Snow in Ohio" and "Minerva, Ohio" in *Poetry*
"Desire" in *Jabberwock Review*
"After Winter" in *The South Dakota Review*
"Mennonite Funeral in Southwest Ohio" in *I Have My
    Own Song For It: Modern Poems of Ohio*
"Riot in New Delhi" in *The Rio Grande Review*
"Whale Song" in *ICON*
"Wild Turkeys at Brokensword Creek" in *The South
    Carolina Review*
"Havana Afternoon" in *Ohio Writer*
"Writing Daddy" in *War, Literature, and the Arts*
"Summer Seduction" appeared as "Invitation" in *Red
    Rock Review*

I am especially grateful for the help of the Akron Poetry
Collective as I wrote many of these poems and developed
this book.

One

*Give us grace, Almighty Father, so to pray, as to deserve
to be heard, to address thee with our Hearts, as with
our lips. Thou art every where present,
from Thee no secret can be hid.*
—Jane Austen, *Prayer Number One*

Wild Turkeys at Brokensword Creek

This afternoon, these grumpy myths
        plow the earth again, feathers full

as the eighteenth century. Their ruby throats
        call autumn's alarm as chicks and hunters

make their pilgrimage to the water of surrender:
        surely they read the day wrong. I want to leave

my truck and climb out of the body, a mad
        messiah demanding they save themselves

from this place. What great giving up happened
        here, so close to Bucyrus? Two men under

a dueling oak, perhaps, bleeding out over
        these fields, or hallowed farmers waiting

for Union sons to return, then breaking swords
        over water as they learned the price of baptized lives.

Some turkeys and chicks bend to drink,
        others preen, showing off after Eden

as their beaks rise to taste the world before them.
        Separate in salvation, they retreat

into disinterested undergrowth, hiding,
        not silencing, their gossip and laughter.

In time, some fly toward new stories;
        I must get to Akron before dark.

Nothing between us, really, except this mystery
        and rifles calling in the coming sky.

Before Houses

I remember wild plum trees
pricking the breath of South Carolina
every day, how Luke and I
ate the small red-and-yellow Augusts
and Daddy said plum worms
would grow inside us wild plum boys.

I remember how pine pitch stuck
our childminds together, how plum tree stickers
wrote our stories in boyblood as we ran
from what we had coming, how we kissed
the girls whose long legs and birthday luck
came before our own, in the time of wild plums.

Now I stand before houses set
on our secret trail, the haunt of arrowheads
and lost Indians the color of small plums,
rooms in which the new boys play, tamed
by computers and a summer waste of games,
where once, in the woods, we tasted wild fruit.

Havana Afternoon

White and dull as wilting blooms,
we wait by long windows
on the second floor verandah,
aware how much the green shutters
plead each day to have their past
aligned with the present, and could
we add two coats of young paint?

Rain disguised as mimosa perfume
washes away our guilt at breaking
the law just by coming here.
Tight-faced old cars sit and grin
as five little hustlers puddle-dance
and try to sell us what they know
of the world. For days we've wandered
lost at all those sites where Hemingway
raised glass after glass to cats and his women
in the damp hauntings of Old Town,

free sounds of love and fights
about lost money, the hot smell
of liquored violence lurching
across the street as the cops come
to put passion to bed. No one needs
the cops now: humidity polices desire,
disrobing reticence one damp button at a time.
Afterwards, we sleep, apart by a foot
or two, then dry in the afterglow of socialism
while cars dream of their long-lost mufflers.

Waiting is what we do best in Havana,
for the dark, the next step in revolution,
a flight to the dirty wonders of Mexico City.
We'll take a whore's bath and go down
before night, to wait with the music
and the unconfident lights, sitting
 in the twilight of borrowed history.

Driving Fast Through Texas, 1973

West of Abilene at seventeen, I couldn't hear
nobody pray except the road runner
who raced me to the exit and sped off
in the dust for whatever we could find
on the El Paso highway and beyond.

At the first gas station my last day on the road,
I wore Daddy's haircut,
so short, so butch,
that a big hat with oily veins
thought I was military and warned me
about the hot pillow joints circling
Fort Bliss like wagons:
Don't let them take you for mo'
than ten dollars an hour, son.
But as a Baptist gentleman,
I knew that, whatever happened,
I'd pay for everything.

Lunch came surrounded by string ties
and boots, men who kept irony in Austin
with the liberals, and let big-hooped earrings
at the cash register seduce their wallets
fat with the hope of condoms and crumpled fives.
They fine-tuned their cussings
and told stories of men getting their nuts cut off
by crotch-warmed beer bottles
as their pickups slammed into the law.
After two minutes, they called me
collitch boy, but punched my arm
for luck on the way out and said
Git all the edjacation you kin.

I lay down my sword and shield
by three o'clock in El Paso—
the pass indeed to small bets
on the dogs, the cliché of turquoise
and tequila sunsets, cigarettes imported
from Juarez under the car seat: *up yours, customs!*
Thirty years on, I wouldn't take
nothin' for my journey now,
down roads the desert fathers made,
a soul with the top down.

Pecan Grove in White Pond, South Carolina

To spite his lupus and forced retirement,
Daddy planted pecan trees on five acres
of chiggers and sand fleas left to Mama.
Hauling water forty summer miles round trip
made no sense, but he was ex-military
and marching to the grave.

One visit before death, I drove us down
the country, passing road signs shot
through with boredom. For miles,
he recited my sins and those
of the *Eyetalians, 'Publicans,* and
Commanist Jews before we stopped
in the clay welfare road. He let out
a rebel yell, then said *Look at 'em trees,
son, jes' look at 'em!*

That Daddy might see without
separation, I reached under
his small breathing and rolled
down the window:
Mighty fine, mighty fine!
and the world went hot with his folly.
Impatient with love, I idled
until he waved us on to Grady's Gas
for a ration of RCs and Moon Pies.
We pulled away in a hell's cloud
of exhaust as the Baptist inside me
prayed *Lord, show us the way home.*

This autumn, guarding the past,
I review his trees in their brown uniforms,
the little ones shadowed in the holy land
between wild plums and scuppernong
vines rusting away. His pecans drop:
five for sorrow, ten for joy.

Some of You Folks Got to Say Amen

God watches a woman sometimes
stand in a house hot and tall
as a tent revival, then rise in the light
of ordinary things to leave the room
she painted on her own terms
and wash her mother's open hair,
each strand a nightmare under water.
Thin ceiling light finds the scars
on the kitchen floor testifying
how hard a woman can work
to clean the road to Jerusalem.

God watches a woman sometimes
give up wearing Baptist slips forever
under her best housedress as she cans
impertinent pickles, her mama's boy son
at her side. Midday, she directs him
to the old church spinet, each hymn
worth two quarters from her damp
pocket, while the house ripens
with vinegar steam, snuff biscuits,
the promise of scuppernong wine
sneaked into the church homecoming.

God watches a woman sometimes
sit on her old bed afghan after dark
as the hard case next door wakes
her dead when he screeches
out his yard, a woman too
knee-tired for much but watching
birds come to the pinewood feeder.
She opens her mouth in time with theirs:
Amen amen sometimes when a woman
turns bronze she just has to say *Amen.*

After Winter

Mulching stays with us
as all work does—
the world
splinters into our hands
in our labor to pull grass
from the iris bed
and spread protection around
the roots, shrubs, and whatever
memory we buried in planting
so long ago.

We depend on mulching,
hymns, old letters, gin, and sweat
to make us cramp, to stretch
our necks in dedication
to dirt and sorrow,
and what failed to survive
February ice. We cramp again
as Barbra Streisand sings from open windows
I love you
while the dog rises
to drool on our dirty legs.

Mulching now makes less work later,
we tell the dog,
mulching stifles gossip
about careless lives and slutty azaleas
nibbled on by love. At dusk,
we'll pick mulch crumbs off
each other's backs before we bathe,
when we are tired
of the earth but not each other,
and the dog will snore by the bedroom door.

Astronomy

I love the planets
he told me
as we drove back
from a Chinese supper
and identical fortunes
in the secret cookies.

On my own
I could never find
the North Star
or either Dipper,
much less see Venus
contemplating my life.

That clear night
he tilted my head
in his garden drive,
and pointed
with his fingerscope
steady on love's arm.

The heavens are this way
he told me
and we entered
the house of all that is
seen and unseen
in the starry dark.

For Ruth

Somewhere on the road from Akron to Canton, I get lost
    between your calling hours and turquoise

earrings, how your hair came back all wild starlings.
    Mounted on your wheelchair throne, you reigned

over our last poetry meeting of the year in that truly
    Ohio Italian café, a Buddha in drag

eating eggplant scrolled into pasta that drooled
    as you showed how your left side refused

that night to rhyme with the rest of you. Then, always,
    you put the freedom in free verse, too Spanish

in ambition and spark to get lost in the heartland.
    Thanks, Ruth, for kissing my poetry

goodbye as I left the table, thanks, just now, for the nerve
    of holding that phallic green-white flower

in your coffin, thanks for winter's tantrum as I drive
    home through January, having signed the book,

shaken hands with the three graces you called my daughters,
    thanks for letting me see your head wrapped one last

time in the colors of what you thought about absolutely
    everything.

Waiting in Key West

Not content with being male or female,
the drag queen deals her cards of gold foil
shining with news of her next show
above another Duval Street bar.
Straight people smile into their fresh hands,
hold her glowing shadow of uncertain sex
and the lights from tropical gems, the choice of identity.

Here in late hours, her exhausted make-up
cakes into squares and falls hard
into the curb asleep with leftover rain.
I want to yell *Go home!* to the moist star,
but who wants home when doused

in passionate emeralds, the sauce of chiffon?
Better to stand for tourists lost in their own
sweat, the cure of midnight, students marinated
in beer and urine who poke each other in love.
As Rich and I pass, her false eyelash drops
in flirtatious salute, revealing above her vision

emerald dust bright with the secrets of palms
crossing her face in the necessity of glamour.
Tonight, at least, she shines with the Chinese
lanterns, kisses the air, and disappoints no one
on the romance toward home.

Winterlust

I respect them more and more each year:
freeway desire, imagined fondlings on communion
Sunday, sneaky ankle glances, a committee meeting
lay, jousting behind a countertenor on stage as he sings;
let's not underrate our lives' moist fictions.

So much greater than porn is the reality
Darling, you send me
especially if *you* is a stranger never
to reveal the lazy belly, set the watch alarm
because of the spouse, or expose the hours

spent in therapy searching for found poems
stolen by mommy. Lock the puritans away
each day at ten and two, then order
the coffee-and-gym break of an erect glance
my way, any way, just get it off in the fantasyland

no Disney mouse ever laid eyes on or got laid in.
Come to Papa, do, you dreamboat sailing through
the February death of life in Ohio or the boredom
of another fucking beautiful Florida day.
I know what perfection is, how it lives

in the fortune unearned or on the flat abs
achieved in spite of drinking, gluttony, and whoring
in the back seat of a convention. I'm one of the
good guys, so are you, but sometimes the other person
inside takes charge. Let me carry you in the lure

of my heart, dream you out of a video or the lecture
on post-colonial Marxist virginity. My impure loves,
you are too good for reality. I'll take my screwings
as I find them, and, baby, I want to make it with
sweet, imaginary you.

Honky Tonk Jesus

We do not choose our subject, we submit to it.

—Flaubert

Laying down my sword and shield for years in the damndest
places,
    I've often found my sins and those of others
    not worth a good spit.

But when I lose faith, my dead Daddy reminds me of our fill-ups
    on Florida's glory road. Eden was still Eden then,
    and our early departures and late leavings testified

To the holy pull of paradise warm on both sides. No matter the
truck stop
    or juke joint, we could walk after midnight with Patsy Cline,
    climb Loretta Lynn's hair out of the coal mines, and let hicks

Tell us about road conditions getting crazy with Willie Nelson.
    Sooner or later, if Daddy talked too much about the war,
    some angelic quarter would find Elvis and slide *How Great
Thou Art*

On the turntable hoarse with country blues. That place,
    every place, would submit to Elvis and my small soul singing
    along to the awesome wonder of poor whites redeemed, as if

Some honky tonk Jesus had come to preach. At the end, you
    could hear gin-soaked *Amens* come out with the lighters
    and orders for *one more, Butch*; the fallen world

Spoke again. Still, that holy voice of praise got us back on
    the road,
  and, decades later, sin-soaked in redemption,
  I know how to drive from cross to cross.

Chicago

That weekend
ended us:
the almond smile
of your beer at the Berghoff,
my cigarette's ruby punctuation,
a cabernet soul-blood
sent by an ivory woman long enough
to eat, who wrapped her metal legs
around a stool before dinner
and made her boyfriend growl.

Leaving *Twelfth Night*,
close as passing trains,
we possessed the demons of the Loop,
art museum handsome,
clothes charged to the Water Tower.
In the haunted charm of our room,
beds separated us for the first time
and you passed out from too much thinking
about somebody else.

I opened the hotel window.
As you dreamed about
what you would not, in the end,
get, I stole two little bottles
you would pay for eternally,
then took the naked night
to heart, every Elyrian light of it.

Three Lesbians Enter a Bookstore, Singing

May I now admit
to the *frisson*
I felt as a young man
in the seventies
when they would take turns
in a mixed bar
lighting my cigarettes,
before they left at midnight
for their own lives?

Hair buzzed and soft as meadow grass,
Lord Byron earrings of turquoise,
these women roamed all worlds in cowboy boots
and sang the rebel yell.
This mocha afternoon,
I want them back beside me, here,
curled in bookstore coffeeland,
between the books for gay men
segregated from those for gay women
across a crowded room so large
you can hear all of Rodgers and Hammerstein.

Long ago, a lesbian friend,
headed toward a grave she dug herself,
held my face and said,
We'll see each other in the Rockies.
On the rocks, all right, we lost touch
many birthdays before her death.
Still, amid the ferns and sandals now,

I hear this trio harmonize—
then lean over, for a light, again.

Snow in Ohio

(for Mary Oliver)

My mooncat's ivory belly
inside the house stretches

as outside the hill turns itself
up to my hand this morning

wanting strokes after the snow
after the day the vet said

he must trust you to let
you rub his belly

and it is the trust I see
between my house and yours

an Amish plainquilt of white luck
I smooth with my palm

this December dawn before
the plow pushes the world my way.

Communion

I borrow other people's children
Sunday mornings at church.
Running from nursery to nave,
the small ones stop by the door,
lazy halos of construction paper
drooping into their eyes.
They charge into waves
of worshipful arms, then
float high above the faithful
sea as their parents raise them
in holy relief. We can all go
forward now while the old people
hum complaints, then doze
to their own lullaby.

Our teens shuffle in packs, bound
to their clothes with silver chains.
Some girls hide their lives
in tents of peasant dresses,
but others bare midriffs
and dare their jeans to drop
while talking of *him* or *Him:*
we can never be sure and fear to ask.
From the back, boys break
their voices over flesh and first base,
then count the number of gay men
to be sure it hasn't grown.

I had no business with kids—or patience.
Yet, each Sunday during communion,
I usher our teens at the end
of the line, slouching toward the altar.
Together we kneel, hands out,
for bread, wine, belief.
Together we pray: *Please don't*
let me catch something from the cup.
Amen.

Back in the pew, I wonder
if I might have found what parents need,
like a conch shell on the beach,
cracked, with a hole in the top.
I would listen to the music,
a song of imperfect prayer.

Two

Illusions are art, for the feeling person,
and it is by art that we live, if we do.
—Elizabeth Bowen, *The Death of the Heart*

Sometimes—there's God—so quickly!
—Tennessee Williams, *A Streetcar Named Desire*

Sunday, Mentor Headlands Beach

All of our sins are strangers here
among the Victorian trees brushing
the laughter of small children inland,
where we sit at a table of beaten boards.
Our picnic basket betrays us because
everything—napkins, cloth, dishes,
cups, cutlery handles—comes in gay blue,
strapped hard in a white wicker basket.
Rich and I unpack with such taste
that a man facing west turns his back
on us before setting his coals on fire.

Free married folks today, we squirt
each other by mistake with mustard
and the memory of giraffes this morning
at the zoo, long-necked in greed, smiling
to us after we'd left the gossipy butterfly
house. Straight men are like zoo animals:
pretty, distant, but keep walking. To the
broiling stranger I want to say: *Yes, we know*
about the gay part of the beach, but
right now we want this democratic shade,
the history of sandwiches and sand.

Sneaking our illegal wine from the turn
of the century, we toast each other
as the sun peeks in to mark the spot.
I want to offer our cherries and drink
to the stranger, then show him the scars
on our bodies—*I almost died here and here,*
Rich was in a terrible car wreck—so he
could see how we drove up on the

interstate Dolorosa, too. But why waste
the effort: we repack, then head for the sun,
Apollo's men, after all, for the afternoon.

Whale Song

Only male whales sing, and they seem to sing
only to each other, to call each other.

—scientist on the radio

That Saturday morning
I cheated my Ohio life
and stood by the kitchen sink
to listen, putting November
on hold for these deep testimonies.

This was the language of men
beneath the surface,
a bass choir of longing
and love knots circling the world,
the sound of steel bending
in good temper, yet I heard
rancor in their call
and response of secret glory.

Even in the other news
that followed too fast, I kept
the low choir close by
in the kitchen as outside
snow silenced everything
and the pink moon disappeared
just before noon.
I know: once you've heard whales
sing in Ohio, you can't stop listening
for what comes next.

Riot in New Delhi

Like some Forster heroine seeing the real India,
we witness brown skins tied into colors
racing like flags, we hear the low-throated voices
of birds deranged by hunger and thirst,
but the noise is nothing to the hotel
clerk who rings his white bell,
white as his clothes and his apology:
This sort of thing goes on all the time,
this hunger in the heat, but do not worry,
your supper will not be late, sirs,
and you do not be late either, please,
like the woman named Bitha
who ran out to the street
in her white skin, flinging
her money and costume jewelry,
and got trampled to death for her love.

She is still in the street,
that woman, a charitable ghost
who gives the nothing she has,
and finds her life in the mad voices
twirling clockwise down the street
into the sewers when the rains come.

Poem for Women Betrayed
by the Music of James Taylor

I've seen fire and rain, all right, on the face
of a woman laid soul-flat in the days of vinyl
when *he* came on Sunday or Saturday afternoons.
He'd held her on beds floating by open windows,
or on winter floors with the fire saying
you can close your eyes.
Stacked records dropped like promises
from his mouth when this woman, any woman,
believed he was sweet baby james
and never tried to sing a post-coital *you're so vain*.

I came in on *you've got a friend*
the day the rent and infant were due.
He had split to cool Mexico, far from his child
screaming at three a.m. I rocked that squalling baby for miles
as my pal told her telephone mother, no,
I wasn't the answer either, I was the gay guy
who suns up on the roof and sings *Mockingbird* with the kid.

There's something in the way she moves, all right,
as she crashes into her chemistry texts and ADC.
She sings how sweet love is
to the toddler, to her homework on welfare,
to the parents offering the security of reproach:
they have Carolina on their minds only twice
a year at Hilton Head; they've worked darn hard
for that, darn hard, and what has she done
except got knocked up by something that probably carried
nine kinds of I-just-can't-say-it-I-just-can't?

The old albums crackled when I picked up the kid
for respite care, and I wanted to ask how

the music could still carry her
beyond food stamps and her parents' tithe.
But who was I to question the life of an Indian blanket
numbed with too many sex stains laid before another fire?
Broken voices spinning for years in my own head had their say:
I hope she's lying beside the greatest hits of her life,
I hope she's lighting a scented sand candle for me, too,
and getting naked while not answering the phone.
I hope she held out for vinyl as long as she could.

Open Lane in the Cuyahoga Falls Natatorium

I prefer most
the old queen,
eighty and crowned
with a circus rug,
bringing to this public pool
the dance classes
he taught for centuries,
the choreography
of his reedy arms,
the history of his closet,
now with an open door.

In swimming briefs
through glasses thick with memory,
he spies on the flab
holding the rest of us afloat,
the secrets that our bodies
show, spots where water
binds to skin with ruby kisses.
Then, he turns his profile to me
with a movie star's precision,
tosses a come hither hook,
and winks.

The Evangelist's Daughter

Just give me Jesus!

Her voice is a plank
leading from the stage
through the big hall,
mute in pastel women.
By reservation only—
tickets required—she
delivers deluxe salvation,
holding that steel of respectability
these suburban sisters imagine
they, too, can lean upon.

Only a few possess
her blonde redemption, the narrow waist
and jewelry of such amazing grace.
Enough for her, pressed in confidence,
to testify of God's presence in Ohio:
Witness those precious nails slitting
the spotlight, before the break.
See that hill far away,
where sunlight brings more
than another damned day.

Her everywhere eyes drill
each woman with holiness:
faith can save their spousal walks
on the Via Dolorosa
with husbands who clear
each truth through their sinuses
at dinner. Believe: only Jesus can
salvage the sheer boredom of living
and driving the Mom's Group, again.

So, they follow
to the end of her prayer
for a second chance to get it right,
this side of Calvary.

Baptist Confidential

At Aiken High, Rachel and I
practiced holy deeds, weekended
with God. Tall as goalposts
and tubbier than Mormons,
we fell into a Sunday school snare
When Baptist Youth Date,
then crossed the Savannah River.

Against the largest small screen
ever invented, Cybil Shepherd
removed her top on a diving board:
water and sex, Lord Help My Christ,
this was yet another full immersion.
Hollywood breasts in front of me,
Baptist breasts to the left of me:
what was I to do?

Afterwards, we shared a communion
of vanilla ice cream and silence
in her living room. Her parents
hid in back, full of prayer as we
parked on virgin vinyl
and wondered *Now what?*

Good church mice, we sneaked
a week later into the sanctuary
at night where Rachel found
a Word prophesying the messiah.
In the dark before God, we almost
kissed, but I heard shotgun steps
of righteousness in the fellowship

hall, so we left seeking milkshakes
and talk of the China missions.

Days of prayer later, as we drove
Mama's car to help the retarded,
Rachel began to cry about her
seizures and future babies
ill-conceived, dropped, or lost.
The car rocked under a dueling oak
with more grief than even God
was good for that night.
I asked Our Saviour how he
was going to get us out of this
one: soon a prophet pointed the way.

The Promised Land was a Texas
college where freedom's just
another word for not saying
bedtime prayers or writing lost
girls living in the sacred.
I had no time for anything
but the unchurched Seventies
and sleeping with *Jesús*.

Unsettling the west took years
in many deserts and rooms
without the Book. Still, I
would visit the underworld
as required: the way of the cross
forever leads home.

One Carolina afternoon, stranded
in a parking lot as Daddy began
his elderly errands, I balanced

my education in the steering wheel.
Bored blind with thought, I raised
my head to see the past get out of a car:

Large with grief and faith,
Rachel crossed two rows ahead.
I knew about the brief marriage,
no kids, her still life teaching
Sunday school in Carolina's gardens
and groves of redemption postponed.

The book closed; the car trembled.
My imagination left and put an arm
around her before asking us both
What are the wages of salvation?

Expert Witness

Beneath the professional tent of mourning,
our family sits on chairs veiled with velveteen.
Two gulls stand guard with friends I don't know
under the live oak older than the Florida dead
surrounding us Christians at work on the sand.

The preacher's prayers shorten themselves this July
as my aunt and cousins shape their grief:
Uncle Van was ninety-one, after all.
We cry before we lay him down beside
Clara, forty years mental in the state hospital,
two aunts lost early to cancer, tall Granddaddy Dukes
who made me tall: we commend our souls to the past, again.

He's on his way to a better place
and I stir with the evangelism of geography:
my Carolina boyhood, Texas, Mexico's beds, London,
born again so often I've lost count, but returning always
for the latest story of the family plot.
I sit in the back row and sweat beyond the last *Amen,*
an expert witness to the grace
of ordinary death, when faith shoulders everything.

Once

Losing you to shopping and sun
     in Florence, I sat between
the ears of a stone gargoyle
     opposite some fountain
where, the night before, you saw him
     the second before he splashed you,
and you laughed back, your teeth
     artful as his in this smelly
city of perfection, you two just drunk enough
     under summer lights,
lost in the glee of secrets.

Eating ice cream, so much better
     over there, I wondered that morning
how forgiveness could so easily be snatched
     from a vacation's long, easy pleasures
and swallowed whole, darling,
     like lovers' lies and public winks.
The cold stone I sat on hurt like first-night,
     all-night sex, raw skin on raw skin,
the whole world burned cold in the dark.

Returning, you carried a blue shopping
     bag with a foulard for me and chocolates
for us both, as if you had to, sweets.
     In your yellow sweater, you were
the pearls of an Italian lover's dream.

We walked easily through this city of metaphors,
        only we were cheap, careless with smiles
to strangers, bows to priests,
        before ending our sentence in a bath
large enough to clean a continent.

Now, this morning is heavy with news
        of your suicide. We lost touch, kid,
except for the odd postcard from art museums,
        always of some fountain in full sonnet,
with whatever we wrote in purple on the back
        meaning the same *Remember?*
I will spend the day sitting on this monster,
        your death, hurting and burning, again,
in the knowing sun.

Summer Seduction

I am the muscadine body.
Sweet inside, skin tough, marked
With crosshairs where the vine
Scratched, where insects
Crawled and lightning almost struck.
Birds broke through to some of my brothers,
Others fell to earth, dark stars rotting.

Eat me in August, I am sweet
From the top of granny's vine rising
Above the old Depression stories,
Up the live oak, high as harp strings.
Drink me at Christmas by the wood stove.
Even in Carolina, we get frost and fear,
The cold violin music rising from rusty graves.

I am a dancing wine for almost anybody,
And good jelly for you, too: spread me as needed.
You will always recall how I taste,
A sweeter friend than your smokes,
Less fatal; give me as a gift if you want.
Best of all, when bad times come,
You will know: you will know you had the truth.

El Paso Elegy

When I find January in the desert,
I visit your graves marked with the question

What were we thinking of?
Hanging denim, we walked our silver studs

through desire and sand, longing for San Francisco
as some covet booze or rough trade, pilgrims in

lavender who invented red wine and the Seventies.
I hopped a bike headed toward Tuscany and

Marseilles without you: forgive me, darlings, but
undiscovered country is a bore. Yet, I return often

to the blow-dried grass of your deaths, looking
down on you perfect queens with, at last, every

blade in place. What I always want is some
black passport letting me tell you *Thanks* for

the lessons you never learned, the desert vowels
of free speech and sex I speak today. But

you cannot hear. I leave you buried and ride
toward the empire Moses never entered.

Persephone in South Akron

(1)

The rubber factories still breathed
when Grandpaw brought us from West Virginia
for the mythic salvations of steady work:
Thursday bowling nights, a better class of drunk,
and food on a formica table that always smiled.
But in the end, he died coughing up a coal mine
into new sheets that resisted every bleaching
a regular check could buy. We gave his body
to a fire that cost seven-hundred-fifty dollars,
plus tax on the past and present,
and promised Mawmaw resurrection of the body.

(2)

Pierogies, live bait, and pork rinds
formed the trinity of my brothers' lives.
What was college on the hill
compared to the golden rams of bike studs
and boys whose courage turned yellow
from too many cigarettes and beer?
Junior lay in rehab and missed his high school
graduation as he dreamed in twelve steps
of Grandpaw's stories about courting
Mawmaw with promises to be her prayer warrior.
The other one sold my books to buy joints:
Mama hit him so hard, he disappeared,
and we didn't bother conjuring his ghost
for three years.

(3)

Holding a curling rod, Mama said
You can divine the truth.

She pulled my hair into different dreams
as she worked for her license: nails, too.
I weren't raised to the Lord, but
a neighbor lady took me to church.
God give me the silent treatment
until one Sunday, I was late. I run
through the cornfield between her land and ourn,
the sun and the corn and my hair was yellow,
and the Lord stopped me and give me the Spirit.
Now, I have the gift of tongues,
and I praise the Lord ever' day even if it means
telling your Daddy to take his lazy snake ass to hell.
She tucked my brain under the plastic dryer cap,
turned the world on *high*, and left
to invent a lexicon from heaven.

(4)

Daddy always walked too fast
to suit the suits, and even the union
gave up on his unemployed plans.
Still, he was the one who stayed up nights
when Mawmaw shriveled from missing the hills.
He rocked his bottle and her so hard that
even through the mind-rape of high school,
I heard him make tracks for heaven.
When she died, he slowed down long enough
to sell his truck for the funeral. Then, he couldn't
go anywhere, and he couldn't be still
until Mama's coffee and cussin' sobered his grief.

(5)

The day of my college graduation,
Mama set me in thirty holy rollers,
then rinsed me in the best crying I'd ever seen.
My brothers shined their bikes and red-neck hair

with the same spray guaranteed
by the auto supply to remove the past.
They found Daddy, pulled him out
the bottle for the afternoon, and trussed
him into one of his Christmas shirts.
On the way, I wanted to explain
that the myth was wrong,
there was no going back to hell
once you've been saved,
but they knew that already.
We parked on the hill next to Calvary
and found our places in time
for the Invocation.
I walked to the stage, and the world
passed the Cross to me.

My First Real Date Happened
When I Was Sixteen

With out-of-state hands, he twisted
the opener around big-and-ready tomato cans,
while Barbra Streisand sang *More Than You Know*
under a five o'clock Georgia hum
serenading the afternoon lace
that kept mosquitoes and morality outside.
He dumped the harvested hearts
of the south into a pan already happy
with tomato paste and browned hamburger,
then set the gas and his voice on red:
This will take a while.

Stripped twice for surgery,
I tried to explain the bumpy roads of my body,
what I knew of the unexpected,
but his non-commissioned mouth
covered all reason. At ease, his fingers rustled
my birthday buttons, belt, and jeans in a room
where polite conversation dared not speak
its name to a life on low boil for the first
time. Then, in a Baptist minute
I had to ask if it would always hurt like this:
A little bit if you're lucky, kid.

I flashed the freedom of my new adult license
and he showed me how to drive, pressed close,
aligned to the back end. Surely he was never
a Christian: he knew to smoke, not eat, in bed
and how *climax* came with at least five syllables
in a room filled with scarlet fever.
He left to lower the heat, while I stretched

into dusk and the surprise of wine I knew
how to drink without training, without
his returning to say what he did in the dark:
It's ready, boy, and so are you.

Three

*Who would have thought the afterlife
would look so much like Ohio?*
—Maggie Anderson, *Beyond Even This*

There'll Be Peace in the Cuyahoga Valley

Every day in the week between two deaths,
I drove through the park to see
winter's wildwood holding out
for better things than the grave.

Inside the covered bridge, three young deer
stayed close as the wise men,
their breaths rising, then spreading
through the cracks.

Another morning, two coyote pups
barked across the plowed-under corn field
where thirty geese, dressed in mourning,
nose for breakfast beneath the snow.

I braked to see them all and braked again
as four women on foot and their binoculars
slid down an icy path to witness
what plumage they could.

Every day now since the week between two deaths,
I count the works of cold faith
and know that Revelation may be wrong:
this heaven, this earth, will save us now.

The Challenge

Tall in his dueler's good looks,
he cut the air with his pensword
while demanding in a demon's voice:
"Write a story beginning with the words
For Sale: Baby Carriage, Never Used.
Make your story without sentiment
for sentiment is the death of art."

As he chattered on about his wife
and her trophy bosom,
we sat in ignorance,
trying to imagine
large, blonde breasts
and the price of a baby carriage.

Later, for a decade, I lived
next door to a couple whose roses
climbed into my trees, so we became
friends with each other's plans.
Then, a premature birth and death
made them huddle with their house,
and grief turned me into the fairy
next door who could be trusted
to smile without speaking across
the thorny fence, heavy with perfume
for months as their trash bags
bulged on the curb, leaning low
with books about the promise of birth.

That last April on block-sale day,
standing among our rusted bikes,
dreams of exercise, and gossip,
I saw them, a procession of two,
put out a bassinet, a walker, and the
baby carriage, wide and deep
enough for a world of congratulations,
the obscene party shine of it blinding
all of us into silence, for once.

Harry sold the things as if
he were selling his hands and hoped
not to caress the world again,
while Sarah, out back,
hid under a new hat,
cutting branches off her smiling trees.

Soon they moved to another country
but not before we wrapped each other
in vows to write.

They did not answer my two letters,
although I reached for months across the ocean,
my hands conjuring the empty wind
of their unspoken goodwill,
always knowing before knowing
what cannot be borne:
that I had failed
the challenge,
unforgivably,
again.

Writing Daddy

Mama whispered bedtime stories of your Korean letters
hidden in a locked cedar casket, your myth kept

out of reach, though I knew early you could barely write
or read the word *impediment* that Mama made from your

misfired Cracker vowels. Later, in some Carolina
woods of wild pines, you aimed your malaria

against my boyhood, the worst a man could get,
you said, so you voted for Stevenson, twice.

Recruited at school, I cracked the secret code
of language, not knowing I had crossed our DMZ.

Angry, you moved Army words against me,
and I learned the maneuver named *goodbye*

on an educational deferment: what else
could protect us so well as *furlough?*

After this truce, you fell first, then Mama
began her great retreat, and I policed the past:

Waiting for her final orders, I took the
forbidden letters to the nursing home cafeteria,

I betrayed the lock with a dying bobby pin
and read your romance, Daddy. Who knew

how dull wartime illiteracy could be?
Cold misspellings, hungry loneliness,

a convoy of *I love you's* crossing the Pacific.
Now, a few years later, the silver and china

rationed to relatives, I have stationed the letters
at my desk. When I need to, Daddy,

I hold this ceasefire of love and wonder
What were you trying to say?

Desire

Still speaking that afternoon, years ago,
we heard from the friendly hotel bartender
spinning midafternoon bourbons and Cokes
that the Key West beaches we came for
did not exist, but we could burn
by the pool, wine-filled,
cuddling next to the outdoor lounge
where money stretched in the sun.
Later, after supper, we walked
to the idea of Cuba and back,
when outside, over drinks,
under the movie-star sky,
you said the guitarist
sang with such gravel in his voice
that you would have been an easy lay
for that stranger, that night.

In your sleep, hours later,
beside my open puzzle book,
you cried *Help! Help! Help!*
as the palm trees prayed outside
to the blue diamond moon,
the lucky night throwing dice
out through open windows.

I did not wake you
as you waited for your guitarist.
You quieted easily.

Then, robing my bare self in white,
I wandered out among leftover drinks,
searching for the whorish music
that made you beg for mercy.

On the rocks where the beach
should have been, he sat
naked with his strings,
looking for something to come.

High Water Warning

Tall as fire, the horses
rose before us in the desert
that night when we five caballeros
tucked stars in the arroyo and bedded ourselves
between sheets of exhaustion and dirty clothes.

Later, after hours, someone yelled
with the lightning we tried to ignore
I love you, Thomas
just as floodwater through the arroyo
threatened to thrill us to a foolish death.

As we climbed the panicked walls of sand,
I remembered the sign *High Water Warning*
on the mountain road. Yes, we laughed
in the small hours. Yes, we slept
too late and too much with each other.

Yes, we ignored the warnings:
anything the horses said now
would be true.

The Horses Next Door

Fixed in winter habits,
lilac, white, blue plaid,
they lean against suburbia,
breathing with the trees
as the snow hides their secrets.

Each November they kneel in prayer
with deer escaping from the great
pursuers. Each spring the horses refuse
to neigh or prance for city people,
slumming, who drive away in thwarted lust.

Once the neighbor saw our cat
astride, sleeping, atop the barebacked
stallion. Each summer, too hot to move,
we imagine how the cat got there
without command of his claws.

In their dreams and ours, the horses
ride from the barn to glory and back
again. They wake to guard the far
end of the corral, then sing, countertenors,
as finches primp in the amber of spying eyes.

Coming in low, an owl scratches the sky
so the horses' songs can rise and leave
the world. Compline completed, the horses
process into the stable, age to youth,
then nod, returning to their holy stalls.

Blessed Assurance

She lies hollow in the metal bed,
sheets bleaching her skin, her hair.
A week ago Mama pointed two raw
fingers to nonexistent robins at the bird bath.
We christened them using the only words
left to her: *Father, Son,* and *Holy Ghost*
Then, everyone but me flew to another fantasy.

For years, her gardeners' hands possessed her,
stewards sorting the saved and the damned.
She gambled on me, her only son, and I became
a croupier of plants, days, books, and people.
Once, as we salvaged a fig tree taller than hope,
I asked about her plans for Eden:
Oh, I've done my traveling,
she whispered as she cut, *you go.*

Now, toward the end, I trim the practical mums
of her room, the phone calls, all holy visitations.
Our Baptist preacher reminds me who put
the whole world in my hands: I know, I know.
He prays us into dormancy, then leaves,
crying. I open her eyes: hard chestnuts,
fixed in coma. Her breathing warns the silence,
Tonight I fly to Beulah land, alone.

Taking His Name to the Lord
(for Lynn Powell and Elton Glaser)

(1)

In curves of youth and music
from the turquoise taverns
of Santa Fe, I lay with him
under pagan quilts before
we all became expensive
cultural artifacts.

He ran his Catholic fingers
up and down two parallel scars
on my abdomen, a Sisyphus
obsessed with the journey
ending at the third scar,
low on the right,
a hardened little manhole cover
where demons had drained.

Aroused, I described
how poisoned beasts inside
tried to kill, twice, but full
immersion under millbrook water
and surgeons' hands saved me,
without much pain,
for our tequila bed and blessings
and the Indian healers on the square,
shaking icons, shaping prayers.

He searched for my guilt
in the sheets, but finding
none, confessed his own
as I held his rosary beads and vows,
wondering what penance he would
discover in the haunting sun.

Afterwards, for months,
I tried to cleanse him
in the sweat after sex,
but he could not
put his head
under water,
or even close his eyes.

(2)

Years later, called home,
I hear Mama say,
even as we lay her down
by the rivers of the family plot,
The Lord is infinitely merciful,
and she should know,
ruined, marked, even crazed
at the end,
but never afraid.

I think of him,
so fine, dying young,
long ago after seas of drink,
in a home for the wayward ones,
somewhere in California:
they were good to him at the end,
I'm told.

Once, after mass,
behind some burly bushes,
I saw three girls become artists
near his beauty
and write
Father-What-a-Waste
with their fingers on his brown velvet face,
still perfect, I heard,
even as he
begged at last
for mercy and water,
and refused both
when brought to bedside
by quiet hands
searching to wash his broken places
in the gravelly dark.

(3)

Now, in the sweet by and by
of this Ohio afternoon,
newly married in Vermont,
motherless, but not really,
I hear him testify
from some unredeemed corner
of the Santa Fe plaza,
where we shook hands goodbye
before I drove to freedom
and beyond.

God, I think,
the duties of paradise.

Tonight,
after supper, I shall rummage
through the artifacts of redemption.

Then, behind this wildwood house,
let us wash his prayer-man
in salvation's melting snow,
and raise him to my mother's arm
so he will know.

Mama Would Be Seventy-Five on Halloween

This year, I shall stop trying
to be careful about her
as if crossing a log over grief.
Let me lose my balance
and fall in the autumn water
always running, always
going somewhere cold.

Let me see October from the bottom
as she did, a girl trapped under
swirling skirts of color, wise
to the rake-work of the world.
Let me witness her signs and wonders,
hear her name wild things again
as once I held her hand, then ran.

I hope I have her patterns
with the china, cookbooks, and verse.
So I testify too much about the habits
of her house, so? This year, I'll keep
the melancholy of mamas' boys,
burn recovery with the leaves,
and let November's table mourn
her custom and call.

Key Deer

Small enough to step
among laws forbidding us
to feed them,
these miniatures
smile into the mouths of open cars,
rush and lurch into our backyards
on legs and cattails,
brown velvet spies every one.

At dusk, these deer unlock
secret doors hinged
to cypress churches
holding rich and famous prayers
sung over hurricanes that shrieked
before swallowing old men and women.

I see their brown eyes in my godson,
my mother, my lover. Tonight,
they inform the violet lace
outside our window that you
will leave both shutters to the future
open, then return to the happy shack
of safety we call Big Pine Key.

Childless

Driving home by an autumn ocean,
I imagine the unstable spaces
where we keep the questions haunting
our lives, where wild sea roses
catch the afternoon light
almost blinding me at the wheel.

Once I had time to listen
to the future, a child holding
a shell to his ear.
I stopped that years ago
except when someone asks
Did you ever want children?
as if I had a choice,
as if the desire to extend our souls
could be turned away like a friend
who wore you out.

We tell the pillows
that, really, we met each other
ten years too late for kids and a new house,
and we have all those bills now anyway.
We hide desire where beach visitors go
when the water is too cold, really,
but they want to swim so much
that the longing drives them
into the cold water and they run
out, screaming, back to shore.

So often we go there,
picking up shells and listening
to the sounds of what we have

and do not have. Rich cradles reeds
and cattails, then digs them up
with a great lover's greed.
I walk the beach to smile at other people
and their busy children, trying to find
another way to save the world.

Minerva, Ohio

Leaves haunt the way from school
for Amish children in Athena's town,
bright ghosts of autumn decorating

and descending into the smile
of walking home. These plainclothes
children do not snatch

testaments of color for home or scrapbook:
They would not mock the Lord
or disobey. But from bonneted

faces and boys' hatbands spring
flags of red oak and gold maple rebellion,
ecstasy riding the trail between schoolwork

and chores at home. As childhood slips
from the dyes of autumn into winter's
white farm labor, these sentries

of innocence march toward duty through
what they see of the changing world.

Mennonite Funeral in Southwest Ohio

(for Gayle King)

On this November hill, once far away,
beside women's hair capped in devotion,
we stand bare as trees and outdoor hymns.

The lives of barns roll into each other
below this churchyard where our prurient eyes
measure the widow's silent life. This morning,

strong people with backhoes and history
part the merciful earth, and the dead farmer
slips away from us, from all the autumns stalks

of work and prayer gathered in the county.
The preacher unfolds the day's passion, returning us
to glory *where we never know despair*,

rocking in the rhythm of the Lord,
with the Father and the Son, with the Spirit
we all feel, so polite and kind that

we have no choice but to disarm death
in the minute before we say *Amen Amen*
and shield our eyes from the cold sun.

Outside the church basement, we pilgrims,
so polite and kind, wait to eat and drink
the mysteries old women heap upon our plates.

We never ask what old women know of life,
the ground, or us. We raise our cups,
our children, our fear, as the women pass, smiling,

cousins, of cousins, sisters, aunts, always willing
to give us more, while the farmers wait for coffee,
the next planting—wait for us to leave.

Midnight

Under the two snarling azaleas,
a fox grits his teeth and warns
the world in a light thrown
by a storm's purple insomnia.

Trespassing our woods, a coyote bites
into Ta-the-cat's last good leg.
She comes to tattle at the patio doors,
bleedings stories of conquest and love.

Robins hit the ground running,
a Norwegian spruce spins its top
to earth, Rich's endless jonquils
twirl madly, tutus flying to Kansas.

A walking rain loses its nerve, then hides
over the barn next door. The fox hurls
itself after a *what-was-that?* as I swaddle
Ta in a towel; we sink into Miss Susie's rocker.

Back and forth, we keep time to danger.
The raunchy horses next door sing
in their blankets, I read diaries
by Anne Morrow Lindbergh:

Even the rocks swear about April.

Florida Reliquary

After the fire before dawn,
the dog and I steer our boat
into bold, wrecked choruses
of flowers melting over ashes,
birds circling, deer crunching underfoot
their scorched food and kin
where even land snakes are lost,
everyone searching for home and water.

What remains are these black tree bones
and a few grasses spearing heaven
with new blades of memento mori,
sharp as any childhood beating or cancer.
Who knew the Everglades
could open death this way,
the swamp rising on its own stench,
even my dog pointing toward home.

Baptism

Stripping to the white underwear of good behavior,
we stand with our fathers in the dressing room,
backs hard against the sight of other boy-bodies.

Haloed in crew cuts, white in white robes,
we know the girls change *over there* in the dressing room
opposite the font dividing us for the first time.

At eight-through-ten years old, we already walk with Jesus.
Yet, just in case, Daddy of the Great Depression,
known to skip church for the bad news and no shave,

made me learn to swim *soz you kin tek care of yo'self boy.*
Now, I stand in steamy gratitude as landlocked Luther
almost cries this side of the widening water.

All daddies make way for sanctity. Third in the alphabet,
I let Mr. Jackson nudge me toward the font. My bare toes
grip the edge of three white steps in turn:

I shall not slip or embarrass the Lord.
Warm water raises the robe hip-high, but no one
can see my underwear, soaked and clinging

to the future. Preacher incants salvation,
puts one hand at the soul of my back, another in front,
and dunks me in full immersion, so it will take.

Rising, I let him turn me as the waterfall of redemption
runs down my face and Daddy pulls me up
He takes off the robe and wipes glory from me

soz you won't git that damned peemoanya.
His sin of honest language so close to the font
makes Luther's daddy frown a Baptist frown.

Pay him no nevermind, whispers Daddy,
so we go, stuck with salvation, hand in hand,
ready to cross Jordan any time.

About the Author

 Thomas Dukes was born in north central Florida and raised in Aiken, South Carolina. He received his B.A. and M.A. in creative writing from The University of Texas at El Paso and his Ph. D. in modern literature from Purdue University. He is currently Professor of English and Associate Provost at The University of Akron. His poetry, scholarship, and other writings have appeared in a variety of journals. He lives near Akron with his spouse, seven cats, and a poodle, Princess Diana.

Shen Fu

Six Records of a
Life Adrift

SHEN FU

Six Records of a Life Adrift

Translated, with Introduction and Notes, by

Graham Sanders

Hackett Publishing Company, Inc.
Indianapolis/Cambridge

Copyright © 2011 by Hackett Publishing Company, Inc.

15 14 13 12 11   1 2 3 4 5 6 7

For further information, please address
      Hackett Publishing Company, Inc.
      P.O. Box 44937
      Indianapolis, Indiana 46244-0937

      www.hackettpublishing.com

Cover design by Abigail Coyle
Interior design and composition by Mary Vasquez
Maps by Tracy Ellen Smith
Printed at Edwards Brothers, Inc.

Library of Congress Cataloging-in-Publication Data
    Shen, Fu, 1763-ca. 1808.
     [Fu sheng liu ji. English]
     Six records of a life adrift / [Shen Fu] ; translated, with introduction
and notes by Graham Sanders.
     p. cm.
     ISBN 978-1-60384-198-6 (pbk.)—ISBN 978-1-60384-199-3 (cloth)
     1. Shen, Fu, 1763-ca. 1808—Translations into English. 2. Authors,
Chinese—Biography. I. Sanders, Graham Martin. II. Title.
     PL2724.H4Z46513 2011
     895.1′448—dc22

                  2011015665

Contents

Acknowledgments vi
Introduction viii
Note on the Translation xvi
Maps xviii

Six Records of a Life Adrift

Record One: *Delights of Marriage* 1
Record Two: *Charms of Idleness* 33
Record Three: *Sorrows of Hardship* 53
Record Four: *Pleasures of Roaming* 83
Record Five: *Experiences of Zhongshan* [missing]
Record Six: *Methods of Living* [missing]

Chronology 136
Shen Fu's Associates and Family Tree 142
Historical Figures Mentioned by Shen Fu 144
Index 146

Acknowledgments

I would like to thank a number of people who made this translation possible, beginning with Shen Fu for writing his memoirs and Yang Yinzhuan for rescuing them decades later from a Suzhou book stall in 1874. There is a mountain of Chinese scholarship dedicated to this slender volume, but I have benefited most directly from the erudition and guidance of Wang Yiting, Cai Genxiang, and Miao Huaiming in their annotated editions.[1] For scholarship in English, I am indebted to the work of Helen Dunstan, Paul Ropp, Stephen Owen, and especially Milena Doleželová-Velingerová, who first introduced me to this marvelous book many years ago.[2] I have consulted the work of previous translators, including Lin Yutang, and Leonard Pratt and Chiang Su-hui in English.[3] I have made every effort to correct previous errors, to provide expanded annotations, and to render Shen Fu's intimate account into a more colloquial and flowing style of English.

I am extremely grateful to my colleagues who took time

1. Wang Yiting, ed., *Shen Fu sanwen xuanji* (Tainjin: Baihua wenyi, 1997); Cai Genxiang, ed., *Jingjiao xiangzhu Fusheng liuji* (Taibei: Wanjuanlou, 2008); Miao Huaiming, ed., *Fusheng liuji* (Beijing: Zhonghua, 2010).

2. Helen Dunstan, "If Chen Yun had written about her 'lesbianism': rereading the memoirs of a bereaved philanderer," *Asia Major* 20 (2007): 103–122; Paul Ropp, "Between Two Worlds: Women in Shen Fu's *Six Chapters of a Floating Life*," in *Woman and Literature in China*, eds. Anna Gerstlacher, Ruth Keen, et al., (Bochum, Germany: Brockmeyer, 1985), 98–140; Stephen Owen, *Remembrances: The Experience of the Past in Classical Chinese Literature* (Cambridge, MA: Harvard University Press, 1986), 99–113; Milena Doleželová-Velingerová and Lubomír Doležel, "An Early Chinese Confessional Prose: Shen Fu's *Six Chapters of a Floating Life*," *T'oung Pao* 58 (1972): 137–160.

3. Lin Yutang, trans., *The Wisdom of China and India* (New York: Random House, 1942), 964–1050; Leonard Pratt and Chiang Su-hui, trans., *Six Chapters of a Floating Life* (Harmondsworth: Penguin, 1983).

away from their own work to look over the manuscript for this book, including Sophie Volpp, Shang Wei, Linda Feng, Sarah Schneewind, and Stephen West. I thank all of them for their expertise and invaluable suggestions for improving the accuracy of the translation and the utility of the notes. I assure them that I am solely responsible for any errors that remain.

I cannot say enough about the patience and dedication of my editor, Deborah Wilkes, who first approached me with the idea for a new translation of *Six Records of a Life Adrift*. Her guidance in producing every facet of this book has made it something of which I am truly proud. She and the staff at Hackett Publishing—especially project editor Mary Vasquez—have made working on this translation a truly rewarding experience.

Finally, I would like to thank my wife Chia Chia and my daughters Mia and Esmé for their understanding and support through the seemingly endless hours that I was adrift in Shen Fu's world.

Introduction

"A skillful man toils, a wise man worries, but a man without ability seeks nothing and is happy to roam about with a full belly; adrift as an unmoored boat, he roams without purpose."

— *Zhuangzi* (Chapter 32)

There is an old Chinese tale about a man who, because he decides to add feet to his drawing, loses a wager to see who can draw a snake the fastest. I feel that I may run the same risk by adding an introduction to a work as simply and beautifully told as *Six Records of a Life Adrift*, so I will be brief in providing some background information that I hope will add to the enjoyment of reading this gem of Chinese narrative.

The book was written in the Qing dynasty (1644–1911) by a man with the surname of Shen and the given name of Fu (hereafter Shen Fu), an unsuccessful scholar, painter, merchant, and private secretary born in 1763 in the renowned garden city of Suzhou. *Six Records of a Life Adrift* is unique in the history of Chinese literature for its unusual approach in telling a life story through a collection of discrete records, overlapping in time but focusing on disparate themes. Shen Fu writes in the concise literary language of poetry, essays, and official histories rather than in the more verbose vernacular language used for the popular lengthy novels and dramas of the Ming and Qing dynasties. This choice allows him to slip readily into a poetic lyrical mode of description when depicting his feelings, his relationships, and the beauty of the natural world. But he is able to use the same terse language to provide many vivid details of daily life, describing topics as far ranging as gardening, finance, social roles of women, tourism, literary criticism, prostitution, class relations, and family dynamics—to name just a few—which makes his book a valuable document about the society and culture of late imperial China.

The modern reader might find surprising the completely open

and frank way in which Shen Fu describes his twenty-three-year marriage to his wife, Chen Yun: their first meeting, their loving partnership, their many years of ups and downs together, their relationships with other people, and Yun's heartbreaking illness and death. Yun is one of the most celebrated female characters in Chinese literature, cherished all the more for being a real person, and Shen Fu's book has been more often read as a tragic love story than as the memoirs of an obscure Qing dynasty private secretary.

The manuscript of this book was discovered in 1874 at a second-hand book stall on the streets of Suzhou, the hometown of Shen Fu. The book was probably completed around 1811, and although its title is *Six Records of a Life Adrift*, only four records were present in the original: "Delights of Marriage," "Charms of Idleness," "Sorrows of Hardship," and "Pleasures of Roaming." The titles of the two missing records—"Experiences of Zhongshan" and "Methods of Living"—were listed, but it is uncertain whether they were lost or left unfinished by Shen Fu.

The book became extremely popular after its initial publication in 1877, so much so that the missing records were reportedly found (also in a secondhand book stall) and a new complete edition of *Six Records of a Life Adrift* was published in Shanghai with much fanfare in 1935. Unfortunately, the restored records were soon proven to be forgeries copied from other works and were poorly written compared to the first four records; I have not included them in this translation. Shen Fu, by his own admission, led an unremarkable, unfulfilled, and itinerant life, so it is somehow fitting that his incomplete manuscript would be set adrift on a sea of old books only to come to light over sixty years after it was written.

Most of what we know about Shen Fu comes from this book. He lived at the turn of the nineteenth century in Qing dynasty China, a time when civil service examinations were still the main path to success for members of the educated classes. Shen Fu and his father both repeatedly claim to be members of a "scholarly family" but neither of them passed the examinations. Shen Fu failed the initial examination at the age of sixteen and gave up his studies completely at nineteen to work alongside his father in occasional employment, for little pay, as a private legal secretary for government officials. He dabbled in painting and calligraphy and supplemented his meager income by selling works of art. When he fell deeper into poverty after becoming estranged from his family, he was reduced to borrowing money from relatives and acquaintances and staying in the houses of friends; he even resorted to that most uncultured of activities—mercantile trade—with little success.

Shen Fu is remarkably candid about describing his personal failures and portrays himself as well meaning but ineffectual, which lends credence to the truth of his account. There is little reason to doubt the main facts of his story, which are corroborated by independent records of the events and people he mentions in his memoirs. There are some chronological inconsistencies in the text, which I have preserved in the translation, but these seem to result from its method of composition as a series of conjoined records rather than as a unitary work from start to finish. Shen Fu remembered things differently at different times in his life and, if we are to believe the portrait he paints of himself as being somewhat feckless, he was not the sort who would take the time to tie up loose ends.

As Shen Fu notes in his opening sentence, he had the good fortune of being born during a peaceful and prosperous era in the city of Suzhou, located in the affluent Yangtze River Delta region of southeast China known as Wu. This area of fertile farmland and extensive waterways in the provinces of Jiangsu and Zhejiang is bounded by the major cities of Shanghai, Yangzhou, Nanjing, and Hangzhou, with Suzhou and Wuxi in its central region around Lake Tai (see the maps in this book). During the Qing dynasty the Wu region supported a large population concentrated in urban centers that boasted a rich cultural life, a thriving merchant class, and an extensive government bureaucracy. The distinctive culture of this southeastern region was marked most clearly by the Wu dialect of spoken Chinese, with its own pronunciation and slang usages that set it apart from the Mandarin dialect spoken in the north. Shen Fu even explains some of the unusual Wu-dialect words that he uses in his story, which suggests that he envisioned a readership for his work beyond his close circle of acquaintances.

Shen Fu's hometown of Suzhou lies sixty miles to the west of Shanghai and has been famous for centuries as a center of literati culture. The area was already home to millions of people in the Qing dynasty; it was known for producing talented calligraphers, painters, and poets; and it still boasts to this day numerous exquisite gardens that once served the wealthy and literate classes as retreats from the hustle and bustle of daily life in a big city. Some of these gardens were open to commoners during the Qing, but many were the domain of powerful officials and were as much a public symbol of their prestige as they were for private enjoyment. Shen Fu was an aficionado of gardens, and he laces his narrative with numerous accounts of notable gardens encountered in his travels, even providing the reader with helpful tips for designing one's own garden and for arranging flowers and raising bonsai.

Shen Fu, his brother Qitang, and their father Shen Jiafu managed to eke out modest livings by serving as private secretaries for local magistrates stationed in government offices throughout the Wu region. It was administrative policy under the Qing to post officials far away from their hometowns to avoid concentrations of power and nepotism, meaning officials might be tasked with overseeing a district with unfamiliar customs and even an unintelligible local dialect. Such officials relied heavily on locally recruited runners, clerks, and secretaries to help them in their daily administrative duties. The private secretary held the highest status among this subaltern class of civil servants, as he worked closely with a ruling magistrate in receiving and responding to legal documents and was paid out of his employer's own pocket. When Shen Fu's father reminds him "we wear the caps and robes of scholars," he is referring to this quasi-official status that he and Shen Fu gained through education and literacy.

Although Shen Fu did not belong to the elite class of government officials, he liked to think of himself as participating in the same high culture. Almost all of the second record, "Charms of Idleness," is given over to detailed and loving descriptions of literati pastimes such as painting, calligraphy, poetry, drinking, and gardening in which Shen Fu uses the technical vocabulary of literary and art criticism. He continues to use the language of literary criticism to discuss the design of gardens seen during his travels recounted in the fourth record, "Pleasures of Roaming." Much of the tension and pathos in *Six Records of a Life Adrift* comes from his struggle to maintain the illusion that he is a scholarly man of leisure when he lacks the financial means to be one. At one point in his story he describes the mock civil service examinations that he and his friends were fond of staging, a somewhat pathetic imitation of the real ones that they never passed themselves. In their version of the examinations they reward themselves for their success with drink rather than illustrious official careers. Even such a modest reward is hard to come by, however, and Shen Fu is often reduced to taking up a collection or pawning possessions in order to purchase the wine.

Shen Fu's dauntless and loving wife of twenty-three years,

Chen Yun, helps her husband maintain the airs of scholarly leisure despite their penury, even pawning her prized hairpins from her own dowry to keep him and his friends in wine for their gatherings. Shen Fu's family had originally arranged a marriage for him when he was a child, but when his betrothed died, the teenage Shen Fu set his heart on marrying his intelligent, beautiful, and talented maternal cousin Yun. Marriage between matrilineal cousins was not unusual at the time, but in an age when arranged marriages were the norm their union stands out as a romantic one based on mutual attraction rather than familial dictates.

The story of *Six Records of a Life Adrift* really is Yun's story from the opening page to the end of the heart-wrenching third record, "Sorrows of Hardship." If we take the titles and supposed contents of the missing fifth and sixth records into account—"Experiences of Zhongshan," on Shen Fu's trip to the Ryukyu Islands, and "Methods of Living," on his philosophical approach to life—we end up with a more balanced work: the first three records being an intimate, lyrical account of the joys and sorrows of Shen Fu's life with his devoted wife and the last three records a more objective, outward account of his travels and his thoughts on health and longevity. It is not certain that the final two records were ever actually written, and the book as it exists today, which reads as Shen Fu's poignant account about his two-decade love affair with Yun, seems all the more powerful without them.

All we know of Yun comes from Shen Fu's depiction of her in the pages of this book. She was orphaned by the death of her father and left on her own to support her mother and younger brother by doing needlework, even making enough to pay for her brother's schooling. She taught herself to read using her brother's books and took to writing her own poetry, thus participating at a young age in the literati culture that provided so much solace for her and her husband over their years of marriage together. In many ways, Yun comes across as having a more refined literary sensibility than her husband. Her deep appreciation of literature, her wit, and her sheer inventiveness are invigorating compared to the stodgy pedantry on offer from her self-conscious spouse. Despite his shortcomings, Shen Fu did support his wife's literary efforts and showed enthusiasm for personally furthering her education. Literary activity among women burgeoned during the Ming and Qing dynasties, and Shen Fu's own mentor, Shi Yunyu (1757–1837)—courtesy name Zhuotang—was a well-known patron of female poets himself.

As a woman in late imperial China, Yun had strictly defined

familial roles: first as a daughter to her mother, then as wife to her husband and mother to her children, and finally as a daughter-in-law to her husband's parents, in whose home she lived after her marriage. Yun is asked to use her literary talents to write letters for Shen Fu's mother to his father, who is working away from home, which leads to a convoluted series of misunderstandings that end up offending both of her parents-in-law. Shen Fu and Yun go through long periods of recurring familial estrangement and financial hardship and must rely on the generosity of friends and acquaintances to survive. These two thematic skeins—turbulent relationships and lack of money—intertwine throughout the delicately layered narrative of this book as Shen Fu and Yun navigate a precarious existence together.

In a pivotal episode, Yun manages to further alienate Shen Fu's family by becoming involved in a controversial affair with a beautiful young courtesan named Hanyuan. Yun says that she loves Hanyuan and wants to arrange for her to become Shen Fu's concubine so that the three of them can live together. Such secondary wives were not unusual among the more privileged classes and were actually seen as a sign of prestige, for they helped ensure more progeny to carry on the family name. The exact nature of Yun's love for Hanyuan is open to interpretation, but acquiring her may also have been a strategy to keep Shen Fu happy at home given Yun's deteriorating health.

Shen Fu's father objects strenuously to the arrangement, outraged that Yun is "swearing herself to a prostitute." Shen Fu, acutely conscious of his own inability to support his family, feels it is imprudent to add another member to it. Yun argues that he needs to maintain face among his colleagues who already have concubines. In the end, they do not have the money to close the deal and Hanyuan is purchased by a wealthier man. The ongoing and stark contrast between what Shen Fu and Yun want to be and what they can afford to be is never far from the surface of the text; it produces a constant tension that draws together these recursive and fragmentary records into a compelling story that is as much about the failures of self-deception as it is about telling the truth.

In his opening paragraphs, Shen Fu promises the reader, "I will do my best to record without omission everything that I did and felt during those times," but he does so with the highly innovative technique of layering episodic narratives atop one another. Each record starts and ends at a different point in his life, yet they all overlap significantly in the time they cover. The narratives proceed chronologically but at different paces, expanding and contracting the time of narration at different points in the plot. (See the Chronology in the appendices for a list of major events and a diagram of the years covered by the records.)

The rhythm of each record depends on its topic—marriage, idleness, hardship, roaming—and its dominant mood—delight, charm, sorrow, pleasure. Extended scenes describing Yun's illnesses in the third record, "Sorrows of Hardship," are glossed over in a few words or omitted altogether in another record. Shen Fu spends pages in the fourth record, "Pleasures of Roaming," describing a trip that is mentioned elsewhere in one sentence. The individual records work together to produce a multilayered collage of Shen Fu's memories; the very structure of the book mimics the shape and behavior of human memory itself. Our memories are selective, inconsistent, recursive, colored by mood; we both recall *and* forget as a way of finding reasons and patterns in the welter of chaotic particulars and emotional associations that are left behind in the wake of our daily experiences. Shen Fu is remembering his life for the reader (and for himself) in four different but complementary ways that end up producing a more satisfying and genuine account together than any single, linear narrative might on its own. He does not try to reconcile the competing versions of his life into a tidy package that would show the artificial "chisel scars" that he detests so much. Instead, he lays out each record side by side and invites the reader to be the fashioner of his life story.

Even with their episodic nature, however, these four records do display a recurring theme with an insistence that suggests it is somehow fundamental to the way Shen Fu viewed and even lived his life. He continually constructs or encounters small, limited spaces—both physical and in his imagination—where he can feel and express his emotions. Yun joins him in doing this during their married life, and they spend some of their happiest moments together in creating and imagining idylls where their romantic love can flourish without external threats of deprivation or disapproval. Such creations are fleeting by nature, however, and Shen Fu is constantly subjected to the pain of losing his small worlds. The grief that he feels at losing his wife and partner of twenty-three years is not only for the loss of her love but also for the loss of being able to share these brief moments of joy with her. This sentiment is captured in a passage that may have inspired

Shen Fu's choice of title for his memoirs: "For in this cosmos we are but sojourners among all things in creation; in time we are but passing travelers through the ages. So in this life adrift as in a dream, how much joy will we find?" The words were written by Yun's favorite poet Li Bai.[1]

Set adrift without Yun in the latter part of the book's final record, Shen Fu becomes a sojourner himself, following his employer and attempting to find a place in the wider world where he can purchase some measure of transient happiness after the death of his beloved. For a short time he contentedly lives in a small garden pavilion called Unmoored Boat but is obliged to move to his next assignment before the chrysanthemums have even blossomed. In the final passage of these brief, graceful, deceptively simple memoirs, Shen Fu mentions his long-held desire to see a famous ocean mirage of a shimmering city that floats over the water off the coast of Shandong near his new posting. In a tone of wistful resignation that speaks to a loss much greater than a missed sightseeing opportunity, he admits, "I never did find a way to see it in the end." After this we hear no more from Shen Fu; no one knows exactly when or where he passed away.

Zhuangzi (Chapter 15) says of the sagely man, "He lives his life as though adrift and dies as though coming to rest." Wherever Shen Fu may have come to rest, all we have left of his unique voice are these four exquisitely written records that capture a fleeting life of beauty, sorrow, love, and regret.

~

---

1. The passage is from a preface written by Li Bai (701–762) for his poem "A Spring Evening Banquet with My Cousins in the Peach Garden" (Chunyeyan congdi taohuayuan xu).

Note on the Translation

The original text for this translation comes from the 2010 edition of *Fusheng liuji*—edited by Miao Huaiming and published by Zhonghua shu ju in Beijing—which is based on the earliest and best editions of the book. (Shen Fu's original manuscript is no longer extant.)

I have tacitly converted units of measurement to the U.S. system and converted dates from the lunar calendar traditionally used in China to the Gregorian calendar in use today, while preserving the mention of years as falling within the reigns of the Qianlong emperor (r. 1736–1795) or the Jiaqing emperor (r. 1796–1820).

The smallest unit of currency mentioned in the text is a copper coin called a "cash" (*wen*), also nicknamed "green beetle" (*qingfu*) for its color. These coins had a hole in the middle and could be threaded onto cords by the hundred for daily use. Ten of these cords joined together made an official "string of cash" (one thousand coins) nominally worth one tael of silver, although the exchange rate varied by time and place. A tael of silver usually took the form of a small ingot or sycee weighing 1.2 troy ounces. In Shen Fu's time, a tael could purchase roughly 1.4 bushels of rice, enough to feed a person for almost three months. Shen Fu also mentions foreign coins, by which he likely means the Spanish silver dollar that circulated in China as a convenient form of silver-based currency beginning in the late eighteenth century. He states in the text that one of these foreign coins could be exchanged for just over seven hundred copper coins.

Names of provinces, cities, towns, mountains, lakes, and rivers are given in pinyin romanization so that they can be located easily on a map, but names of hills, bridges, temples, gardens, and streets are translated to convey their local character. All proper names are also rendered using the pinyin system, which is pronounced largely as one would expect in English with the following exceptions: "zh" is pronounced as "j" in *jungle*; "q" as "ch" in *ch*eap; "x" as "sh" in *sh*eep; "c" as "ts" in ra*ts*; and "z" as "ds" in frien*ds*.

Shen Fu and his friends consume much "wine" in the course of this book, but what they are actually drinking is alcohol fermented and/or distilled from grains such as rice, sorghum, or millet rather than grapes or other fruits. It was usually warmed before serving, as is normally done with Japanese sake. I have retained the conventional use of the misnomer "wine" for this type of alcohol because the alternatives of "ale" or "liquor" sound a bit jarring in this context.

There are two maps in the front matter of the book showing where Shen Fu lived and traveled; the back matter includes a chronology of Shen Fu's life, a diagram of his associates and family tree, and a list of historical figures mentioned in the book. The illustrations at the beginning of each record are from the *Painting Manual of the Mustard Seed Garden* (*Jieziyuan huazhuan*), a popular Qing dynasty guide to painting techniques that Shen Fu may have used in his own early training as a painter.

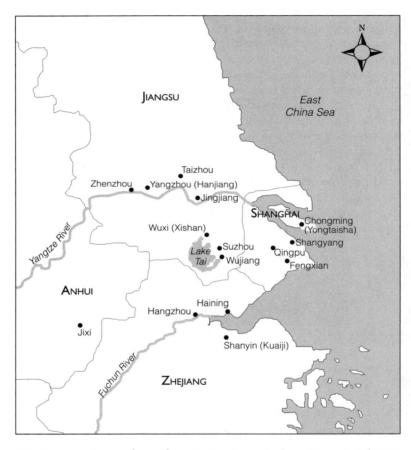

Wu Region: places where Shen Fu lived, worked, and traveled (1763–1805). Modern provincial boundaries are shown for reference.

Shen Fu made trips to Lingnan (1793–1794); Jingzhou, Tong Pass, Laiyang, and Beijing (1805–1807); and Ryukyu Islands (1807). Modern provincial boundaries are shown for reference.

Six Records of a Life Adrift

RECORD ONE

Delights of Marriage

On December 26, 1763, in the twenty-eighth year of the Qianlong reign, I was born during a time of great peace and prosperity into a scholarly family living by the Pavilion of Azure Waves in the city of Suzhou, so one might say that Heaven has been very generous to me.

But as the poet Su Shi once wrote, "The past is a spring dream that fades without a trace," so if I do not record my story with brush and ink, then truly I would be turning my back on Azure Heaven's generosity.[1]

Now, keeping in mind that the three hundred verses of the *Classic of Poetry* begin with a song of courtship called "Osprey's Cry," I will begin my book with my marriage and proceed from there.[2] I will do my best to record everything that I did and felt during those times, though I am somewhat ashamed to admit that I strayed from my studies when I was young and that I am not very good at writing. If you would look for skill in my composition, you may as well demand light from a filthy mirror.

~

I was first betrothed as a child to a young girl of the Yu family in the city of Jinsha, but she died at the tender age of eight, so instead I took a bride from the Chen clan by the name of Yun (Rue), who used the courtesy name Shuzhen (Lovely Treasure).[3] She was the

---

1. Su Shi (1037–1101), also called Su Dongpo, was a renowned poet, lyricist, essayist, artist, and official of the Northern Song dynasty. This line comes from his poem: "On the Twentieth Day of the First Month, I Accompanied Pan and Guo on a Spring Outing to the Suburbs . . ." (Zhengyue ershi ri yu Pan Guo er sheng chujiao xunchun . . .), which begins: "The east wind will not yet enter East Gate, / on horseback we return to find the village of yesteryear. / People are like autumn geese bringing word again, / but the past is a spring dream that fades without a trace."
2. The *Classic of Poetry* (*Shi jing*) is a collection of 305 poems of folk and court origins that reached a stable form around 600 BCE. Confucius praised the moral purity of the collection as "having no untoward thoughts" and it entered the canon of Confucian learning. The collection begins with "Osprey's Cry" (Guan ju), which is traditionally read as a song of proper royal courtship and was often cited as a rationale for discussing conjugal matters in literature.
3. Chinese people of the educated classes traditionally had several names: a personal name (*ming*) given at birth, a courtesy name (*zi*) used among peers in adulthood, and one or more sobriquets (*hao*), which were

1

daughter of my maternal uncle, Mr. Chen Xinyu.

Yun was born with a quick mind and learned to recite all of Bai Juyi's "Mandolin Ballad" when she was still learning to speak.[4] At the age of four she lost her father, which left only her mother, a woman of the Jin clan, and her younger brother, Kechang, in a house with little more than four bare walls.

As Yun grew older, she learned the art of needlework and was able to provide for a family of three relying on nothing more than the effort of her ten fingers, even making enough extra money to send her brother to a tutor for his studies.

One day, she found a copy of "Mandolin Ballad" in Kechang's book chest and was able to make out some of the characters in the piece that she knew so well by heart and thus taught herself to read. When she took a break from her stitching, she would often compose and chant poetry of her own. One of her memorable couplets reads: "Autumn encroaches on my shadow wasting away; / frost paints the chrysanthemums growing full."

When I was thirteen, during a trip with my mother to visit her side of the family, Yun and I got along famously, and I was even able to see some of the poems she wrote. I sighed aloud over her talent and elegance of expression, but I secretly worried that her exceptional talent might mean that her good fortune would not last. Even so, I could not get her out of my mind and declared to my mother, "If you would choose a wife for me, let it be Sister Shuzhen or I will not marry at all!"[5]

My mother was also fond of her gentle manner, so she promptly took a gold ring from her own finger and presented it to Yun as our engagement ring. This was on August 11, 1775, in the fortieth year of the Qianlong reign.

~

---

invented at will and used as playful pseudonyms for cultural activities such as poetry and painting. The normal sequence of names is the family name followed by whichever of the first names is appropriate for the circumstances.

4. Bai Juyi (772–846) was a renowned and prolific Tang dynasty poet. His poetry was easily understood and widely circulated orally. His "Mandolin Ballad" (Pipa xing) is a long narrative poem that he wrote during his exile when he met a retired mandolin performer who told him of her glory days as a courtesan in the capital before her beauty faded and she ended up marrying an itinerant tea merchant.

5. The appellation "sister" was used as an affectionate form of address for female relations of the same generation.

In winter of that same year, I returned with mother for Yun's older female cousin's wedding.

Yun and I were close in age—she was only ten months older—and we had always called each other Elder Sister and Younger Brother ever since we were young, so I continued calling her Sister Shuzhen just like old times.

The whole house was filled with people dressed up in the latest fashions—save for Yun, who wore subdued colors over her entire body except for a new pair of embroidered slippers. I saw the exquisite needlework on them, and when I found out that they were her own handiwork I realized that her intelligence was not limited to wielding brush and ink alone.

Yun had slender shoulders and a graceful neck and was quite slim without being gaunt. Her eyebrows arched delicately over her lovely eyes, and she was always looking about brightly in high spirits. Her front teeth did show a bit too much, which is an unlucky trait, but she had such a winning way about her that one was soon lost in her charms.

I asked to see the poems she had been working on, and it turned out that some were just one couplet, others just three or four lines, and most were unfinished. When I asked her why, she just laughed and replied, "I did them without a teacher, but I would like to find someone discerning who might guide me in whipping them into shape." So I playfully inscribed her notebook with the title, "Brocade Pouch of Fine Verses." Little did I know at the time that this concealed an omen of her life being cut short.[6]

~

Later that night I saw my newly married cousin off to her new home in the outskirts of the city, and by the time I got back the water clock was showing past midnight.

My stomach was empty, so I asked for a little something to eat. One of the serving girls presented me with some dried dates, but they were too sweet for my taste. Then Yun quietly took me by my sleeve and led me to her own room, where I saw that she had set

---

6. This is an allusion to the Tang dynasty poet Li He (791–816), who was known for his precocious talent and ghostly imagery. As a boy he would roam about on a donkey in search of poetic inspiration, writing down any lines that came to him and tossing them into an old brocade pouch to finish later. When his mother saw how many poems he was working on, she lamented that his obsession would drive him to "spit out his heart." He died at the age of twenty-seven.

aside some warm rice congee with pickled garnishes for me.

I happily picked up my chopsticks to eat when I suddenly heard Yun's older male cousin, Yuheng, calling out, "Sister Shuzhen, come quick!"

Yun rushed over to shut the door, calling back, "I'm exhausted and was about to lie down," but Yuheng squeezed his way into the room.

When he saw me there, ready to eat the congee, he looked askance at Yun and laughed, "Hey! Just now when I was looking for some congee to eat, you told me that it was all gone! But you were saving it as a special treat for your little 'husband' here, right?"

Yun was so embarrassed that she ran straight from her room, trailed by loud laughter from everyone in the house. I was so upset for her that I called for my old servant and left before she could return.

After the mockery over the "congee incident," whenever I went back, Yun would hide herself away from me, and I knew it was because she was afraid of having everyone laugh at her again.

~

On February 26, 1780, in the forty-fifth year of the Qianlong reign, I could see by the flickering light of our wedding candles that Yun's figure was just as delicate as before.

When her bridal veil was lifted, she looked at me and smiled warmly. After we had sipped wine together from the wedding cups, we sat down next to one another at our banquet table with our shoulders touching. I secretly took her hand into my own beneath the table, and her warm, smooth, delicate touch set my heart to thumping wildly within my chest.

I invited her to eat first, but she had just started her vegetarian fast, which she had been doing at regular intervals for the past several years. I did a mental calculation and realized that the first time she went on one of these fasts was when I had chickenpox, so I laughed and teased her, "Now that my skin has cleared up without a spot left, surely you can give up your vow of abstinence?"

Yun smiled at my request with a glance of her eyes and assented with a nod of her head.

~

On the twenty-eighth, my own elder sister was also to be married and as the day before was a memorial day in honor of our previous emperor during which celebrations were not permitted, my sister had to hold her farewell banquet on the same night after our wedding on the twenty-sixth.

Yun went out to attend the banquet, but I stayed behind in our wedding chambers and lost repeatedly at an odds-and-evens drinking game with the bridesmaids until I was so drunk that I fell asleep. When I came to the next day Yun was already putting on her makeup for the morning. All that day an endless line of kinfolk and friends arrived until the wedding lanterns were lit that evening and the celebration could finally begin.

At midnight on the twenty-eighth, as a newly minted brother-in-law, I escorted my sister to her new home. I returned in the wee hours to find the celebrations over, the lanterns burned low, and the household silent. I made my way quietly back to our room only to find the servant woman dozing at the foot of the bed while Yun herself was undressed but still wide awake. A candle shone brightly beside her as she bent her pale neck to read with rapt attention a book I did not recognize. I stroked her shoulder and said, "You've been so busy these past few days, Sister. What are you studying there so diligently?"

Yun quickly turned to face me, then got to her feet, saying, "I was going to bed just now when I found this book in the bookshelf and started to read it straight through without giving a thought to being tired! I've heard about *Romance of the Western Chamber* many times, but this is the first time that I've actually seen a copy. It really does deserve its reputation as a work of genius even if it is a touch risqué in places."[7]

I laughed and replied, "Only a genius could be risqué purely through his writing."

The old servant woman interrupted to suggest that we go to sleep, but I told her to leave and shut the door behind her. Then Yun and I sat down next to each other on the bed, our shoulders touching, laughing and teasing each other like old friends newly reunited. I playfully reached for her breast and felt that her heart was thumping as wildly as my own, so I bent close to her ear and whispered, "Sister, why is your heart pounding so quickly?" She

---

7. *Romance of the Western Chamber* (*Xixiang ji*) was an extremely popular Yuan dynasty play attributed to Wang Shifu (ca. 1260–1336) that details an illicit love affair between a young woman and a young scholar staying at a Buddhist monastery. It was controversial for its explicit depiction of premarital sex and for its condoning of a freely chosen marriage based on passion rather than familial arrangements. The plot of the play (with a revised happy ending) was drawn from the famous Tang dynasty classical tale "Yingying's Story" (*Yingying zhuan*) by Yuan Zhen (779–831).

glanced up at me and smiled in a way that sent a jolt of passion into my very soul. I took her in my arms and we went behind the bed curtains, where we stayed, oblivious to the brightening of the sky in the east.

~

As a newlywed, Yun was very quiet at first and would never look upset about anything through the course of a day, just smiling back whenever anyone spoke to her.

She served those above her with respect and treated those below her with kindness. She was always well organized and never let anything slip in the slightest. Each morning, when the sun first peeked in the window, she would throw on some clothes and leap into action as though someone were shouting at her to get moving. I would smile when she did this and say, "It's not like the 'congee incident' anymore. You can't still be afraid that people will laugh at you?"

"Ever since I saved some congee for you, it has been a joke in our family," she replied. "I'm not afraid of being laughed at anymore; I'm afraid that your parents might say your new wife is lazy."

I would have loved for her to stay in bed with me longer each morning, but I had to admire her integrity, so I began to get up early with her. From then on we stuck together as close as a body and its shadow and the love we shared was beyond the power of words to describe.

~

Times of joy pass quickly and the first month of our marriage was gone in the blink of an eye.

At that time, my father, Jiafu, was serving as a private secretary in the government offices at Kuaiji (Shanyin). He sent word for me to join him there to study with a teacher by the name of Master Zhao Xingzhai from Hangzhou. Master Zhao was the most patient of teachers and it is thanks to his efforts that I am able to use this writing brush now.

I had agreed that I would serve at my father's side after my wedding ceremony, but I still felt extremely disappointed reading his letter. I was afraid that Yun might burst into tears when I told her that I would be going away, but she put on a brave face, urged me to go, and even prepared everything for my journey. That evening all I noticed was a subtle change in her demeanor and expression. As she was seeing me off, she said to me in a small voice, "There'll be no one there to take care of you, so make sure to look after yourself."

As I boarded the boat and they cast off the moorings, the peach and plum blossoms were each vying to be more beautiful than the other and yet I suddenly felt as though I were a bird lost from its flock and the whole world seemed drained of its color. Right after I arrived at my father's offices, he set off on an eastward journey across the river.

~

I stayed there for three months; but it felt as though I had been separated from Yun for ten years.

She wrote occasionally, but her letters contained twice as many questions as answers and I was frustrated that they were mostly words of encouragement with polite civilities filling out the rest. Every time I heard the breeze in the bamboo outside or saw the moon rising through the plantain leaves in the window, she would be called to my mind until my very dreams and soul were shaken.

My teacher knew how I was feeling, so he wrote a letter to my father informing him that he had assigned ten essay topics for me and sent me home on temporary leave. I was as elated as a solider being dismissed from frontier duty.

On the boat home, every quarter hour seemed a year. When I finally arrived at our house, I paid my respects to my mother and then made my way straight to our room. Yun rose to meet me and we clasped hands, barely able to speak a word as our souls suddenly seemed to dissolve and flow together like mist and clouds, leaving nothing but a clear ringing sound in my ears and the feeling that I had left my body.

~

The heat indoors was stifling in July.

Luckily, our home was next to the Pavilion of Azure Waves, just west of the Lotus Lover's Abode. By a wooden bridge overlooking the water, there was a banquet hall called My Choice after the song that says you can choose to rinse your cap strings when waters run clear or to rinse your feet when waters run muddy.[8]

---

8. "Fisherman's Song" (Yu ge) is an ancient folksong cited in the Confucian classic *Mencius* (*Mengzi*) (4A.8) that speaks of suiting one's actions to the tenor of the times: "If azure waters run clear, they may serve to rinse my cap strings; / if azure waters run muddy, they may serve to rinse my feet." In times of peace one serves a capable ruler by wearing

Just in front of the hall was an old tree that cast shade across the windows so deep that it painted the faces of the people inside with emerald hues. All day people would stroll back and forth on the opposite bank. My father, Jiafu, would entertain his guests at private functions in this spot, and I was able to get permission from my mother to take Yun there to while away the hot summer days.

It was too hot for Yun to do her needlework, so she kept me company instead while I studied my books and we talked about the olden days and did nothing more than enjoy the moon and flowers. Yun was not a big drinker, but if I coaxed her she would have a few cups, so I taught her how to play a few drinking games involving poetry. We felt that no one else's delight in this world could surpass our own.

~

One day, Yun asked me, "Of all the works of classical prose, which would make the best model to follow?"

"Well," I replied, "I would borrow from the cleverness of the *Schemes of the Warring States* and *Zhuangzi*,[9] the elegance of Kuang Heng and Liu Xiang,[10] the erudition of Sima Qian and Ban

---

the cap of an official; but in times of chaos one retreats into reclusion. The Pavilion of Azure Waves is also named after this passage.

9. *Schemes of the Warring States* (*Zhanguo ce*) was compiled from received materials by Liu Xiang (79–8 BCE) in the Western Han dynasty and includes almost five hundred short anecdotes, organized by region, purporting to record memorable speeches made at the different courts of the Warring States era (402–221 BCE). *Zhuangzi* is a famous canonical work of Daoist philosophy compiled by many hands over centuries with a core set of chapters by a thinker named Zhuang Zhou (fourth century BCE). The book uses fanciful parables and paradoxical arguments to explore the nature of personal freedom and was often a source of escape for people who felt constrained by conventional mores.

10. Kuang Heng (fl. first century BCE) was an influential Western Han dynasty Grand Councilor and scholar of the *Classic of Changes* (*Yi jing*) who memorialized the emperor on how to encourage peace and harmony in the land. Liu Xiang (79–78 BCE) was a royal prince and bibliographer of the same era who compiled and edited many famous collections such as *Biographies of Virtuous Women* (*Lienü zhuan*) and *Classic of Mountains and Seas* (*Shanhai jing*).

Gu,[11] the rusticity of Han Yu and the austerity of Liu Zongyuan,[12] the ease of Ouyang Xiu, and the disputation of the Three Sus.[13] Furthermore, there are the proposals of Jia Yi and Dong Zhongshu,[14] the parallel prose of Yu Xin and Xu Ling,[15] and the memorials of Lu Zhi.[16] There are countless models to learn from, but you really learn how to write from your own heart and mind."

"Classical prose lies in the realm of deep understanding and powerful spirit," Yun replied. "I'm afraid studying its intricacies

---

11. Sima Qian (?145–?86 BCE) of the Western Han dynasty was China's greatest historian. He completed a work of private history started by his father (Sima Tan) called *Historical Records* (*Shi ji*)—a 130-volume comprehensive, categorized history of China from earliest times to the reign of Emperor Wu (r. 141–87 BCE). It provided a model for Ban Gu (32–92 CE), an Eastern Han dynasty historian who compiled China's first history dedicated to a single dynasty: *History of the [Western] Han* (*Han shu*).

12. Han Yu (768–824) was a towering Tang dynasty literary figure who advocated a move away from the overly ornate, abstruse style of parallel prose writing (*piantiwen*) popular in his time in favor of returning to a simpler, more lucid "old-style prose" (*guwen*) based on early exemplars such as *Mencius* and Sima Qian's *Historical Records*. His contemporary, Liu Zongyuan (773–819), was also a celebrated master of this minimalist prose style.

13. Ouyang Xiu (1007–1072) was a powerful Northern Song statesman, historian, and arbiter of literary taste who was famous for his poetry, prose, and calligraphy. He was a fervent advocate of Han Yu's "old-style prose" and sought to convey a free and unrestrained quality in his own prose writing. The Three Sus refer to Su Xun (1009–1066) and his two sons, Su Shi (see n. 1) and Su Che (1039–1112), who both passed the imperial examinations under the patronage of Ouyang Xiu. The Three Sus were skilled essayists and, along with Han Yu, Liu Zongyuan, and Ouyang Xiu, are counted among the Eight Great Prose Writers of the Tang and Song dynasties.

14. Jia Yi (201–169 BCE) was a famous poet, essayist, and Confucian scholar of the Western Han dynasty known for his rhapsodies (*fu*) and essays. Dong Zhongshu (179–?104 BCE) was an official instrumental in establishing Confucianism as state doctrine during the Western Han dynasty and was famous for writing lucid, compelling political essays.

15. Yu Xin (513–581) and Xu Ling (507–583) were both Southern dynasties' (420–589) writers known for their poems, rhapsodies (*fu*), and essays in parallel prose.

16. Lu Zhi (754–805) served as Grand Councilor under Emperor Dezong (r. 780–805) in the Tang dynasty and was acclaimed for his graceful and lucid memorials to the throne.

poetry, a means of entertainment, is considered a lesser art form

is beyond the grasp of a woman. The only path left to me is poetry, for I do have a slight grasp of that."

"Poetry was used during the Tang dynasty to select men of talent to become officials, but the great masters of poetry were certainly Li Bai and Du Fu.[17] Who would you prefer as your model?"

Yun opined, "Du Fu's poems are forged with purity, while Li Bai's poems are carefree and unrestrained. When it comes to emulating their style, I would take Li Bai's liveliness over Du Fu's severity."

"But Du Fu is a paragon among poets, and all students of poetry revere him! Why would you alone choose Li Bai?"

"For precision in prosody and aptness of diction it's true that Du Fu reigns supreme, but Li Bai's poetry seems to come from a divine hand; it has the charm of a fallen blossom carried away by a stream and captivates a person. I wouldn't say that Du Fu is second to Li Bai, just that fondness for Li Bai runs deeper in my heart than reverence for Du Fu."

"I never suspected," I said with a smile, "that Blue Lotus Li would speak to the heart of my Lovely Treasure Chen!"[18]

Yun smiled back and said, "There is still my very first teacher, Master Bai Juyi, whom I have always cherished with unchanging devotion."

"What do you mean?"

"Well, didn't he write 'Mandolin Ballad'?"

"Extraordinary!" I exclaimed with a laugh. "Li *Bai* speaks to your heart, *Bai* Juyi is your first teacher, and I—with the courtesy name of San-*bai*—am your husband. Are you fated to have some sort of connection with the word *bai* [white]?"

"If I do have a connection to the word *bai*, I'm afraid it might mean that I will leave many white spots in my compositions!" In our regional Wu dialect we called incorrectly written characters,

---

17. Li Bai (701–762) was the most famous poet in Chinese history. He was known as the Poetry Immortal and was loved for his eccentric and outrageous style, which drew upon fantastic images from history and myth, and for his near constant state of drunkenness. His more staid contemporary, Du Fu (712–770), eventually came to be recognized as the greatest poet in Chinese history. He was called the Poetry Sage or the Poet Historian in later ages and was revered for his technical prowess and moral commitment.

18. Qinglian Jushi (Blue Lotus Hermit) was one of Li Bai's many sobriquets. Shen Fu calls Yun by her own courtesy name here—Shuzhen (Lovely Treasure).

"white characters."[19]

We both laughed out loud at this and then I asked her, "As you already know so much about poetry, you should also know the ins and outs of the rhapsody form."[20]

"It is descended from *Songs of Chu*, but my knowledge beyond that is slight and I find it very difficult to understand.[21] Among the rhapsody writers of the Han and Jin dynasties who had a command of euphony and refined language, it seems to me that Sima Xiangru stands out as the best."[22]

I teased her by saying, "So perhaps *that's* why Zhuo Wenjun ran off with her lover, Xiangru, and not because of his prowess with the zither." We finished our conversation with a good laugh about this.

~

Now, while my nature is to be quite direct and uninhibited, Yun tended to be a bit old fashioned and a stickler for rules of etiquette.

Whenever I helped her into a jacket or adjusted her sleeves for her, she would always thank me repeatedly. If I handed her a handkerchief or a fan, she would always rise to receive it. At first, I was annoyed by this and told her, "Are you trying to keep me at bay with all this politeness? Don't you know the saying, 'Too much courtesy must mean treachery?'"

Yun's cheeks flushed red and she said, "I treat you with respect and courtesy and you repay me by speaking of treachery?"

"But respect lies within one's heart, not in empty formalities."

---

19. White is also the traditional color of mourning in China.

20. The rhapsody (*fu*) was a genre of showy, complicated, lengthy rhyming prose that came to prominence during the Han dynasty as a means of displaying literary talent at court.

21. *Songs of Chu* (*Chu ci*) is an anthology of poetry that originated in the Warring States kingdom of Chu in south China. The most prominent pieces in it are attributed to Qu Yuan (?340–?278 BCE), a Chu culture hero who was exiled from the court of King Huai of Chu (r. 328–299 BCE). The extravagant Chu style of poetry, distinct from the more sober northern *Classic of Poetry*, was imitated in the Western Han court.

22. Sima Xiangru (179–117 BCE) was a colorful Western Han dynasty literary figure and the undisputed master of the rhapsody form who wrote some of the genre's most famous pieces. He was involved in a controversy when a young widow, Zhuo Wenjun, the daughter of a wealthy salt merchant, eloped with him after hearing him play the zither. The couple were estranged from their families and were forced to open a wine shop to make ends meet until Sima Xiangru was called to court and awarded a post by the emperor, who admired his poetic talents.

"No one is more dear to us than our parents; could we actually respect them in our hearts alone while being reckless in our actions and words?"

"I was only joking when I said that!"

"Many a falling out in this world start with a single joke. You must be kinder to me from now on or I shall die of frustration."

I took her in my arms and after I comforted her she relaxed and began to smile. From that moment on the expressions "May I?" and "Thank you" became part of our daily conversation. We were to live together as a devoted husband and wife for three and twenty years, and our feelings for one another grew more intimate with each passing year.

At home, if we met each other in a darkened room or bumped into one another in a narrow hallway, we would clasp hands and ask each other, "Where are you off to?" Our secretive hearts would be aflutter as though we feared someone might see us at any moment. The truth is that we started out not letting anyone see us walk together or sit side by side, but after a while it did not concern us anymore. If Yun happened to be sitting down to chat with someone and she saw me come into the room, she would always stand up and move over to let me sit down next to her. Neither of us really thought about why we were acting this way, and we were even sheepish about it at first; but after a while it just seemed to happen naturally. I have always found it odd when older couples look upon each other as sworn enemies and have never understood the thinking behind it. Some people say, "If they didn't act like that, how could they last until they were old and white-haired together?" I wonder if this is really true.

~

On August 6, 1780, during the Seventh Night Festival of that year, Yun set up a small altar with incense sticks and pieces of melon and fruit in My Choice Hall, where we made our obeisance to the Weaving Girl star.[23]

---

23. Legend has it that the Weaving Girl star (Vega) fell in love with the Herd Boy star (Altair), but the Heavenly Emperor forbade their love and slashed the sky to form a River of Stars (the Milky Way) to keep the lovers separated for eternity. Once a year, on the seventh night of the seventh month in the lunar calendar, magpies took pity on the lovers and flew up into the sky to form a bridge, allowing them to be reunited. Young women would pray to the Weaving Girl for skills in the domestic arts and to find a good husband.

I carved two square seal stamps with the words "May we be together now and forever as husband and wife." I took the seal carved in relief and gave Yun the incised seal so that we might use them to mark our letters to one another.

That night the moonlight was particularly lovely and we turned our eyes down to the river, where we saw the light shimmer upon the waves like fine white silk. We sat there together in that small window overlooking the water, dressed in summer robes, fanning ourselves gently. Then we raised our eyes to see scudding clouds break into countless shapes as they crossed the sky.

"The cosmos is so vast," said Yun, "yet we all share this same moon. I wonder if there is another couple in this world at this very moment who share a love equal to ours."

"People everywhere like to take the cool evening air beneath the moon," I said. "When it comes to savoring splendid clouds, you might find quite a few women in their boudoirs admiring them secretly in their hearts to be sure, but I wager when a couple views them together what they end up savoring is not found in the splendid clouds." Before long, the candles burned low, the moon sank in the sky, and we cleared away the plates of fruit and went to bed.

~

August 14, 1780, was the full moon in the middle of the month, known as the Ghost Festival, so Yun prepared a small tray of wine and snacks to invite the moon to drink with us.[24]

But the sky suddenly grew overcast and as dark as a moonless night. Yun's face looked troubled and she said, "If I'm meant to grow old and white-haired with you, then the full moon should show itself!"

I too was saddened, but then I caught sight of fireflies flickering as countless points of light against the far bank, weaving their way through the willow fronds and wild grasses on the island in the river. So I started up a game of linked verse with Yun to chase away our bad mood.[25] After just two turns, we already found

---

24. During the Ghost Festival on the full moon of the fifteenth day of the seventh lunar month the gates of the underworld were opened to allow the souls of the deceased to return home, where family members set out offerings of food for them.

25. Producing linked verse (*lian ju*) was a popular literary pastime that could be extended indefinitely in which one participant would improvise the first line of a couplet and the next would come up with a matching line to complete it.

ourselves feeling more relaxed with each new couplet and even got a little carried away, calling out whatever silly thing came to mind. Yun nearly choked with laughter, and tears were streaming down her face as she laughed her way right into my arms, unable to get another word out. The rich fragrance of jasmine-scented hair oil rose to my nostrils as I patted her on the back and spoke of something else to help her calm down.

"I always imagined that women in the olden days used jasmine buds to adorn their hairstyles because they looked like pearls. I never knew that when this flower is mingled with the smell of hair oil and makeup its fragrance becomes even more captivating. It leaves the scent of a citron offering far behind."

Yun stopped laughing to say, "The citron is a gentleman among fragrances and lingers with the utmost subtlety, while jasmine is a commoner, borrowing its influence from other scents while it toadies and simpers."

"If that's true, then why do you hold yourself apart from the gentleman and stay with the commoner?"

"Because I'm mocking the gentleman for loving a commoner, that's why!"

While we were chatting, the water clock had advanced to midnight. Slowly, much to our delight, we saw the wind sweep away the clouds to reveal a full moon. We leaned on the windowsill and drank to the moon, but before we finished our third cup, we suddenly heard a great splashing noise from beneath the bridge as though someone had fallen into the water. I thrust my head out the window and scanned the waters carefully, but they were as flat and bright as a mirror in the moonlight and I could not see anyone. All I heard was the sound of a duck scurrying away on the sandy shoals. I knew that the area around Azure Waves was the favorite haunt of ghosts of people who had drowned, but I did not dare to mention this to Yun for fear of her timid constitution.

"Oh!" Yun cried. "That noise! Where did it come from?"

We could not stop ourselves from trembling, so we hurriedly shut the window and brought the wine back into the room. The oil lamp was sputtering, casting spooky shadows on the bed curtains that made it hard for us to calm down. I cleaned the lamp wick to make it brighter and brought it into bed, but Yun was already having an attack of feverish chills. I fell ill soon after, and the two of us suffered for almost three weeks. It was truly a case of disaster arriving at the height of delight as well as an omen that we were not destined to grow old and white-haired together. ⌉

~

With the arrival of the Mid-Autumn Festival on September 13, 1780, I was on the mend.[26]

By then, Yun and I had been married for half a year and she had yet to set foot in the Pavilion of Azure Waves next door. So I sent one of our old servants to arrange with the gatekeeper to turn away any visitors to the pavilion. As evening came, I accompanied Yun and my younger sister, with a servant woman and a servant girl to help us along. Another old servant led the way as we crossed over the stone bridge and entered the main gate, then veered eastward, making our way into the garden along a winding pathway. There we found boulders piled up into mountains, surrounded by lush forests of green vegetation, with the pavilion itself perched atop an earthen hill. We climbed up to the very center of the pavilion, where one can survey for miles around as far as the eye can see. Smoke from kitchen chimneys rose on all sides in the burning afterglow of the day. There was a spot on the far shore named Mountainside Forest where high-ranking officials used to gather on their outings. In those days, the Academy of Orthodox Teachings had yet to be built on the site.[27]

We had brought a blanket with us that we spread out in the middle of the pavilion so that we could all sit in a circle together and enjoy freshly brewed tea brought to us by the gatekeeper. Before long the full bright moon peeked out over the treetops and we felt our sleeves begin to flutter in the breeze. The moonlight touched the heart of the rippling waters below and all our mundane worries and dusty concerns were washed away.

"Today's little outing has been so delightful!" exclaimed Yun. "If only we could hire a small boat to drift to and fro down there; wouldn't that be even more wonderful?"

But it was already time to light the lanterns for the Mid-Autumn Festival, and, mindful of our frightening experience the month before, we decided to help each other down from the pavilion and return home.

---

26. During the Mid-Autumn Festival on the fifteenth day of the eighth lunar month people celebrated by going on outings to enjoy the full moon and to see elaborate displays of lanterns.

27. The Academy of Orthodox Teachings was a school established in Suzhou by powerful government officials in 1805.

During the festival it is our custom in the Suzhou area that all the women come out in groups to stroll on this evening, from wealthy and poor families alike. We call it "Walking by Moonlight." The grounds at Azure Waves are laid out with great elegance and generous proportions, but not a single person was there that evening.

~

My father, Jiafu, was fond of taking on protégés, so I actually have twenty-six older and younger "brothers" with surnames different from my own.

My mother also took on nine sworn "daughters," two of whom—Second Sister Wang and Sixth Sister Yu—got along well with Yun. Wang was a foolish girl who liked to drink, while Yu was a bold girl who liked to talk. Every time they got together with Yun, they would shoo me out of my own room and sleep together in the same bed, which was Yu's idea.

"Just wait until *you* get married, little sister," I said to her with a laugh. "I'll invite your husband over to stay here for at least ten days!"

"Then I'll come here too," Yu replied, "and sleep in your wife's bed! Wouldn't that be grand?" Yun and Wang just smiled at this and said nothing.

~

Around the time my younger brother, Qitang, was getting married, we moved to Granary Lane by Watering the Horse Bridge.

Although the rooms were spacious, they were not as tasteful as our quarters by the Pavilion of Azure Waves. For my mother's birthday, we hired an opera troupe to put on a performance and Yun found it to be quite a spectacle at first. My father was not superstitious about taboos, so among other pieces he requested an excerpt called "Tragic Parting." The veteran actors gave vivid performances and everyone in the audience was moved.[28]

Through the gauze curtain I spied Yun suddenly get up and leave.[29] She did not come out for a long time, so I went inside

---

28. "Tragic Parting" likely refers to "Tragic Sight" (Can du), a popular excerpt from an early Qing dynasty play called *Slaughter of the Loyalists* (*Qian zhong lu*), about a violent purge of officials at the end of the Ming dynasty.

29. A sheer curtain was suspended in front of female spectators during the performance to shield them from public view.

to look for her. Sisters Yu and Wang soon followed. We saw Yun seated alone at her dressing table with her chin in her hand.

"Why so unhappy?" I asked her.

"Watching an opera performance is meant to be a way to relax, but today's show is really quite heart wrenching!" Yun replied.

Both Yu and Wang laughed at her.

"It's because she feels things so deeply," I explained to them.

"Are you just going to sit here alone like this all day?" Yu asked her.

"I'll wait until there's something I can bear to watch before I go back," Yun replied.

After Wang heard this, she went back to ask mother to request "Assassinating Liang," "A Sequel to Seeking," and other excerpts; then she convinced Yun to come back out and Yun finally started to feel better.[30]

~

My eldest paternal uncle, Sucun, passed away early in life before having any children of his own, so my father designated me to act as his heir.

My uncle's grave site was at the edge of our ancestral burial grounds at the Western Span Embankment on Longevity Hill. Every spring I would take Yun with me to pay my respects and to sweep the gravesite. Sister Wang heard that there was a famous scenic site in the area called Halberd Garden, so she asked once if she could come along with us.

While we were there, Yun spotted a small pile of stones on the ground that were streaked with a mossy pattern and mottled with lovely hues. She pointed them out to me, saying, "If we arrange these in a basin in the shape of a tiny mountain, they would have a better air of the ancient than the usual white rocks from Xuanzhou."

---

30. "Assassinating Liang" (Ci Liang) is an excerpt from the drama *Delight of the Fishing Family* (*Yujia le*), by the prolific early Qing dynasty playwright Zhu Zuochao. It tells the story of an old fisherman's courageous daughter who avenges her father's murder by assassinating the most powerful and corrupt official of the Eastern Han dynasty, Liang Ji (d. 159 CE). "Sequel to Seeking" (Hou suo) is an excerpt from the play *Sequel to Seeking Lost Relatives* (*Hou xun qin*) by Qing playwright Yao Ziyi (fl. 1692), which tells a convoluted tale of financial intrigues. In this excerpt the wife of an impoverished man in exile is able to reclaim a debt owed to her husband.

"I'm afraid we won't be able to find enough of them," I replied.

Wang chimed in, "If you really like them so much, then I'll gather some for you." She went straight to the grave keeper to borrow a gunnysack and then began to step carefully over the ground as deliberately as a crane picking out the stones. Each time she got one, I would say "Fine!" and she would put it in the bag, or I would say "No!" and she would toss it away. Before long, her powdered face was glowing with perspiration and she brought the sack back to us, saying, "Any more and I won't be strong enough to carry this!"

Yun set about choosing the best stones and told us, "I've heard that if you want to harvest fruit from the mountainside, it's best to avail yourself of a monkey's services. Now I see how true this is!"

Wang curled her fingers up in rage and made as though she were about to tickle Yun when I stepped between them and scolded Yun, "She was doing all the work while you were taking it easy, then you say something like that? No wonder she's upset!"

On our way back, we took a stroll through Halberd Garden, where tender green leaves and lovely red blossoms vied to be the most beautiful. Wang has always been a silly girl and she just had to pluck every blossom she came across.

Yun scolded her, "We don't have a vase for those and you're not putting them in your hair, so what's the point in snapping off so many?"

"They don't feel any pain," replied Wang, "so what's the harm in it?"

I laughed and said, "When you are punished by having to marry a tassel-bearded man with pocks blooming on his face, then the flowers will have their revenge!"

Wang glared at me, flung the flowers to the ground, and kicked them into the pond with her dainty feet. "How can you be so mean to me!" she cried. Yun laughed and calmed her down before we left.

~

In the beginning, Yun was quite reticent and enjoyed simply listening to my disquisitions on various topics.

But I was able to coax her into speaking more, as one might use a slender reed of grass to prod a cricket into song, and she slowly began to voice her own opinions.

Every day Yun would soak her rice in tea and she was fond of having it with a kind of fermented bean curd in mustard sauce that people in Suzhou commonly call "stinky bean curd." She also liked a kind of pickled cucumber as a garnish for it. I have truly hated both of these things all my life, so I teased her about them by saying, "Now, a dog has no palate and will even eat dung because it doesn't realize how foul it tastes. But a dung beetle rolls up dung because it longs to transform itself into a cicada to ascend to a loftier position. So, my dear, which are you? A dog or a cicada?"

"This type of bean curd is inexpensive," she explained, "and it goes well with congee or plain rice. I've been eating it since I was a child and have acquired a taste for it. Now that I am living in your esteemed abode, it truly is as though I have transformed from a dung beetle into a cicada and yet I still enjoy eating it, for it reminds me of my humble roots. As for the pickled cucumber, I'd never tasted it before coming *here*."

"Oh, so my home is a doghouse, is it?"

Yun was embarrassed and tried to explain, "You can find dung in every household. The important distinction lies in whether one eats it or not. Now, you love to eat garlic, so I force myself to eat it. I wouldn't force stinky bean curd on you, but you could hold your nose and try a little pickled cucumber. Once you swallow it, you will realize how nice it is. It's like the Lady of Saltless Town, who was ugly in appearance but lovely in virtue."[31]

"Are you trying to turn me into a dog?" I asked with a laugh.

"Well, I've been eating like a dog for a while now, so it's high time we got you to try a taste."

She popped a piece of cucumber into my mouth with her chopsticks. I held my nose and chewed it over and found it to be wonderfully crisp, so I let go of my nose, continued to chew it, and actually found it especially tasty. From then on I enjoyed eating it too.

Sometimes Yun would mix a little sesame oil and vinegar and sugar in with salted bean curd, which was delicious. Or she would mash up pickled cucumber and mix it with salted bean curd and call it her "twice as tasty" sauce, which was quite outstanding. I once told her, "I started out hating this and ended up liking it, but I'm not sure how it happened!"

---

31. The Lady of Saltless Town (Wuyan) was a shockingly ugly woman named Zhong Lichun who gave useful political advice to King Xuan of Qi (r. 319–300 BCE). The king was so impressed with her virtues that he made her his queen despite her physical shortcomings. Her story is recorded in the *Biographies of Virtuous Women*.

"If you are fond of something, you don't mind if it's ugly," was her reply.

~

The betrothed of my younger brother, Qitang, was the grand-daughter of Mr. Wang Xuzhou.

When it came time to send her the groom's gift of jewelry and cosmetics before the wedding day, my brother happened to be short a few pearl hair ornaments, so Yun brought out some from her own betrothal gifts and presented them to my mother. All the servant girls thought it was such a shame to lose them, but Yun explained to them, "All women already belong to *yin* by nature, and pearls are the essence of *yin*. If I wear them in my hair, then any *yang* energy I have will be overpowered by them, so of what value are they to me?"[32]

Yun did, however, treasure all sorts of tattered books and damaged paintings to an almost excessive degree. She would gather up all kinds of loose pages from old books, sort them out into separate categories, collate them, and then bind them into new covers. She referred to these books as her "bits and pieces" of literature. When it came to torn scrolls of calligraphy and paintings, she would look for some matching old paper on which to remount them, then ask me if I might restore the missing places with my brush before she rolled them up again. She called these scrolls her "scraps of appreciation." Whenever she had time off from her sewing and cooking, she could spend an entire day working diligently at these pastimes without feeling tired in the least. When she was lucky enough to find a piece of paper with something worthwhile on it in a worn out chest or between the pages of a moldering book, it was as though she had acquired a priceless treasure. Old Woman Feng next door was always collecting an assortment of old books and scrolls to sell to her.

~

Yun and I had the same likings, so we were able to discern thoughts in each other's eyes and understand the language of each other's brows; in every move we made we could communicate with just

---

32. Traditional Chinese cosmology holds that the entire universe, including human beings, is made up of a carefully balanced, constantly shifting mixture of active *yang* and passive *yin* elements. Health and prosperity are more likely if one acts in accordance with these natural principles to keep them in balance.

the expressions on our faces and all would be perfectly understood between us.

I once told her, "It's a shame that you have to hide away at home as a woman. If only you could transform yourself into a man, we might visit famous mountains together, seek out ancient historical sites, and just roam beneath the sky. Wouldn't that be splendid?"

"What's so hard about that?" she replied. "Just wait until my hair turns gray and, although we won't be able to go as far as the Five Sacred Peaks, we could still visit nearby Tiger Hill and Lingyan Mountain, or even go south to West Lake or north to Mount Ping and visit all sorts of places together."[33]

"I'm just afraid that by the time your hair turns gray, you won't be able to get around very well."

"Well, if we can't do it in this life, then let's agree to do it in the next."

"If you are a man in your next life, then I will be a woman to stay with you."

"That would only appeal to me if we could still remember this life."

"We are still talking about the 'congee incident' from our childhood in this life," I laughed. "If we still remember this life in the next, then we will end up talking about our past life so much on our wedding night that we won't even have time to sleep!"

Then Yun remarked, "People say there is an Old Man beneath the Moon who is in charge of arranging marriages in the world of mortals. We were brought together in this life thanks to him, so we will have to look to his divine powers to destine our union in the next life too. Shouldn't we have an altar portrait made of him so that we can provide him with offerings?"

At that time, there was a skilled portrait artist, Qi Liudi—personal name Zun—living near Tiaoxi. We asked him for a portrait of the Old Man beneath the Moon with his red silk threads in one hand and in the other hand a staff, atop which was tied

---

33. The Five Sacred Peaks (Wuyue) refer to Mount Tai in the East, Mount Hua in the West, Mount Heng in the South, another Mount Heng in the North, and Mount Song in central China; adherents to Daoism made pilgrimages to all five. Tiger Hill (Huqiu) is a famous landmark in Suzhou said to resemble a crouching tiger. Lingyan Mountain is just southwest of Suzhou. West Lake (Xihu) is a famous scenic lake in Hangzhou, and Mount Ping is in Yangzhou.

the Register of Destined Unions.[34] In the painting, he had a youthful face with the flowing white hair of a crane and was gliding through a misty landscape. Master Qi was very proud of this particular portrait. My good friend Shi Zhuotang wrote an inscription praising the work at the top of the scroll.[35] I hung it in our room and on the first and fifteenth day of each month, Yun and I, as husband and wife, would burn incense and pray before the altar.

Afterward, because of all the trials we went through, I lost track of this painting and now I do not know in whose house it may have ended up. "The next life is unfathomable as this one draws to a close."[36] Can two people who were so madly in love really request that the gods judge in their favor again?

~

When we moved to Granary Lane, I hung a scroll over our bedroom door that read "Honored Guest's Fragrant Gallery" to capture both the aromatic qualities of Yun's name (Rue) and the old saying that a husband and wife should treat each other as respectfully as guests.

The courtyard of this new home was quite cramped and surrounded by tall walls so there was really nothing desirable about it. There was a wing of rooms at the back that led to a small library, but the windows opened onto an abandoned garden of the Lu family, which made for a bleak view. Yun began to sorely miss the lovely scenery of the old Azure Waves place.

---

34. The Old Man beneath the Moon was a mythical figure who used red silken thread to join the ankles of people as children who were destined to be married later in life. He recorded the predestined marriages in his register.

35. Shen Fu provides a brief biography in Record Three of his illustrious childhood friend Shi Zhuotang (1757–1837), who placed first in the imperial examinations of 1790, served in a series of high official posts, and employed Shen Fu after Yun's death.

36. This is a line by the Tang dynasty poet Li Shangyin (813–858), who was known for his highly cryptic and densely allusive style of poetry laced with striking and suggestive images. His poem "Mawei" describes the tragic love affair between Tang Emperor Xuanzong and his favorite concubine, Yang Guifei, who was executed to save the empire. The poem captures the longing of Emperor Xuanzong for his lost love: "In vain I hear of other lands beyond the seas; / the next life is unfathomable as this one draws to a close."

There was an old woman who lived east of Golden Mother Bridge, just north of Ridge Lane. Her house was surrounded by vegetable gardens and she had a rustic gate woven from twigs. Just outside her gate was a sizeable pond in which the reflections of the flowers and trees at the water's edge would mingle with that of the hedges. Her house sat on the site where the palace of the late Yuan dynasty rebel Zhang Shicheng once stood.[37] A few steps to the west of her house there was a rubbish heap the size of a small hill that one could scale to the top for a clear view of a sparsely populated expanse of land quite rich in natural beauty.

The old woman once spoke of all this to Yun, who could think of nothing else afterward. Yun told me, "Ever since we left Azure Waves, I return there in my dreams constantly. I know we cannot go back there, but I've been thinking about something almost as good. What about that old woman's place?"

"Well this endless late summer heat *has* been scorching," I replied, "and I've been thinking about finding a cool place to spend these long, hot days. If you want to go there, then let me go to take a look at her place first, and if it's livable, we can pack up our things and go there for a month or so. What do you think?"

"I'm afraid your parents might not allow us."

"I'll ask them myself."

So the next day I went to the old woman's house and found that it had only two rooms, but if they were each divided into front and back chambers to make four rooms and the windows were papered over and a bamboo divan were added, the place could have a refined charm to it. When the old woman found out what I had in mind, she very cheerfully let out her own bedroom to us. I papered all the walls with white paper, which immediately changed the whole look of the place. Then I informed my mother and brought Yun to live there.

The only neighbors we had were an elderly couple who made a living from tending the gardens. When they found out the two of us had come there to escape the summer heat, they came over to welcome us, bringing a fish that had been caught in the pond and some vegetables from the garden as a gift for us. We wanted to pay for these things, but they would not hear of it, so Yun made

---

37. In 1353, the salt merchant Zhang Shicheng (1321–1367) led an uprising called the Red Turban Rebellion against the Mongol rulers of the Yuan dynasty and briefly established his own fiefdom in 1356 with its capital in Suzhou.

them some shoes in return, which they refused at first but then eventually accepted.

~

[In late August, the verdant trees gathered deep shade, a breeze came across the face of the water, and the singing of cicadas buzzed in our ears.]

The old man fashioned a fishing rod for us, and I went fishing with Yun in a spot deep beneath the shady willows.

[As the sun sank, we climbed the nearby hill and took in the rosy clouds streaked by the glow of the setting sun, chanting whatever lines of poetry came to mind, such as: "The beastly clouds gulp down the setting sun, / The bow-shaped moon looses shooting stars."]

Before long the shape of the moon was imprinted on the surface of the pond and the sound of cicadas rose up on all sides. We brought out the bamboo divan and set it beneath the hedge. The old woman let us know when the wine was warmed and the food was ready so that we could toast each other in the moonlight and enjoy our meal under the pleasant spell of the wine. After an evening bath we put on comfortable sandals and fanned ourselves with palm leaves, sitting or lying down as we pleased as we listened to the old man tell tales of karmic retribution. Around midnight we went to bed, our bodies utterly cool and refreshed, feeling almost as though we did not live in the city at all.

We asked the old man next door if he might buy some chrysanthemums for us to plant all along the hedge. They bloomed in mid-October, so we stayed on there to enjoy them for an extra ten days. Even my mother was delighted to come to see them and indulge in eating crab claws by the chrysanthemums for an entire day of sheer enjoyment.

Yun said to me happily, "One day you and I should pick a spot here to build a home and buy an acre or two of land around it for gardens. We would have our servants plant melons and vegetables for us to live on. You could paint and I could do my needlework to keep us in wine and poetry. We'd be able to live out our days in delight with humble clothes and simple food and never have to think about leaving again." I had deeply hoped to make all this come true. Now the place is still there, but the one who knew me is gone and I can do nothing but sigh deeply.

~

About a quarter mile from our home there is a temple in Vinegar House Lane that was built to honor the Lord of Lake Dongting.

Most people call it Water Spirit Temple and it has winding verandas and a modest arbor.[38]

On the Lord's birthday the prominent local families each claim a spot to hang up special glass lanterns, set up elaborate thrones, and put out vases on stands with flower arrangements in a sort of competition. The whole day is given over to opera performances and the night brings all sorts of candles of different shapes and sizes scattered among the flowers, which is known as the Floral Illumination. Aromas waft forth from the elaborate incense burners amid the glowing flowers and flickering lanterns, making it really seem like a night banquet in the palace of the Dragon King. The heads of the families play the flute, sing songs, or chat idly over tea, while onlookers gather around like ants in such numbers that they have to put up a fence beneath the eaves of the temple to keep them out.

I was once invited by a group of friends to arrange flowers with them at the temple, so I was able to see the splendor of the occasion for myself. When I returned home, I told Yun how wondrous it was and she said, "It's such a pity that I can't go just because I'm not a man."

"Why not put on my hat and clothes to transform yourself from female to male?" I suggested. And so she switched her hairstyle from a woman's bun to a man's plaited queue hanging at the back and painted her eyebrows to make them look thicker. When she put on my cap, some of her hair still peeked out at the sides, but we were able to tuck it in. When she put on my robe, it was about two inches too long, but she was able to sew it up at the waist and cover everything up with a riding jacket.

"What should we do about my feet?" she asked.

"In the street market, they have butterfly shoes in all sorts of sizes," I suggested. "It would be easy to buy you a pair and later you could even wear them as slippers in the house. Wouldn't that be perfect?" Yun was overjoyed with our plans.

After dinner she put on the whole disguise and spent a long time imitating the gait of a man, taking long steps with her hands clasped in front of her. She had a sudden change of heart though and said, "I won't go. If I were discovered, it would cause too

---

38. Lord of Lake Dongting was the honorific title of Liu Yi, the title character in a Tang dynasty classical tale by Li Zhaowei called "The Story of Liu Yi" (Liu Yi zhuan). Liu Yi ends up marrying the daughter of the Dragon King and occupies his throne at the bottom of Lake Dongting.

much trouble, and if your parents heard about this, they would certainly disapprove."

I urged her on and said, "All the family heads at the temple will know who I am. Even if they were to find out, they would just laugh it off. And my mother is over at Ninth Sister's place right now; if we go and come back in secret how would she ever find out about it?"

Yun took a look at herself in the mirror and burst into uncontrollable laughter. I grabbed her hand and the two of us stole out of the house. We strolled around the temple grounds without a single person realizing that she was a woman. Whenever anyone asked who she was, I would just say that she was a younger cousin, and she would clasp her hands before her in greeting and move on.

Finally, we arrived at a spot where some young wives and their daughters were seated behind a decorated throne. They turned out to be the members of the Yang family. Yun went straight over to them and struck up a friendly conversation. She leaned in to say something and placed her hand unawares on the shoulder of one of the women.

One of their servant girls leapt to her feet in indignation, crying out, "What kind of madman are you to behave so rudely?"

I tried to say a few words to smooth things over, but Yun could see that things were taking a bad turn, so she pulled off her hat and stuck out one of her dainty feet for them to see, saying, "I'm a woman too!"

They all looked at each other in stunned silence for a moment, then their anger turned to amusement and they asked us to join them for some tea and snacks before calling for sedan chairs to see us home.

~

When Mr. Qian Shizhu died of illness in Wujiang, my father sent news by a letter home instructing me to attend the funeral on behalf of the family.

Yun said to me in private, "To get to Wujiang, you must travel by Lake Tai. I'd like to go with you to broaden my view of this world."

"I was just thinking how lonely it would be to travel on my own. It would be wonderful if you could come with me! But we need some excuse for me to bring you along."

"We could say that I'm leaving to visit my family. You could get on the boat first and then I would join you later."

"If we do that, we could even stop the boat at Eternity Bridge on our way back and relax together in the cool moonlight and pass the time as we used to do during our days at Azure Waves."

It was a cool morning on August 7 when I took my servant with me to the ferry dock at Crab River. I boarded the boat to wait for Yun, who showed up soon after in a sedan chair. We cast off and emerged from under Tiger Roar Bridge, gradually catching sight of sails and gulls, with the blue water stretching out to meet the blue sky.

"Is this really what they call the great Lake Tai?" Yun asked. "Now that I've witnessed the vastness of this world, this life is not in vain! And to think that many a woman spends all her days in her room without ever getting the chance to see this." We chatted idly and before long the wind was rustling in the willows along the shore as we had already arrived at Wujiang.

I went ashore to attend the funeral. I returned to find that the boat was deserted. I quickly questioned the boatman as to Yun's whereabouts and he pointed her out, saying, "Don't you see them over there on the long bridge, under the shade of the willows watching the cormorants dive for fish?" It turned out that Yun had accompanied the boatman's daughter ashore. I came up quietly behind them to find Yun glowing with perspiration as she leaned on the other girl, rapt in watching the birds.

I tapped on her shoulder and said, "Your flimsy blouse is soaked through with perspiration!"

Yun turned her head and replied, "I was afraid that someone from the Qian family might come with you back to the boat, so I thought I would stay out of the way for a while. What are you doing back so soon?"

"I really wanted to get away!" I said with a laugh and helped her back to the boat.

We made our return trip to Eternity Bridge, before the sun had set. We opened the window shutters on the boat to let in a cooling breeze, brought out round silk fans, changed into comfortable clothes, and cut up some melons to help dissipate the late summer heat. After a while glowing clouds shone on the reddening bridge, mist enveloped the darkening willows, the silvery moon began to rise, and fishing boat lanterns filled the waters.

We sent our servant to have a drink with the boatman in the stern. The boatman's daughter was named Suyun. I found her personality refreshing when I had shared drinks with her in the past, so I called her over to sit with Yun. There were no lanterns lit at the bow of the boat, so we were able to enjoy our wine under the moonlight and play our favorite poetic drinking game. Suyun could only blink her eyes at us in bewilderment as she listened for a good while, until she finally said, "I'm an old hand at running drinking games, but I've never heard of this one before! Can you teach it to me?"

Yun tried to explain it to her using some examples, but she was still confused. I laughed and said, "Enough of your lectures, Lady Tutor. I have a brief analogy that should clear this whole matter up."

"And what might that be, sir?" replied Yun.

"A crane is good at dancing but cannot plow. An ox is good at plowing but cannot dance. That is the natural order of things. As a teacher, when you try to go against that order, are you not just wasting your efforts?"

Suyun laughed and punched me on the shoulder, saying, "You're making fun of me!"

"You may move your lips, but not your hands!" commanded Yun. "Anyone caught breaking this rule must drink a flagon of wine." Suyun had a heroic capacity for drink, so she simply poured out a flagon of wine and polished it off in one gulp.

"Not moving your hands just means no punching; surely it must be all right to caress someone?" I inquired.

Yun laughed and pulled Suyun over to my lap, saying, "Here, caress her all you like!"

I laughed, "You don't understand these sorts of things. Caressing has to be done without the appearance of intent. If you just grab a woman and rub her all over, then you're acting like a coarse farm boy."

By now the fragrance of the jasmine blossoms pinned in their hair was being carried on the bouquet of the wine and mingled with the scent of their makeup, creating a powerful perfume that penetrated my nose. I teased them by saying, "The smell on you commoners is stinking up the whole bow of this boat and making me ill!"

Suyun could not keep from clenching her fists and pummeling me with blows, crying, "Who told you to come sniffing around here so rudely?"

"You broke the rule! Two flagons for you!" called out Yun.

"But," Suyun protested, "he insulted us by calling us commoners! Shouldn't I punch him for that?"

"He had a reason for using that term," Yun explained. "Finish these flagons off and I will tell you what it is." Suyun drained the two flagons of wine one after the other, and then Yun told her all about the time at our old place, Azure Waves, when we had been enjoying the cool air [and she had called jasmine the commoner of scents].

"Oh! If that's the case," said Suyun, "then I was truly wrong to blame you and I had best have another penalty." And with that, she drank one more flagon.

"I've long heard about the fine singing of Suyun," said Yun. "Might we hear your lovely voice?" Suyun tapped an ivory chopstick against a dish to keep time and began to sing. Yun joyfully drank her fill and, before she knew it, she was stone drunk and had to be taken home in a sedan chair. I stayed to chat with Suyun over tea for a while, then strolled home in the moonlight.

At the time, we were staying in the Tower of Tranquility at the home of my friend Lu Banfang. A few days after our trip, Mrs. Lu had the wrong idea from some idle talk that she passed on to Yun in private, saying, "Two days ago, I heard that your husband had a singing girl on each arm while drinking at Eternity Bridge. Did you know about this?"

"That's right," replied Yun. "And one of those singing girls was me!" She told her the whole affair in detail, after which Mrs. Lu gave a great laugh at the misunderstanding and went about her business.

~

In August, 1794, in the fifty-ninth year of the Qianlong reign, I returned from Guangdong with my traveling companion—my cousin's husband, Xu Xiufeng—who brought a concubine back with him.

He sang the praises of his new woman's beauty to everyone and invited Yun to come meet her. Later, Yun mentioned to Xiufeng, "She may be beautiful, but she isn't very charming."

"Ah, so if your husband were to take a concubine, she would have to be both beautiful *and* charming?" Xiufeng retorted.

"Of course," Yun said. From that point on, Yun became obsessed with hunting down a beauty, even though we were so short of money.

Just then, staying in Suzhou there was a courtesan of some renown from the Zhejiang region surnamed Wen, who went by the name Lengxiang. She had composed four verses about willow catkins; the verses were sweeping the region and winning many poems in response from her admirers. A friend of mine from Wujiang, Zhang Xianhan, had long appreciated the talents of Lengxiang. He brought by her poems on willow catkins to ask us to help him write a response to them. Yun did not think much of the woman and set aside the poems, but I was itching to show off my skills and wrote some verses matching her rhymes. Among them was one couplet that read: "They touch me with spring sorrow ever more softly; / they stir in her tender longing even moreso." Yun clapped her hands at this one to show her appreciation.

~

The next year, on September 17, 1795, my mother was going to take Yun on an excursion to Tiger Hill, when Zhang Xianhan suddenly showed up and said to me, "I'm also on my way to Tiger Hill, and I came here with the express purpose of inviting you along to find ourselves some beauties to go with us."

So I asked my mother to go on ahead with Yun and arranged to meet with them at Half Dike near Tiger Hill.

Xianhan brought me to where Lengxiang was staying and I saw for myself that she was already well into middle age. She had a girl named Hanyuan, who was not yet sixteen years old, but she was slim and graceful and truly had eyes that could "cool you as an expanse of clear autumn waters."[39] As they received us, it became readily apparent that she was quite cultured. She had a younger sister named Wenyuan, who was still a girl.

I had no rash ideas at first and was only thinking of chatting with them over a cup of wine. A humble scholar like me could not afford to do more, so when we first went in I was a bit nervous in my mind about what might happen and had to force myself to respond normally in my conversation with them. I whispered as an aside to Xianhan, "I'm only a poor scholar—how can you let such bewitching beauties trifle with me?"

"No, no, no," Xianhan laughed. "A friend of mine invited me here today to repay a favor, but he was called away to receive some important visitors. I've stepped in as host and invited you as my guest, so don't give it another thought." After hearing this, I was able to relax.

When we reached our meeting place at Half Dike and our

---

39. This is a variation on a line from "A Gift" (You zeng) by Tang dynasty poet Cui Jue (fl. 859) describing a beautiful singing girl, who could "cool you with a single glance of springtime waters."

boat met up with the other one, I told Hanyuan to go over to my mother's boat to pay her respects. When Yun and Hanyuan met each other, they immediately hit it off like old friends and went hand in hand to climb Tiger Hill to take in all the famous sights. Yun was particularly fond of the high, airy feeling at Thousand Acre Clouds, and they sat there admiring the vista for quite some time. When they got back to Wild Scent Shore, we tethered our boats together and drank to our heart's content.

When it came time to cast off, Yun came over to ask me, "Would it be all right if you go back on Mr. Zhang's boat and Hanyuan stays here to go back with me?" I agreed to this. We got as far as Capital Pavilion Bridge and there we returned to our own boats and said our farewells.

It was already past midnight when we got home and Yun said to me, "Today, I have met a girl who is both beautiful and charming. Just now, I asked Hanyuan to pay us a visit tomorrow so that I can make some plans for you."

I was somewhat shocked and said, "This is not a golden palace for royal concubines! How can a lowly scholar like me even dare to entertain such a rash notion? Besides, we have a very strong bond as husband and wife—why would we go looking for someone else?"

Yun laughed, "But I love her myself. You just wait to see how it turns out."

The next day around noontime Hanyuan did indeed arrive at our door. Yun received her with great enthusiasm. While we were eating, we played a number-guessing game with the rule that the winner would chant a poem, while the loser would take a drink. By the end of the meal, we still had not talked about our plans.

After Hanyuan went home, Yun said to me, "We just made a secret pact together that on the thirtieth she will come back here to become my sworn sister. You had best prepare some animals for the ceremonial sacrifice." Smiling, she pointed to a kingfisher jadeite bracelet on her arm and said, "If you see this bracelet on Hanyuan then you will know that she has agreed to our arrangement. I just blurted it out to her before she left, and I'm not sure that she's made up her mind completely yet."

I just listened to everything Yun said for the time being.

~

There was a big rainstorm on the thirtieth, but Hanyuan braved the rain and made it to our house.

She and Yun went into another room for a good while, then they came back out holding hands. Hanyuan looked at me somewhat bashfully and I saw that the kingfisher jade bracelet was indeed on her arm! After we had burned the incense and they took their oath of sisterhood, we had planned to pick up our drinking where we had left off before, but it turned out that Hanyuan was going on a trip to Stone Lake and had to leave straightaway.

Yun was delighted and said to me, "Now you've got your beauty; how are you going to thank your matchmaker?" I asked her about all the details of the arrangement.

"Just now," she recounted, "I spoke to Hanyuan in confidence, because I was afraid that she might already have feelings for someone else. After a few inquiries, I realized that she didn't, so I said to her, 'Little sister, do you know why you are here today?' She replied, 'To be the recipient of praise from a lady like you truly makes me feel like a lowly weed leaning against a magnificent tree of jade. But my mother considers me very valuable and I am afraid that I am not at liberty to make up my own mind in these matters. I would like to take things one step at a time with you.' Then I took my bracelet off and placed it on her arm with these words: 'From this jade bracelet, understand that our bond is as strong as the stone and as endless as the round shape. Keep it close, little sister, as a sign of our future together.' Then she said to me, 'The power to bring us together is completely in your hands, my lady.' So the way I see it, Hanyuan's heart is already with us. The hard part will be winning over her mother, Lengxiang, but I will come up with a plan for that too."

I laughed and said, "Are you trying to reenact Li Yu's play, *Loving the Fragrant Companion*?"[40]

"That's right," she replied.

And from then on not a day went by that she did not have something to say about Hanyuan. But afterward, Hanyuan would be snatched away from us by a powerful man and all our plans would come to naught. In the end, it was because of this that Yun was to die.

---

40. Li Yu (1611–1680)—courtesy name Liweng—was a prolific and flamboyant literary figure of the late Ming and early Qing dynasties who made a name for himself as an iconoclastic playwright, essayist, critic, fiction writer, and garden designer. His play *Loving the Fragrant Companion* (*Lian xiangban*) is about a wife who falls in love with a young woman and arranges for her to become her husband's concubine so that they can stay together forever.

RECORD TWO

Charms of Idleness

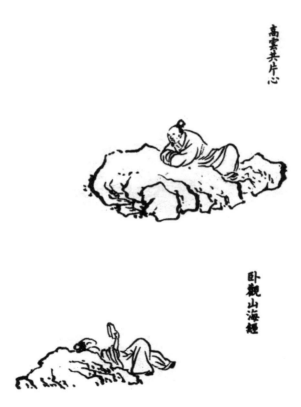

高雲共片心

卧觀山海經

I REMEMBER THAT WHEN I WAS A CHILD MY EYES WERE STRONG ENOUGH TO stare directly at the sun and I could see the tip of a fine hair with great clarity.

When I saw tiny and insignificant things, I just had to examine the patterns on their surfaces in minute detail; and often I would be transported by their otherworldly charms.

When summer mosquitoes thrummed in great swarms, I would pretend to myself that they were flocks of cranes dancing in the air. If I let my mind dwell on them, they really would appear to me as hundreds upon thousands of cranes. I would lean my head back and stare up at them until my neck was stiff. Or I might keep a few mosquitoes behind some white gauze and slowly blow incense smoke at them until they were flying and buzzing awash in a haze and appeared as white cranes soaring through blue clouds. They really did seem like cranes calling from the cloud tops, and I would cry out with delight.

I would often crouch down in the ditches by the earthen walls or among the thickly growing plants in flower beds, my eyes level with the ground. I would watch patiently until the plants appeared to me as a forest, insects as great beasts, small mounds in the gravel as mountains, dips as ravines—I would let my spirit roam over all of them without a care in the world.

One day, I saw two insects struggling among the blades of grass; I was observing them intently when a gigantic monster suddenly arrived on the scene, pulling up mountains and knocking over trees in its path. It was actually a toad, and it gulped down both insects with a flick of its tongue. I was still young at the time and had been so enrapt in the scene that my mouth fell open in shock. Once I calmed down, I caught the toad and gave it a good thrashing before banishing it from the yard. Now that I am older, I think back on that battle of the two insects and realize that it was likely an act of rape in progress. The old saying has it that "rape is close to killing." Could this be true for insects as well?

Once, while I was engrossed in these living worlds, my "egg" was breathed upon by an earthworm.[1] "Egg" is the common word we use in Suzhou for penis. It swelled up so much that I could not even urinate. The maidservants seized a duck and held its

---

1. Earthworms neither bite nor breathe, so it is unclear what actually happened to Shen Fu as he was crouching down in the garden—he may have been bitten by a venomous centipede.

beak open to breathe on my "egg," but one of them lost her grip on the bird and it lunged out its neck as though it might swallow my "egg" whole, which made me scream in terror![2] This became a favorite story to tell in my family.

All these things were the idleness of my childhood.

~

When I was older, my fondness for flowers turned into an obsession and I loved nothing more than to raise miniature bonsai plants.

It was only when I befriended Zhang Lanbo, however, that I perfected the art of pruning branches and raising cuttings, and from him I even learned methods for grafting flowers and arranging marvelous stones and pebbles.

The orchid is the paragon of flowers because of its delicate fragrance and charming beauty, but a flawless specimen worthy of the record books is hard to come by. When Zhang Lanbo was nearing the end of his life, he gave me a potted spring orchid with lotus-shaped flowers that had pure white centers. The outer leaves were smooth and broad, and the thin stems delicately supported the spotless petals. This was a plant for the record books and I cherished it as I would a fine piece of antique jade. When I was working away from home, Yun would water it for me, and it flourished under her care. But before even two years had passed, one day it suddenly wilted and died. I dug it up to examine the roots and found them all as white as nephrite, and the plant was putting forth new shoots. I could not explain it at first and thought that I was just not fated to deserve such a flower and could do nothing but heave a deep sigh over my misfortune. Afterward I found out that someone who had wanted a cutting from the plant had poured boiling water over it when I turned down his request. From that moment on I swore that I would never raise orchids again.

My next choice of flower would be the azalea. It may not have much of a fragrance, but it does have a most attractive color and is quite easy to raise. But because Yun pitied the branches and felt sorry for the leaves, she could not bear to let me prune them properly, which made it hard for me to raise them to maturity. She was like that about all of my potted plants.

~

---

2. The duck is the earthworm's natural predator so its breath would supposedly counteract the earthworm's breath.

Each year, east of our fence, chrysanthemums would burst into bloom and become my obsession for the autumn.

I preferred to pluck the blossoms and place them in vases rather than raise them in pots. Potted chrysanthemums are pretty enough, but our house lacked a proper garden in which to raise them. And the plants for sale in the market are so motley and charmless that I would never get them.

When arranging chrysanthemum blossoms in vases, you should use an odd rather than even number of flowers. Each vase should contain only one variety in one color. The opening of the vase should be wide rather than narrow, as the extra room allows the flowers to unfold naturally, without constraints.

Whether you are arranging just five or seven or as many as thirty or forty blossoms, you must always arrange them to spring upward from the mouth of the vase in a single cluster. For the best effect, do not let them fall over sloppily, squeeze them together too tightly, or let them lean on the lip of the vase for support. This is known as a "rising bunch properly close," in which some of the flowers stand erect while others seem to float and dance at various angles.

The flowers should vary in height and be separated by some that are still budding to avoid the mistake of making them look like straight rows of "spinning plates on sticks" [as you might see in an acrobatics show].

The leaves should not be messy nor should the stem be too stiff. If you do decide to use pins, they should remain concealed and any protruding bits snipped off so that not a single pin is visible in the stems. This is known as a "vase mouth properly clear."

Select the appropriate size of display table for the flowers and place from three to seven vases on it, but no more. Any more and it becomes difficult to tell the "eyes" from the "eyebrows," and it starts to resemble one of those chrysanthemum folding screens found in the market.

The stands for the vases should be from four to five inches high up to two and a half feet, but no taller. They must be of various heights that go well with one another so that there is a genuine feeling of unity about the whole arrangement. If there is a tall stand in the middle flanked by two lower ones, or if the back row is tall while the front row is low, or if they are all lined up in matching pairs, then you are making the mistake of fashioning a "brocade rubbish heap."

Whether the flowers are closely gathered or spread apart,

whether they face forward or away: when all these considerations are made by a connoisseur with a sense of painterly composition, then the arrangement will be acceptable.

~

As for the various pots, platters, and basins used for flowers, you can make a glue for them out of painter's pigment, pine resin, elm bark, and flour mixed with tung oil heated over the embers of burning rice husks.

Then you push pins up through a thin slip of copper and affix it to the inside of a pot using the hot glue. After the glue cools down, tie up a bundle of flowers with fine wire and stick them onto the pins at the bottom of the pot, making sure that they are at angles for maximum effect and not just sitting in the middle. Then spread the stems apart and ensure that the leaves are clearly separated and not all crammed together. Finally, add water and a small amount of decorative sand to cover up the copper slips at the bottom. The ideal effect has been achieved when the viewer mistakes the arrangement for live flowers actually growing in the pot.

~

There is also a method for pruning branches of tree blossoms and fruit to arrange in a vase—assuming that you have not been able to gather them for yourself and knowing that those cut for you by other people invariably fall short.

You must first hold a branch in your hand and tilt it this way and that to get a sense of its lines, then turn it around until you have a firm grasp of its overall shape. Once you have made your appraisal, cut away any stray twigs that do not belong until you have a specimen of sparse and extraordinary beauty. After that you must consider how the branch will fit into the vase, bending or twisting it when inserted to avoid the disastrous effect of squishing all the leaves to the back and the flowers to the side. If you just take any branch, straighten it out, and stick it in a vase, then the effect will look sloppy and forced, with flowers facing the sides and leaves facing the back, making it impossible to grasp the overall look of the arrangement and rendering it completely devoid of charm and beauty.

Now for the technique of putting a subtle bend in a branch: carefully saw halfway through the shaft and insert a tiny piece of stone into the incision; then the straight shaft will have a bend in it. If you are worried that the shaft might fall over, then insert one or two pins to reinforce it.

Even maple leaves, bamboo stalks, and random bits of grass and bramble can be part of what you choose for your arrangements. If you take something like a single stalk of green bamboo and place it with several wolfberries and a few blades of slender grass along with one or two branches of bramble and arrange them all properly, you will have something with an ethereal charm to it.

~

When newly planting flowers and trees, do not worry if they appear crooked or askew.

Just let the leaves slant to one side; after a year or so, the branches and leaves will stand up on their own. If you plant them all perfectly straight, they will never have a natural appearance.

~

When it comes to pruning bonsai trees, first choose plants with roots showing above the soil like chicken claws, then cut off all the branches from the first three segments or so of the trunk and let the rest spread out from there.

Each branch should stem from one segment of the trunk, with a total of seven to nine branches by the time you reach the top of the tree. Never allow two branches to be joined directly opposite one another like two shoulders and never allow the joints to swell up like "crane knees." The branches must radiate from all around the trunk, not just from one side, or the tree will suffer from a "bare chest and exposed back"; neither should they stick straight out from the front and back. Some trees are called "double growth" or even "triple growth" when two or three trunks rise from a single root. If the roots do not resemble claws, then the tree will look like it is just stuck in a basin and no one will want it.

To bring a tree to maturity properly takes at least three or four decades. In my entire life I have seen only one old man from my hometown, by the name of Wan Caizhang, who was able to raise several trees successfully during his lifetime. Once, I saw a boxwood and a cypress bonsai that had been brought as gifts by a visitor from Yushan to the house of a merchant in Yangzhou, but I regret to say that they were pearls cast into the darkness and I have not seen any specimens as fine since then. If you let the branches spread out too much like a pagoda or curl around too much like worms, then your tree will have an artificial quality to it.

When you adorn your bonsai with stones and flowers, you can fashion miniature scenes to lose yourself in and expansive scenes to strike wonder in you. Then when you enjoy a cup of fresh tea in your secluded studio, you can be amused by letting your spirit wander freely in the scenery before you.

~

Once when I was planting some narcissus, I found myself without any pebbles from Lingbi to go with them, so I had to substitute pieces of coal that looked like stones.[3] If you take five to seven stalks of various sizes from the heart of a bok choy as white as pure nephrite and plant them in a rectangular pot full of sand covered with bits of black coal in place of rocks, the contrast between the white and black will be quite distinct and intriguing. You can come up with other refined charms such as these on your own, ones too numerous to mention.

~

You can take sweet flag grass seeds, chew them up in your mouth with some cold rice gruel, and spray them onto pieces of charcoal. Keep them in a dark, damp spot and soon delicate sweet flag filaments will grow on them. Place the pieces of charcoal in any bonsai basin you fancy and they will grow a lovely moss-like covering.

~

You can also grind the ends off old lotus seeds, place them in an eggshell, and let a chicken sit on them until hatching time, after which you take them out and plant them in a small pot using a combination of eight parts mud from an old swallow's nest mixed with two parts mashed white asparagus. Water the seeds with river water and warm them in the light of the rising sun. Tiny flowers will bloom the size of wine cups, with leaves shrunken to the size of a rice bowl—graceful and adorable to behold.

~

When it comes to the best placement of garden elements such as gazebos, towers, alcoves, verandas, mountains of stone, and flower beds, you should see the small in the large, the large in the small, the real in the illusory, and the illusory in the real, with some things hidden and others exposed, some things obvious and others profound.

It is not just a matter of the four rules of circling, winding, curving, and bending, nor is it just having many rocks across a wide area—these alone are simply a waste of effort.

---

3. Stones from the Lingbi region of Anhui province were prized for their dark, lustrous color.

You need to dig up an area and pile earth into a small hill that you can then break up with pieces of stone interspersed with flowering plants and grasses; for the fence, use interwoven plum trees and have a wall with vines climbing up it, and then a mountain will appear where there was none before.

As for seeing the small in the large: you can take an untended spot and plant it with swiftly growing tall bamboo, then plant an interwoven profusion of smaller plum trees as a sort of screen in the foreground.

As for seeing the large in the small: the wall surrounding a modest courtyard garden should have nooks and alcoves here and there that can be adorned with greenery, bedecked with climbing vines, and inset with larger stones inscribed with characters after the manner of stelae and tablets. When you open the windows to look out it will feel as though you are facing craggy cliffs with an unending range of peaks.

As for the real in the illusory: if there is some place where the "mountains" and waters seem to taper off, then have a bend around which a whole new scene bursts forth. Or situate within a pavilion a cabinet that actually leads to an adjacent garden when it is opened up.

As for the illusory in the real: have a doorway open onto an inaccessible yard and arrange bamboo and stone in it so there appears to be a garden where there really is none. Or erect a low railing on top of the garden wall so there appears to be a balcony overlooking the garden when actually there is nothing there.

~

Poor scholars with too few rooms for too many people should arrange things after the layout of living quarters in the aft sections of the Taiping boats of my native region, which have beds on stepped platforms to make the most of available space.[4]

You can make three berths this way, dividing them with planks covered in white paper so that they are all neatly separated from one another. In such a room it seems as though you are taking a stroll on a long road without feeling cramped in the least. When Yun and I were staying in Yangzhou together, we used this method once. Our house only had two rooms, but we managed to make an upper and lower bedroom, a kitchen and a sitting room, all

---

4. Taiping boats were found on the waterways around Suzhou and had permanent living quarters in covered cabins on the sterns of the boats.

neatly laid out with generous proportions. Yun laughed about it once and said to me, "This arrangement may be refined, but it still doesn't have the feel of a wealthy family's house." I suppose it was true!

~

Once, when sweeping the family graves in the mountains, I picked up some lovely stones with ridge-shaped patterns on them.

When I got back home, I consulted Yun about them, "When I use putty to cement a pile of white Xuanzhou pebbles into a basin of white ceramic, the pale shades all go together.[5] These brown mountain stones have an old, rustic quality to them, but if I use the light putty, the brown and white will offset each other and the gaps between the stones will be highlighted. What do you think I should do?"

"Pick out the inferior stones," replied Yun, "and pulverize them until they are as fine as ash; then sprinkle the dust over the wet putty and when it dries the colors might match."

So we did as she suggested and piled up the stones into a miniature mountain inside a rectangular basin from the Yixing kilns.[6] The mountain rose up at the left side of the basin with some hillocks to the right. Along the back of the mountain we made rows of angled patterns akin to Ni Zan's technique for depicting stones.[7] The craggy ridges jutted up and down like the rocky outcroppings over the Yangtze River. We cleared one corner and planted a white mille-feuille duckweed plant in river mud, and among the rocks we planted cypress vines, otherwise known as "cloud pine." We worked on it for several days before it was finally finished. By late autumn the cypress vine had spread over the entire mountain and was hanging from the rocky cliffs like wisteria. Its flowers bloomed a brilliant red and the white duckweed burst through the water with glorious blossoms as well. The red and white complemented each other, and when you let your

---

5. Xuanzhou pebbles were pure white stones from a region to the west of Suzhou.

6. The Yixing kilns were known for producing distinctive red, brown, and black unglazed ceramics since the Song dynasty.

7. Ni Zan (1301–1374)—courtesy name Yunlinzi—was one of the Four Masters of Yuan dynasty painting and was from Wuxi (northwest of Suzhou). He loved to paint the scenery of the region and was especially esteemed for his striking depiction of mountains and stones.

spirit wander among the flowers, it was as though you were visiting the enchanted isle of Penglai.[8]

We placed the basin outside under the eaves, where Yun and I could appreciate and comment on various spots: here we would build a waterside pavilion; here was perfect for a thatched gazebo; here was a nice spot for an inscription reading, "Betwixt falling blossoms and flowing water"; here we could make our home; here we could fish; and from here we could survey it all. We harbored these mountains and ravines in our hearts as though we might actually be able to move there one day.

But one night a pair of worthless cats slipped from the eaves while fighting over some food and smashed the basin and stand to pieces in the blink of an eye. I sighed and said to Yun, "Even this small effort of ours has made the Fashioner of Things jealous!"[9] The two of us could not hold back our tears.

~

To burn incense in a quiet room is an elegant and charming form of idleness.

Yun would place aloeswood and other fragrant woods into a large rice pot to steam thoroughly.[10] Then she would set up a holder made of copper wire on the stove about an inch or so above the flames to warm the pieces of wood gradually, producing a delicate fragrance without any smoke.

The Buddha's hand citron should not be smelled by someone with alcohol on his breath or it will spoil soon after. The quince should not be allowed to sweat; if it does, you should wash it off with water. Only Yichang lemons can be handled without special precautions.[11] There are also particular methods for arranging

---

8. Penglai was a mythical island supposedly in the Bohai sea off the east coast of China and was said to be home to the Eight Immortals of the Daoist pantheon.

9. The Fashioner of Things (*zaowu*) is a personification of the creative force that leads to the emergence of material objects in the universe. Shen Fu and Yun incurred its jealousy because they presumed to create their own miniature world.

10. Aloeswood is an aromatic resinous heartwood of Aquilaria trees used to make incense. It is known as "sinking incense" because it is too dense to float in water.

11. The Buddha's hand citron is a fragrant fruit shaped like a many-fingered hand that was used to perfume rooms, tea, and clothing and for offerings at Buddhist temples. The Yichang lemon is a hardy, aromatic,

an offering of Buddha's hand citrons and quinces, but I cannot write about them here. I find there is always someone who will grab something from a finished offering of fruit to sniff at it and then just shove it back in again. These people have no grasp of the proper method for arranging an offering.

~

When idle at home I never fail to have a vase of flowers on my desk.

Yun once told me, "Your flower arrangements can appear as though they are in the wind, sun, rain, or dew. They really are exquisitely captivating. There is a school of painting devoted to insects on blades of grass. Why not try imitating that in your arrangements?"

"Insects are always moving around," I replied, "and won't allow themselves to be restrained. How am I supposed to imitate that style?"

"There is a way. But I'm afraid that it may start a wicked practice for me to suggest it."

"Just tell me what it is."

"Well, insects don't change in appearance after they die. You could find a praying mantis, cicada, or butterfly or something like that, kill it with a pin, and fasten its neck to a flower or blade of grass with a piece of fine thread. Then you could arrange its legs so that some are clasping the stem while others are stepping on the leaf, just as they would in real life. Wouldn't that be perfect?"

I was delighted and set about following Yun's method. Without exception, everyone who saw the results proclaimed their excellence. I'm afraid that were I to search among women these days, I would find none who could understand these things as well as she did.

~

While Yun and I were staying with the Hua family at Mount Xi, Mrs. Hua had her two daughters take instruction in reading from Yun. The summer heat grew oppressive in that open courtyard out in the country, so Yun taught them the truly wonderful trick of making sunscreens out of living flowers.

For one screen she took two twigs about five to six inches long and ran four crosspieces between them about a foot wide, so that it looked like a low bench with empty spaces. Then she drilled round

---

inedible yellow-green citrus fruit about the size of a grapefruit.

holes in the four corners of the frame and inserted two sections of bamboo latticework with squared pegs at the bottom. The screens were six to seven feet high and at the bottom of each one, between the two sections of latticework, she placed a pot of sandy soil planted with hyacinth beans, which would climb up the latticework as they grew.

Two people could move a screen quite easily and put them alongside one another to cover up a window, filling it with a cool green shade that kept out the sun while letting in a breeze. They also lined them up to form curving pathways that could be changed on a whim, which is why they are called "living flower screens." This method can be used anywhere, with any kind of climbing vine or sweet smelling plant. It really is a boon to country living.

~

A friend of mine, Lu Banfang—personal name Zhang, courtesy name Chunshan—is a master at painting pine and cypress trees as well as plum and chrysanthemum blossoms. He is also accomplished in writing ancient scripts and carving seal stamps.

We once stayed at his home for a year and a half in quarters called the Tower of Tranquility. We occupied three of the building's five eastward-facing rooms, from which we could enjoy the distant vista day or night, in wind or rain. In the yard there was a sweet osmanthus tree that gave off a delicate, alluring fragrance. There were even verandas and side rooms; the whole place had a supremely secluded and restful air about it.

When we moved there, we brought a servant and his wife and young daughter with us. The husband could tailor clothes and the wife could spin thread for fabric. Yun embroidered, the woman spun, the man tailored, and in this way we were able to provide for our basic needs.

I loved having company over, which meant always having snacks and drinks on hand for the drinking games. Yun was excellent at thrifty cooking; simple melons, vegetables, fish, and shrimp would all take on sublime flavors in her hands. My friends knew that I was poor and they would usually come up with the money for wine so that we could while away our days lost in conversation. I have always liked to keep things clean, so our place never had even a speck of dust; but I am fairly relaxed on the whole and would never resent someone for letting loose occasionally.

My friends at the time included Yang Bufan—personal name

Changxu—who excelled at painting portraits; Yuan Shaoyu—personal name Pei—who was a master of landscape painting; and Wang Xingcan—personal name Yan—who was good at painting flowers and birds. All three of them adored the quiet refinement of our Tower of Tranquility and would often bring over their brushes and inks so that I might study painting with them. I could also write characters in ancient script and carve seal stamps for people to make a bit of extra money, which I would then entrust to Yun to provide tea and wine for our guests. We would spend entire days talking about poetry and painting and nothing else.

In addition to these three close friends, there were also the Xia brothers, Dan'an and Yishan; the Miao brothers, Shanyin and Zhibo; as well as Jiang Yunxiang, Lu Juxiang, Zhou Xiaoxia, Guo Xiaoyu, Hua Xingfan and Zhang Xianhan—a group of gentlemen who would come and go from our place as swallows flit to and fro from the rafters. Yun would even remove her own hairpins and pawn them to buy us wine without batting an eye, for such lovely scenes were not lightly passed up.[12] But now we all live in different corners of the world, scattered like so many clouds in the wind. And Yun is now shattered jade and buried incense. I cannot bear to look back on all this now!

~

There were four forbidden activities in the Tower of Tranquility: discussing promotions, doing office work, composing examination essays, and gambling with cards or dice.[13]

Anyone who broke these rules was fined six pints of wine. We also had four worthy attainments: heroic magnanimity, tasteful refinement, untrammeled freedom, and peaceful tranquility.

Without much to do during the long summer days, we would hold examination couplet parties attended by eight people, who

---

12. The Tang dynasty poet Yuan Zhen (779–831) wrote three "Dispelling Sorrows" (Qian beihuai) poems mourning the death of his young wife who came from a wealthy family but married him even though he was a poor scholar. Yun's selfless behavior in pawning items from her dowry recalls a couplet from the first poem, which reads, "She saw I had no clothes and went to her garment chest, / I pestered her to buy wine with her golden hairpins."

13. Examination essays during the Ming and Qing were written in a rigidly structured form in eight parts (*baguwen*) that took a great deal of practice to master.

would each contribute two hundred coins of copper cash.[14] We would draw lots, and the winner would get to be the provisional chief examiner, who would sit apart to keep watch on the proceedings. The runner-up would act as the official record keeper and also sit apart from the others, who would act as the examination candidates.

Each candidate would receive a slip of paper from the record keeper, who would stamp it with an official seal. The chief examiner would then produce a line of poetry in five syllables and another in seven syllables that the candidates would have to match in the time it took to burn through one stick of incense. They could walk around or stand still, as they wished, when thinking of their compositions, but they were not allowed to put their heads together to whisper to one another.

When their couplets were completed, they would place them in a small box and then be allowed to take their seats again. After all the slips of paper were handed in, the record keeper would first open the box and copy each of the entries into a single booklet in his own hand and only then present them to the chief examiner, which was a means of curtailing favoritism.

The best three couplets in five syllables and three in seven syllables would be chosen from among the sixteen couplets.[15] Whoever of these six finalists wrote the best couplet would become the next chief examiner and the runner-up would be the next record keeper. Anyone who did not have either of his couplets chosen as a finalist would be fined twenty cash. Those who only had one couplet chosen would pay a reduced fine of ten cash, but those who exceeded the time limit would be fined double. In one sitting, the chief examiner could stand to make a hundred cash in "incense money," meaning that over the course of ten sittings in one day we could accumulate a thousand cash, which was an ample amount for buying wine.

Only Yun was considered to be writing an "official examination,"

---

14. A "cash" was a small copper coin with a square hole through the middle that was often threaded onto one-hundred-coin cords. These coins were nicknamed "green beetles" (*qing fu*) because of their color and because an old myth said that if you smeared beetle blood on them they would come flying back after being spent.

15. Shen Fu seems to have forgotten that the two people supervising the "examination" would not submit couplets so there should only be twelve couplets in total.

so she was permitted to remain seated while thinking of her compositions.[16]

~

Yang Bufan once painted a small portrait of Yun and me amid the flowers and it really did capture a true likeness of the two of us.

The moonlight was particularly beautiful that night, casting shadows of orchid blossoms upon the whitewashed walls, lending the garden an atmosphere of extraordinary elegance. Xingcan was already a bit drunk, and he suddenly blurted out, "Bufan may be able to do your portrait, but *I* can capture the shadows of these flowers."

I laughed and said, "Ah, but will your flower shadows compare to the image of the two of us?"

So Xingcan took a sheet of white paper, spread it out on the garden wall, then traced the orchid shadows, using darker or lighter shades as appropriate. We looked at his work later in the light of day, and while it was not really a painting as such, it did create the charming impression of flower petals spread out beneath the moonlight. Yun adored it, and each of us inscribed it with lines of poetry.

~

There were two areas in Suzhou, known as South Garden and North Garden, where the yellow colza flowers would bloom, but unfortunately there were no wine houses there for refreshments.

If we were to bring along our own hamper of provisions, we would have to toast the flowers with tepid wine, which is not at all flavorful. We considered looking for something to drink nearby or even viewing the flowers first and then going home to have a drink, but neither of these options seemed as enjoyable as toasting the blossoms themselves with freshly warmed wine.[17]

None of us had made up our minds about what to do, when Yun smiled and said, "Each of you bring your drinking money tomorrow and I will bring a stove with me!"

Everyone laughed and said, "All right then!"

---

16. An "official examination" was a preferential examination given to sons of high officials under favorable conditions and was not counted in the regular quota of imperial examinations.

17. Shen Fu and his friends are likely planning to drink liquor derived from fermented rice, which is best enjoyed warm to enhance its flavor and potency.

After they left, I asked Yun, "Are you really going to show up with a stove?"

"No," she replied. "But I have seen wonton sellers in the market who carry a pot and a small stove with them, which is all we really need. Why not hire one of them to go with us? I'll prepare some nice treats for us beforehand, and when we get there I can warm them up in the pot to have along with the tea and wine."

"That will work for the food and wine, but we still won't have a proper teapot."

"Let's bring one of those clay teapots, put an iron hook through the handle, move the cooking pot off of the stove, hang the teapot over the open flame, and build up the fire to boil the tea. Wouldn't that do?" I clapped my hands together and told her that it was a wonderful idea.

On our street there was a man named Bao who sold wontons for a living, so I hired him for a hundred cash to bring his stove and he readily agreed to come with us the following afternoon. The next day when everyone had arrived at our place to go see the blossoms, I told them the arrangements and they all sighed in anticipation.

After lunch, we set off together, carrying mats and cushions, to go to South Garden. We chose a shady spot beneath the willows and sat in a large circle. First we brewed some fine tea, and after enjoying it we warmed up the wine and snacks. It was a beautiful sunny day with a warm breeze; everything was covered in a blanket of yellow and gold blossoms crisscrossed with the blue gowns and red sleeves of passersby on the paths as butterflies and honeybees darted to and fro—an intoxicating scene even without the wine.

Once the food and wine had been warmed up, we sat down for a grand feast. The man who brought the stove was not a rough sort at all, so we invited him over to drink with us. The passersby who saw us were all filled with envy at our marvelous idea.

Afterward, with the cups and plates strewn about, each one of us was completely content. Some were sitting; others were lying down. Some were singing; others were whistling. As the red sun sank in the sky I had a craving for congee, so the wonton seller bought some rice and boiled it for us so that we all could return home with full stomachs.[18]

---

18. Shen Fu's description of the end of their lovely outing recalls the closing of Su Shi's "First Rhapsody on Red Cliff" (Qian Chibi fu): "My guest laughed with delight as he rinsed out his cup and poured another. The

"Wasn't today's outing delightful?" asked Yun.

"If it were not for the lady's efforts," I replied, "we would not have achieved this." With that everyone had a good laugh and we went our separate ways.[19]

~

When it comes to a poor scholar's daily clothing, food, tableware, and lodgings, they should be spare, elegant, and immaculate.

The way to be sparing is to make do with what you have.

I love to have a drink with a modest meal, but I am not fond of having a multitude of dishes. Yun once fashioned a plum blossom platter by using six white porcelain plates two and a half inches in diameter, placing one in the middle and five around the edges in the shape of flower petals. She painted them with a pale gray lacquer and then covered them with a lid curved to match the blossom shape. On top of the lid was a handle that resembled a flower stem. When you set down this special platter, it looked just as though a plum blossom from an ink painting had been turned over on the table. Then when you lifted the lid to look inside, it was as though the food were resting on flower petals. One platter could hold six different dishes, which was enough for two or three close friends to snack on, and it could be replenished as needed. Yun also made a round tray with a low lip around it that was perfect for carrying things such as cups, chopsticks, and wine pots, which made it very easy to set out or tidy up things wherever you wished. These are just some examples of being sparing when it comes to food.

My caps, collars, and socks were all handmade by Yun. If I had a hole in my clothing, she would borrow a bit of cloth from elsewhere on the garment to patch it up. Clothes must be tidy and spotless and one should choose somber colors to avoid showing stains and because they can be worn when going out on special occasions or every day at home. These are just a few brief examples

---

snacks and nuts were done and the cups and plates lay strewn about. We leaned against each other in the boat and were oblivious to the brightening of the sky in the east."

19. Yun's question echoes one asked by a Daoist priest who appears in a dream in Su Shi's "Second Rhapsody on Red Cliff" (Hou Chibi fu). Shen Fu answers with a subtle pun on a passage from the ancient historical classic *Zuo Tradition* (*Zuo zhuan*), in which he changes the words "that man" to "the lady" by altering the spoken tone of one word.

of being sparing when it comes to attire.

When Yun and I first arrived at the Tower of Tranquility we hated the gloomy rooms, so we pasted white paper on the walls, and it brightened up the whole place. During the summer months we removed the coverings from the downstairs windows, but there were no lattice screens on them, which made them feel too open and exposed.

"What about those old bamboo blinds," Yun asked. "Couldn't we use them in place of screens?"

"How would that work?" I asked.

"We could take several slats of bamboo and paint them black, then fashion a latticework from them, leaving empty spaces. Then we could cut a blind in half and hang it from a horizontal slat at table-height down to the ground. Then use twine to tie four short pieces of bamboo upright in the opening and find some old strips of black cloth to sew around the crosspiece holding the blind up. It would be more private, look decorative, and we wouldn't have to spend any money!" This is yet another way of making do with what you have. This example proves that there really is something to the old saying, "Even bamboo slips and wood chips have their uses."

~

During those summer months when the lotus flowers first started to bloom, they would close up in the evening and open up again with the dawn.

Yun would place a few tea leaves in a tiny gauze bag and put it at the very center of the flower. The next morning she would retrieve it and steep the leaves in boiling rainwater. The charm of its fragrance was truly exquisite.

> Much of Shen Fu's attention to and love for beauty, and his need to create 'spaces' that are immaculate, perhaps is his way to deny his poverty and financial woes

RECORD THREE

Sorrows of Hardship

亂石疊累法
亂石疊累欲使其磈磈有聲。須將
泉力向石之虛處致亂處積

W<small>HY MUST HARDSHIP COME TO US IN LIFE?</small>

Often we are the authors of our own misfortunes, but surely that is not the case for me. I am caring, reliable, plainspoken, and easygoing, yet somehow it is these very traits that have brought me trouble. It was just the same with my father, Jiafu. He was a grand, big-hearted man who worried over other people's troubles, helped other people achieve their goals, found husbands for other people's daughters, and supported other people's sons. On occasions too numerous to mention he threw away money as though it were dirt, all for the sake of other people.

When my wife, Yun, and I were living at home we were sometimes forced to pawn something when the need arose. At first we were able to make ends meet, but it became more and more difficult to go on in that fashion—as the saying goes, "Without cash one soon finds both house and home in decline." What started out as petty gossip among nobodies eventually brought us the ridicule of our own family.

~

The old saying "Lack of talent in a woman is a virtue" really is a timeless truth.

Although I am the senior son in my family, I am the third child, so everyone used to call Yun Third Lady. One day someone happened to call her Third Madam in jest and though it began as a joke it became a habit until everyone, of every station and age, was calling her Third Madam. Sometimes I wonder if this was when all our troubles began.[1]

In 1785, the fiftieth year of the Qianlong reign, I was away working under my father in the Haining administrative offices. Yun used to slip in a small note to me among the letters from home, so my father said, "As your wife is so adept with brush and ink, you can let her handle your mother's letters too."

Soon afterward, though, there was some gossip in the household. My mother suspected Yun of relaying something inappropriate and stopped dictating letters for her to write.

When my father saw that the letters were no longer in Yun's

---

1. "Madam" (Taitai) was a title reserved for the wives of high officials and was inappropriate for the wife of a commoner such as Shen Fu. The "Third" designation also implied that Shen Fu had at least two other wives. It was being used as a form of ironic mockery that violated the basic Confucian principle that everyone should occupy a properly defined role.

hand, he asked me, "Is your wife ill?" I wrote a quick note to see what was wrong, but Yun never responded.

After a while, my father grew furious and said, "I wonder if your wife thinks that writing letters for us is beneath her?"

It was only when I got back home that I found out the full story. I wanted to explain things gently to my father, but Yun rushed to stop me, saying, "I would rather shoulder the blame from my father-in-law than risk losing the favor of my mother-in-law." She never did explain herself to him.

~

In the spring of 1790 I went to work under my father again, this time in the government offices at Hanjiang in Yangzhou.[2]

One of his colleagues, by the name of Yu Futing, had brought his family to live with him. My father once said to Futing, "I lead a hard life, always on the road, and would like to find someone to live with me and to serve me, but I haven't be able to. If my son could bring himself to respect my wishes, he might find someone to come here from our hometown who could at least speak with me in my own dialect."

Futing passed this sentiment on to me and I secretly wrote a letter to Yun asking her to look for a suitable companion for my father. She found a girl from the Yao family. Yun thought it best not to inform my mother until the matter was settled, so when the girl first came Yun said that she was just the neighbor's daughter going on a sightseeing trip.

Later, when my father ordered me to bring her to stay with him permanently in Hanjiang, Yun again listened to other people's thoughts on the matter and told my mother that my father had actually been fond of the girl for quite some time. When my mother saw her, she asked, "Isn't she that neighbor's girl who was just sightseeing? How could he possibly be taking *her* in as a concubine?" And so it was that Yun also fell out of favor with her mother-in-law.

~

In the spring of 1792 I was working in Zhenzhou when my father fell ill back in Hanjiang.

When I went to check on him, I also got sick. At the time, my younger brother, Qitang, was also working under father.

---

2. Hanjiang was a smaller district in the greater Yangzhou area and Shen Fu often uses the two place names interchangeably.

Yun sent me a letter telling me, "Your brother, Qitang, borrowed money from the lady next door some time ago and asked me to act as his guarantor. She has just called in the loan and is pressing me for repayment." When I asked Qitang about it, he turned the whole affair around and said that this was just his sister-in-law causing trouble. So at the end of my letter back to Yun, I simply said, "Father and I are both sick and have no ready cash to make good on the loan. It will be fine if you just wait for my brother to get back to take care of things himself."

Before long my father and I were both feeling better and I returned to Zhenzhou. Soon after, a letter to me from Yun arrived at Hanjiang and my father tore it open to have a look at it. In it, Yun mentioned the affair between my brother and the neighbor and then went on to say, "Your mother thinks that your old man's illness all started with his concubine from the Yao family. When he's feeling better, it might be best to secretly urge the girl to tell your father that she misses her family. Then I will ask her parents to go to Yangzhou to take her home. This way no one has to take the blame."

When my father saw all of this in the letter, he was enraged. He questioned Qitang about the matter with the neighbor, but Qitang said that he knew nothing about it. So father wrote to set me straight, chastising me. "Your wife borrowed money behind your back and put the blame on her brother-in-law," he said. "And then she referred to her mother-in-law as 'your mother' and even called me, her father-in-law, 'your old man'—this is all simply disgraceful! I have already dispatched someone to Suzhou with a letter dismissing your wife from the family and if you have the least bit of human sentiment left, you will acknowledge the error of your ways!"[3]

His letter struck me like a thunderbolt out of the clear blue sky. I immediately wrote a respectful reply to father admitting my guilt and found a horse to ride back home as fast as I could. I was afraid Yun might try to commit suicide. Just as I arrived at the house and was trying to explain everything to my mother, a servant came in holding the letter of dismissal from father, which condemned Yun for each of her transgressions in turn and declared that she must leave the house for good.

---

3. Chinese familial relationships were delineated with very specific forms of address and propriety. Yun was showing a lack of respect with her overly familiar terms and was meddling in the affairs of her in-laws.

Yun began to sob, "It's true that I shouldn't have said those reckless things, but my dear father-in-law should forgive this ignorant woman!"

A few days later, another letter arrived from my father. "I shouldn't be so hard on you," he wrote. "Take your wife to live somewhere else with you; as long as I don't have to see the two of you again you may avoid my wrath."

I was going to send Yun back to her family home for a while, but her mother had passed away, her younger brother had left the household, and she was not willing to impose on her extended family. Luckily, my friend Lu Banfang heard about our plight and took pity on us. He invited us to stay in the Tower of Tranquility at his house.

~

During the two years we spent there, my father gradually became aware of what had really happened.

One day when I had just returned from a trip to Lingnan, my father himself arrived at the Tower of Tranquility. "Now I've gotten to the bottom of everything that happened before," he told Yun. "Why don't you come back home?"

We were overjoyed and returned to our old home together with my father, where flesh and blood were reunited at last. How could I have foreseen then the misfortune that Hanyuan would soon bring upon us?

Yun had always suffered from a bleeding disorder ever since her younger brother, Kechang, had run away from the family and never returned.[4] Mother Jin had actually died from pining away for her son, so great was her sorrow at his loss. But, ever since meeting Hanyuan over a year ago, Yun had not suffered a recurrence of her condition. I was just marveling at Yun's good luck in finding such a miraculous cure, when Hanyuan was forcibly taken from us by a powerful man who paid a thousand taels of silver for her and agreed to support her mother as well.[5] It was a

---

4. The nature of Yun's disorder is not specified, but as Shen Fu describes Yun "discharging blood" (*fa xue*) rather than coughing it up, it seems to be a form of chronic vaginal bleeding, perhaps caused by uterine cancer.

5. Shen Fu actually uses the word "gold" (*jin*) as the unit of currency here and elsewhere in the book. It was a vernacular term for a silver ingot or sycee weighing one tael, approximately 1.2 troy ounces. It seems that Yun and Shen Fu had not yet paid the money needed to redeem Hanyuan when her "mother" received a better offer from someone else.

case of "the beautiful maiden going to General Sha Chili."[6] I knew all about it but did not dare to tell Yun. She found out when she went to visit Hanyuan one day and returned home sobbing.

"I never would have imagined that Hanyuan could be so unfaithful!" she cried.

"You yourself became infatuated," I said to Yun. "How can you expect someone like her to have the same depth of feeling? Besides, she will be wearing silk brocade and eating fine foods there and never would have stayed satisfied with the thorn hairpins and plain clothing we have here. It's better that we break it off now rather than she regret it later."[7]

I tried to console her again and again, but her resentment at being duped by Hanyuan was so intense that it finally erupted as a massive bout of bleeding. She began to waste away in bed and her medicine stopped working. Her episodes of bleeding would come and go and she grew gaunt and emaciated.

After a few years our unpaid debts were increasing every day and criticism of us began to mount. My own parents grew to loathe Yun more and more because she had become sworn sisters with a singing girl. I was the one who had to mediate between them and it really became an unlivable situation.

~

Yun had given birth to our daughter, Qingjun, who was already fourteen years old at this time and quite adept at reading and writing and extremely capable in all respects.

We were lucky to have her to manage the chore of pawning our clothes and hairpins to cover our living expenses. Our son, Fengsen, who was twelve years old, was pursuing his studies with a tutor.

I was without a place of employment for several years running, so I set up a small painting and calligraphy shop in our home, but the money I would take in over three days was not even enough to cover one day's expenses and the work and worry of it wore me to the bone.

That winter we found ourselves without any warm clothing

---

6. A famous Tang dynasty classical tale "Willow's Story" (Liushi zhuan) by Xu Yaozuo (fl. 790–820) tells of a beautiful consort named Willow who is stolen from a poet, Han Yi, by a ruthless frontier general Sha Chili.

7. The thorn hairpin and plain clothing are symbols of a faithful wife remaining loyal in the face of poverty.

and we just had to steel ourselves to suffer through it. Qingjun's legs were shivering beneath her thin garments, but she still forced herself to say, "I'm not cold." Yun even swore that she would not buy her medicine anymore because of our situation.

Once when Yun was able to get out of bed for a spell, one of my friends, Zhou Chunxu, stopped by on his return from Prince Fu's secretariat and mentioned that he was looking for someone to embroider the Heart Sutra. Yun felt that embroidering a holy sutra would be a good way to ward off bad luck and invoke blessings and also bring in some profit from her handiwork, so she agreed to do it.[8]

Chunxu was in a hurry and could not stay in the area for long, so Yun completed the job in just ten days. In her weakened condition she overexerted herself and ended up with back pains and dizziness that grew worse each day. Who knew that even the Buddha would show no mercy to one so unfortunate as her? After Yun finished embroidering the sutra her illness took a turn for the worse and she was constantly calling out for water or asking for broth, until everyone grew tired of her requests.

~

There was a man from the western provinces who rented rooms to the east of my painting shop, where he made a business of lending out money.[9]

He would occasionally hire me to do a painting for him, so I knew him a little. A certain friend of mine once borrowed fifty taels of silver from him and asked me to act as his guarantor. I felt badly about refusing him, so I agreed to do it, but then he made off with the entire loan! The westerner next door only had the guarantor to pursue for recourse and was always coming by to make a fuss. At first I was able to compensate him with paintings, but I eventually ran out of things to give him. Near the end of the year, my father was at home with us when the westerner came looking for payment and started shouting outside our gate. My

---

8. The *Heart [of the Perfection of Transcendent Wisdom] Sutra* (*Prajñāpāramitā Hṛdaya*) is a brief but central text in the Mahāyāna school of Buddhism and was often reproduced in various media to accumulate good karma. Its most well-known line reads, "Form *is* emptiness, and emptiness *is* form."

9. Shen Fu uses the term "Westerner" (*xiren*), but in this case it probably means someone from the western provinces of Shanxi and Shaanxi, which both have the word "west" (*xi*) in their names.

father heard him. I was summoned and berated.

"We wear the caps and robes of scholars. How can we owe money to a nobody such as him?" he demanded.

Right when I was going to explain the whole affair to him, a messenger arrived to inquire after Yun's health. He had been sent by a sworn sister from her childhood who had married into the Hua clan at Mount Xi.

My father mistook him for a messenger from Hanyuan and grew even more enraged, shouting, "Your wife does not act as a proper woman should, swearing herself to a prostitute! And you have no wish to associate with your betters. Instead you freely consort with these base people! I would take you to the execution grounds, but I cannot bear it in my heart. I will be lenient and grant you three days to make your plans to leave. But do it quickly or I will report you for disobedience!"[10]

Yun heard this and wept, "Your father is so angry and it is all my fault. But if I were to die and leave you to go on, you couldn't bear it. And if I were to stay while you leave—you couldn't abandon me. Go secretly tell the messenger from the Hua family to come here. I will force myself to get up so that I might ask him something."

So I told Qingjun to help Yun out of the bedroom, whereupon she summoned the messenger from the Hua family and asked, "Did your mistress send you just to see me, or are you stopping in on the way somewhere else?"

"My mistress has long heard that you have fallen ill," he replied. "She wanted to come herself to inquire after your health, but as she has never called on your house before, she did not want to presume. As I was leaving to come here, she instructed me to tell you that if you do not despise the rustic country life, you might come to recover at her home in the countryside and fulfill the oath sworn by the ladies beneath the lanterns when they were young." This referred to a promise that Yun and her friend had made while embroidering together one day—that they would help one another if either of them should ever fall ill.

So Yun instructed the messenger, "Please go back quickly to request that your mistress secretly send a boat for us in two days time."

After he left, she turned to me and said, "My sworn sister in the Hua family is dearer to me than my own flesh and blood. If

---

10. Lack of filial piety was listed as one of the Ten Abominations in the Qing legal code and was punishable by death.

you are willing to go to her house, then we should travel there together. We can't bring our son and daughter with us, but we shouldn't burden your family with them either. We must find a suitable place for them in the next two days."

At the time, I had an elder male cousin named Wang Jinchen, who had a son called Yunshi and wanted to make Qingjun his daughter-in-law.

"I have heard that young Master Wang is weak and somewhat useless," Yun said. "Though he might be able to maintain the family fortune, there really isn't much of a Wang fortune to maintain. At least they are a family of culture and learning and only have the one son to inherit their property. I suppose we should allow the marriage."

I told Jinchen, "You have a bond with my father of nephew to uncle and if you wished to make Qingjun your daughter-in-law, he would not refuse you. But we need to wait until she is grown up and ready for marriage, and we aren't able to do that in our present situation. After Yun and I have made it to Mount Xi, you could inform my parents that you wish to make Qingjun your future daughter-in-law. What do you think?"

"I will follow your instructions with care," said Jinchen happily.

With that decided, I entrusted my son, Fengsen, to my friend Xia Yishan, who was to recommend him to an associate to study the trading business.

~

No sooner were all our plans settled than the boat from the Hua family arrived on February 8, 1801, in the fifth year of the Jiaqing reign.

Yun said, "If we try to set out alone now, not only will the neighbors mock us but I'm afraid that the westerner won't let us leave without repaying our debt. We must go quietly tomorrow before daybreak."

"But can you bear the chilly dawn air in your condition?" I asked.

"Whether I live or die rests with fate. Don't worry about me so much," was her reply. I secretly informed my father of our plans and he agreed to them.

That night I took the little luggage we had down to the boat and told Fengsen to go to bed. Qingjun was sobbing at her mother's side. Yun gave her the following instructions: "Your mother has had a hard lot in life, and is too passionate about things, which is why I've come to this desperate state. Luckily, your father is always there for me, so you don't need to worry about me when I go. We will arrange to see both of you again in two or three years. Now go to your new home and try your best to be a proper woman; don't be like your mother. Your new parents-in-law feel lucky to have you and will surely look upon you kindly. As for everything we've left behind, take it all with you. Your little brother is still so young that we haven't told him about all this. When I'm leaving, I will tell him that I'm going to see a doctor and that I will back in a few days. Wait until I am far away from here and then you can tell him why we had to go, and let your grandfather know too."

Nearby was the old woman I mentioned earlier, who once rented us her own rooms to escape the summer heat. She wished to see us off to the countryside, so she stood beside us, wiping away her tears again and again.

When it was time for us to go, we warmed up some congee and sipped it together. Yun forced a smile onto her face and said to me, "Long ago it was a bowl of congee that brought us together and now it is a bowl of congee that sees us leaving. If this were made into a play, it could be called *A Tale of Eating Congee*."

Fengsen woke up when he heard her voice. "Mother, what's happening?" he groaned.

"I'm just going out to see a doctor, that's all," Yun replied.

"But, why are you up so early?"

"Because it's a long way off, that's why. You and your sister be good here at home. Don't annoy your grandmother. Your father and I are going together, but we should be back in a few days."

A rooster crowed three times outside as Yun held back her tears and leaned on the old woman for support. She opened the back door and was about to go out when Fengsen suddenly cried out, "No! My mother's not coming back!" Qingjun was afraid that he would wake everyone up, so she quickly covered his mouth and spoke soothing words to him. Yun and I were being torn apart inside and could not manage to say anything more than "Don't cry!"

Qingjun shut the door behind us and Yun took about a dozen steps into the lane before she was too exhausted to walk. I handed the lantern to the old woman and carried Yun on my back the rest of the way. As we neared the docks, we were almost arrested by a curfew patrol, but fortunately the old woman claimed that

Yun was her sick daughter and I was her son-in-law. The boatmen who had arrived for us all worked for the Hua family and when they heard our voices, they came to greet us and helped us down to the boat. Only after we cast off did Yun finally let herself cry out in painful sobbing. After we left mother and son never saw each other again.

~

Mr. Hua was named Dacheng, and he and his family lived in a house facing Eastern Heights Mountain in Wuxi.

He made his living farming there and was truly a man of simplicity and integrity. His wife was of the Xia clan and it was she who was the sworn sister of Yun.

We arrived at their home before noon that day to find Mrs. Hua waiting at the gate. She brought her two young daughters down to meet the boat and everyone was overjoyed to see us. She helped Yun ashore and treated us with warm hospitality in their home. Soon the wives and children of the neighbors all around noisily crowded into the room to get a good look at Yun. Some asked how she was and some commiserated with her, while others put their heads together to whisper about her, until the whole room was filled with their chattering.

"Today," Yun said to Mrs. Hua, "I really do feel like the fisherman who found Peach Blossom Spring."[11]

"Don't laugh at us, sister," replied Mrs. Hua. "Country folk get to see few new things and marvel much when they do, that's all."

And so we settled in to spend the New Year with them.

~

By the time of the Lantern Festival, almost three weeks after our arrival, Yun began to get up and to walk around a bit.[12]

On the night when we went to see the dragon lanterns at the

---

11. "Peach Blossom Spring" (Taohuayuan ji) is a well-loved story by the famous poet Tao Qian (365–427) of the Eastern Jin dynasty. The story tells of a fisherman who follows a stream lined with peach trees to its source behind a cliff, where he finds a hidden village that has been cut off from the outside world for centuries. The villagers are astonished by his arrival and treat him with great hospitality during his stay. After he returns home he reports his discovery to the local officials but is unable to find his way back again.

12. The Lantern Festival is during the first full moon of the New Year. In this year it fell on February 27, 1801.

threshing grounds she seemed to have regained some of her former spirit and color, which set my mind at rest. I said privately to her, "Staying here is no plan for me. I wish I could go elsewhere, but we are so short on funds. What can we do?"

"I've been considering this too," Yun replied. "Your brother-in-law Fan Huilai is now in charge of the accounts at the Jingjiang Salt Bureau. Ten years ago he borrowed ten taels of silver from you, but we didn't have that much so I pawned my hairpins to make up the difference. Don't you remember?"

"I had forgotten about that!"

"I've heard that Jingjiang is not far from here. Why don't you go there?" said Yun. So I did as she suggested.

~

The weather was unseasonably warm and I felt hot in my woolen gown and serge jacket on that February 28, 1801, in the sixth year of the Jiaqing reign.

That night I stayed at an inn near Mount Xi where I rented linens and lay down to rest.

In the morning I got up early to catch the boat to Jiangyin, but we were traveling against the wind the whole way in an unending drizzle. By the time we reached the mouth of the river at Jiangyin that night, the early spring had turned cold and chilled me to the bone, so I emptied my purse for some wine to warm up. I hemmed and hawed the entire night about whether I should pawn my inner jacket for the ferry passage.

By March 3, the wind from the north had grown fiercer, bringing thick blankets of snow, and I could not keep from shedding a tear in misery and frustration. I calculated in my head the cost of lodging and ferry passage and did not dare to buy another drink. I was downcast and shivering with cold when I suddenly spotted an old man come into the inn. He was wearing straw sandals and a felt rain hat and had a brown sack slung over his shoulder. He cast his eye over me as though he might know me.

"Old man," I said. "Aren't you Mr. Cao from Taizhou?"

"That's right," he replied. "And if it weren't for you, sir, I would be lying dead in a ditch somewhere! My young daughter is in good health and is always singing your praises, sir. I never imagined that I'd bump into you today! What are you doing staying in this place?"

When I was working in Taizhou as a secretary, there was a man of humble origins named Cao who had a beautiful daughter. He had already betrothed her to his future son-in-law when a powerful man with designs on his daughter lent him money at interest, which led to a lawsuit. I used my position to intervene on Cao's behalf and saw that his daughter was returned to her betrothed. Cao showed up at the court to volunteer his labor and kowtowed repeatedly in thanks, which is how I came to know him. I told him that I was at the inn because I had encountered the snowstorm on my way to visit relatives.

"It will clear up by tomorrow," Cao said. "I'm going that way too, so let's travel together." Then he brought out some money to buy wine and treated me most generously.

On the morning of March 4 I was already stirring with the dawn bell and caught the sounds of the ferryman shouting at the river's mouth. I leapt up and called to Cao that we should go across together. "Don't be in such a hurry!" he said. "We should have full stomachs before getting on the boat."

Then he took care of my food and lodging costs and took me out to buy something to eat. I wanted to cross as soon as possible because I had been delayed for several days already, and I only managed to get down a couple of sesame cakes, as I was not really up to eating.

When we finally got on the boat the wind on the river was whistling and my whole body started to shiver. Cao said, "I heard that a local man from Jiangyin hanged himself in Jingjiang and that his wife has hired this boat to go over there, so we'll have to wait for her before we can set off." I had to bear the cold on an empty stomach until we finally cast off at noon.

When we reached Jingjiang, the smoke from the evening cooking fires was gathering on all sides. "Jingjiang has two government headquarters," Cao told me. "Are you visiting the one inside or outside the city wall?"

"I don't really know whether it's the inside or outside one," I admitted as I trudged along behind him.

"In that case," suggested Cao, "Let's just put up for the night here and go pay them a visit tomorrow."

By the time we entered the inn my shoes and socks were already soaked through with filthy mud, so I asked for them to be dried by the fire while I ate and drank greedily. But then I fell into a deep sleep from exhaustion, and when I got up in the morning, my socks were half-burned by the fire! Cao took care of my lodging and dining expenses again.

When I arrived to pay my visit at the headquarters in the city center, my brother-in-law, Huilai, was not even up yet, but when he heard that I was there he threw on some clothes and came out. He looked shocked when he saw me.

"Brother-in-law! How did you end up such a mess?" he exclaimed.

"Don't ask right now," I replied. "First, can I borrow two taels of silver from you to repay this fellow who accompanied me here?"

Huilai handed two round foreign silver coins to me instead and I presented them to Cao.[13] At first he refused them strenuously, but finally accepted one coin and went on his way. Then I told Huilai my whole story about everything that happened to me and why I had come to visit him.

"You and I are close relatives by marriage and even if I didn't owe you anything, I would exhaust my last bit of strength for you," he said. "Unfortunately, our salt ships were just captured by pirates at sea and I would need to straighten out all of the accounts before I could transfer any funds to you. I might be able to arrange for twenty coins of foreign silver to make good on my old debt. Would that do?" I was without great hopes in coming to him in the first place, so I agreed to this.

I stayed for two more days, until the weather cleared up and grew warmer, then started making my plans to return home. I made it back to the Hua residence on March 9.

"Did you run into the snowstorm?" Yun asked me. I told her everything I had suffered and she grew sad and said, "When it was snowing, I thought you must have reached Jingjiang already, but you were stuck at the river's mouth. It was lucky that you met Old Cao to help you out of such dire straits. I guess it is true when people say that Heaven helps a good person."

After a few days we received a letter from our daughter, Qingjun, who told us that our son, Fengsen, was already employed in a shop through my friend Yishan and that my cousin Jinchen had asked my father for Qingjun's hand in marriage and had chosen March 8, 1801, to bring her into his home. Even though the affairs of our son and daughter were mostly settled, we were still sorrowful in the end because we remained apart from them.

~

---

13. Foreign silver coins made their way into China through international trade and were more convenient to carry than Chinese ingots or sycees. The Spanish silver dollar (often minted in Mexico) was a widespread form of currency in China beginning in the late eighteenth century.

By mid-March the days had grown milder with warm breezes and I was able to use the funds from my trip to Jingjiang to make preparations for a trip to visit my old friend Hu Kentang in the local salt office at Hanjiang to look for work.

The director of the tax office there hired me to be the clerk in charge of correspondence, so my body and mind were somewhat calmer after that.

~

In September 1802, I received a letter from Yun in which she wrote, "I'm fully recovered now, but I don't think my continuing to rely on these people who are neither family nor close friends is a good long-term solution. I'd like to come to Hanjiang and take in the sights of Mount Ping."

I rented a place with two rooms overlooking the river outside of Hanjiang's Early Spring Gate and went myself to the Hua's to meet Yun so that we could travel together. Mrs. Hua gave us a young serving boy nicknamed Shuang to help prepare our meals and made a pact with us that someday we would live as neighbors.

~

It was already November when we returned to Hanjiang, and Mount Ping was so cold and desolate that we made plans to visit it in the spring instead.

We were full of great hopes of restoring Yun's fragile state of mind and were even making cautious plans to reunite our family, but before the month's end, the director of the tax office suddenly cut fifteen people and I was let go as I was only a friend of a friend. Yun seemed to have a hundred different plans to help me and forced a smile onto her face as she consoled me without ever blaming me in the slightest.

By March 1803 Yun's bleeding disorder erupted again. I wanted to make another trip to Jingjiang to ask for help from my brother-in-law, but Yun said, "It would be better to ask for help from a friend than from a family member."

"That may be so," I replied. "But all our closest friends, while they may care about us, are also out of work and too busy trying to look after themselves."

"In that case, we are fortunate that the weather is already getting milder and you won't need to worry about snowstorms on the road ahead. I only hope that you can go there and come back swiftly without fretting about my being sick here at home. If you were to get sick too, I would be all the more to blame."

My salary had already run out by that point, but to put Yun's mind at ease I pretended that I was going to hire a mule for the journey. I actually just put some flat cakes in my pockets and set out on foot, eating as I went along. I headed southeast for twenty-five miles, crossing two forks of a river, until I came to a deserted area without a single village in any direction.

It was already evening and all I could see was vast stretches of brown sand with sparkling stars overhead, until I happened upon a small shrine to the local earth god. The shrine was just over five feet high and was surrounded by a low wall with a pair of cypress trees planted by it.

I made a kowtow to the god with the following entreaty: "I am Shen of Suzhou. I lost my way on a journey to visit relatives and have ended up here. I wish to avail myself of your shrine for one night's stay and hope to be fortunate enough to receive your pity and assistance."

Then I shifted the small stone incense burner to one side and stretched out in the shrine, which barely covered half of my body. I turned my wind cowl around to cover my face and situated myself inside with my knees and legs poking outside. I closed my eyes and listened quietly to nothing but the sounds of the breeze gently soughing. My feet were so sore and my spirits so exhausted that I drifted off to sleep as darkness fell.

When I awoke in the morning, the sky was already brightening in the east. Suddenly there were sounds of footsteps and voices coming from outside the shrine wall, so I hurried out to take a look and found some locals passing by on their way to the market.

I asked one person which way to go and he replied, "Go south for three miles and you will be at the county seat, Taixing. Go straight through the city and head southeast for another three miles until you reach a mound. After you pass eight such mounds, you will be at Jingjiang. It's all on main roads."

I turned myself around and shifted the stone incense burner back into its original spot, made another kowtow to the god in thanks, and went on my way. Passing through Taixing, I was able to engage a barrow as transport and arrived at my brother-in-law's compound in Jingjiang late that afternoon. I sent in my visiting card and after a long while the gatekeeper returned to tell me, "Master Fan had to go to Changzhou on business."

I could tell by the way he said it that this was just a pretext, so I questioned him. "What day might he be returning?"

"I don't know," was the reply.

"Well," I said. "I will wait for him for a year if necessary."

The gatekeeper recognized my determination and whispered, "You are Master Fan's wife's younger brother, are you not?"

"If he were not married to my sister, I would not be waiting for him to return!"

"Then, sir, please wait for him," he said.

After three more days, I was told that my brother-in-law had returned to Jingjiang and that he had requisitioned twenty-five taels of silver for me.

I hired a mule and rushed back home only to find that Yun had taken a terrible turn for the worse: her breathing was labored and she was sobbing. When she saw me come back, she blurted out, "Did you know that Shuang ran off with our valuables yesterday afternoon? I asked everyone to look all over for him, but they still haven't found him. I don't really care about losing our things; it's just that his mother told me over and over again to look after her son when we were leaving the Hua's. And now if he is running back home, he will have to cross the wide Yangtze River and I know how dangerous that can be. Or what if his parents hide him away and try to swindle us? What will we do then? How can I face my sworn sister again?"

"Please don't get so anxious," I told her. "You are thinking about it too much. If they really were concealing him to swindle someone, they would need to do it to someone who actually has money. The two of us can barely support ourselves! And for the six months he was with us, we gave him clothing, we shared our food, and we never once beat or even scolded him. Everyone in the neighborhood knows that! The truth is, he's just an ungrateful little slave taking advantage of our hard circumstances to run off with whatever he can steal. Your sworn sister from the Hua family presented us with a scoundrel! She is the one who won't be able to face you; how could you say that you can't face her? Now, let's report this to the county court so that it won't cause us problems later."

Yun calmed down a bit after listening to what I had to say. But from that moment forward, when she would talk in her sleep she would often call out, "Shuang has run away!" or, "How could Hanyuan betray me?" and the course of her illness grew worse with each passing day.

I wanted to call for a doctor to treat her, but Yun stopped me and said, "My sickness began when my brother ran away and my mother died and my grief was too much to bear; it persisted because of my passionate feelings; and then it was inflamed by my anger. Through it all I have worried too much, always trying my best to be a good daughter-in-law, but I couldn't do it. And now my head is dizzy, my heart beats too quickly, and I have a host of other symptoms. This illness is too advanced now and I am beyond the help of even the best doctors. Please don't waste money when it won't do any good.

"When I think back on our twenty-three years of harmony together—the undeserved love you've given me, the tenderness you've shown me in so many ways, your devotion to me even when I've been difficult or stubborn, the way you truly understood me—to have had someone like this for a husband means that I can leave this life without regrets! We have enjoyed warm clothing, full stomachs, a peaceful home, and leisurely strolls among rocks and streams in the Pavilion of Azure Waves and the Tower of Tranquility, truly as though we were immortals amid the smoke of cooking fires. But one needs several lifetimes of religious practice before becoming an immortal. What sort of people are we that we might hope to become immortals? In striving for it, I have provoked the jealousy of the Fashioner of Things who torments me with the demons of passion. In the end it was because you loved me so much more than I deserved that my fate was to be so unlucky!"

She began to sob, "After a full life, we all end up in death. But to leave you now midway on this journey, to suddenly part forever, to be unable to carry out my wifely duties or to see our son's wedding with my own eyes: this is what truly upsets me in my heart." As she finished speaking, tears rolled down her face.

I struggled to console her by saying, "You haven't been well for eight years now; you were often so sick that you were on the verge of leaving me before, so what makes you suddenly speak with such agony now?"

"These past few days," she replied, "I've been dreaming that my father and mother have sent a boat for me. When I close my eyes, I feel as though I am floating through the air, walking on the clouds and mist; could it be that my soul is about to depart, leaving only the shell of my body behind?"

"This is just your spirit being disturbed by illness," I said. "If you take your medicine, rest, and eat well, you will get better on your own."

Yun choked through her tears, "If I had even one last thread of life to hang onto, I would never upset you with this sort of talk. But the path to the underworld is already so close that if I don't speak to you now, there will never be another day for these words. You have lost the love of your parents and fallen into hard times, all because of me. After I die you can regain their love and live a life free from worry. Your parents are already well advanced in their years, so it is only right that you hurry back to them after I am gone. If you don't have the strength to take my bones back with you, then you can just leave my coffin here for now and come back for it later. I want you to marry someone else who is kind and attractive, so that she may serve your mother and father and look after the children I am leaving behind. Only then will I be able to rest in peace." When she said this it tore me apart inside and I could not keep from weeping in anguish.

"If you must truly leave me midway on our journey," I said, "then I cannot think of marrying another, for 'Having seen azure oceans, rivers are nothing to me; apart from the mists of Mount Wu, there are no clouds.'"[14]

Yun took my hand in hers and wanted to say something more, but she could only manage to whisper "next life" a few times. Then she let out a gasp and closed her lips, her two eyes staring into emptiness. I called to her over and over again, but she could no longer speak. Tears of pain streamed down her cheeks. Then her breathing began to fade and her tears ran dry. Her soul drifted away and she was gone forever. This was on May 20, 1803, in the eighth year of the Jiaqing reign. In that moment a lone lamp flickers in its basin; I lift my eyes but I see no one; in my two hands I hold nothing; my heart is about to shatter. This pain is everlasting—when will it ever end?[15]

~

---

14. This couplet is from the fourth quatrain in a famous series called "Thoughts on Parting" (Li si) written by the Tang dynasty poet Yuan Zhen (779–831) after the death of his wife. Mount Wu forms the gateway to the Three Gorges in Sichuan and was said to be the home of a goddess who would bring clouds to the peaks in the morning and rain in the evenings.

15. After Yun dies at the age of forty-one, Shen Fu echoes the closing line of China's most famous narrative poem, "The Song of Lasting Pain" (Changhen ge) by Bai Juyi. It tells the story of the tragic love affair between Tang Emperor Xuanzong and his favorite concubine, Yang Guifei, who was put to death to save the empire from rebellion. The poem ends: "One day Heaven and Earth will be no more, / but this pain is everlasting without end."

With the help of my friend Hu Kentang, who loaned me ten taels of silver, and by selling off everything I owned down to the bare walls, I was just able to cover the expense of a coffin on my own.

Alas, my poor Yun! She had all the breadth of mind, ability, and talent of a man but was born a woman. After she came to live with me as my wife, I was rushing about every day to keep us fed and clothed, and even though we often ran short of money, Yun was always careful not to be resentful. Whenever I was at home, we would pass the time with nothing more than our discussions and debates about literature. That she should end her days in illness and poverty and die with a heart full of pain—who brought this about? It was I who betrayed my true companion among women; is there anything more that I can say? I have some advice for the husbands and wives of this world: while you must not hate one another, nor should you love one another too much. They say that "a loving couple never makes it to the end"; the path I took could certainly serve as a lesson to others.

~

During the Time of the Returning Ghost, custom has it that the spirit of the dead will return home as a ghost on a certain day and that the house must be arranged exactly as it was while the person was still living.

The old clothes should be spread out on the bed with the old shoes placed at the foot of it so that the spirit might return to see them there. In the Suzhou region we call this "drawing the eye" of the spirit. A Daoist priest would be invited to perform the ritual, which involved first summoning the spirit to the bed and then sending it on its way in a rite called "receiving the ghost." The custom in Hanjiang, however, was to set out wine and food in the deceased's room and then have the entire family leave the house in a rite known as "avoiding the ghost." This sometimes led to houses being burglarized when the owners were away.

When it was time for Yun's ghost to return, my landlord, who was living in the same house, went out to avoid it. The neighbors all advised me to set out an offering of food and to get as far away as possible, but I was hoping for a glimpse of Yun's returning spirit, so I was indefinite in answering them. A friend of mine named Zhang Yumen, who was also from Suzhou, admonished me, "You can become bewitched when you are involved with these other-worldly things; it's best to just believe that they actually exist and not to try to test it out."

"Oh, I *do* believe they exist," I replied. "That's why I'm going to wait for her rather than avoid her."

"But to offend a ghost upon its return can be harmful for the living. Even if your wife's spirit does return, the two of you are already separated into the worlds of the living and the dead and I fear that the one you long to see may not even be in a form that you can accept. You should avoid her altogether rather than provoking her to attack you."

But I was mad with unshakeable grief and snapped back, "Whether I live or die is a matter of fate! If you really are worried for me, why not stay with me?"

"I will stand guard outside the door," Zhang replied. "If you see anything out of the ordinary, just give a shout and I will come right in."

I took a lantern into the room and saw everything laid out just as it had been when Yun was alive; only the sight and sound of her were missing, and I could not stop crying from the heartache. My eyes were so bleary that I was afraid that I might not see her, so I held back my tears and opened my eyes wide as I sat on the bed to await her. I caressed the clothes that she left behind, inhaled the lingering fragrance of her perfumed hair oil, and before I knew it I was drifting off into the darkness of heartrending sorrow. But then I remembered I was here to wait for her spirit; how could I let myself go to sleep so easily?

I opened my eyes and looked around. A pair of candles on the table guttered with blue flames that were no larger than beans. My hair stood on end and my entire body started shuddering all over. I rubbed my hands together, wiped my forehead, and kept a close watch on the candles. The pair of flames started to grow until they were over a foot tall, and the paper covering the ceiling was almost singed. I took the chance to look around in the brightness, but suddenly the flames shrunk down to their former size.

By then my heart was pounding and my limbs were trembling in fear. I wanted to call in my friend, standing guard, to witness this, but then I changed my mind because I was afraid that Yun's delicate female spirit might be scared off by another man's *yang* presence. I quietly called out Yun's name as an invocation, but the entire house remained silent with absolutely nothing to see. Then the candles grew brighter again, although they did not shoot up as before. I went out to tell Yumen, who was convinced that I was fearless; what he did not know was that I was mad with longing for Yun.

~

After Yun was gone I recalled a saying by the poet Lin Bu, "the plum trees are my wives, the cranes are my sons," so I took the sobriquet Meiyi, meaning "Bereft of Plum Trees."[16]

I buried Yun temporarily at Cassia Bark Hill outside the Western Gate of Yangzhou at a place commonly called the Hao Family Pagoda. I bought a plot big enough for only one coffin and placed Yun there for the time being, as she had requested in her dying words. Then I took her wooden tablet back to my home in Suzhou, where my mother joined me in mourning Yun.[17] Qingjun and Fengsen also came home and wept bitterly as they donned their mourning clothes.

Qitang came in to inform me, "Father is still angry with you, brother, so I think it would be best if you went back to Yangzhou. I will wait for father to return home and smooth things over with him, then write for you to come back." So I paid my respects to my mother and said farewell to my children, crying bitterly the whole time.

~

I arrived back in Yangzhou, where I spent my days selling paintings.

During that time, I often wept at Yun's graveside, a lonely, solitary, and utterly desolate figure. Whenever I happened to pass by our old home, it was too painful for me to even look at it. By October 24, 1803, the time of the Double Ninth Festival, all the adjacent grave sites had turned brown; only Yun's grave was still green.[18] The grave keeper told me, "This is a good location for a grave and the life force of the earth here is strong."[19] Secretly, I prayed to Yun, "The autumn winds are upon us and I am still wearing thin garments on my body. If you have any spirit powers at all, please help me find a position so that I can spend the rest of the year here waiting to receive a letter from home."

~

16. Lin Bu (967–1028)—posthumous name Hejing—of the Northern Song dynasty lived as a recluse raising plum trees and cranes on Solitary Hill by West Lake in Hangzhou.

17. The wooden tablet with Yun's name engraved on it would be used to make offerings in her memory in the absence of her coffin.

18. The ninth day of the ninth month in the lunar calendar was a festival when chrysanthemums were in full bloom and people would visit the graves of loved ones and drink tea made from chrysanthemum blossoms to increase their own longevity.

19. Life force or energy (*qi*) was thought to course through the entire cosmos, and people would use geomancy (feng shui) to select places with high concentrations of auspicious *qi* on which to situate their homes or graves.

Soon afterwards Mr. Zhang Yu'an, an aide in Yangzhou, wanted to return to the Zhejiang region to bury one of his parents and asked me to take his place for three months, which provided me with a means of warding off the cold for the winter.

After I had made my report and finished the assignment, Zhang Yumen invited me to spend some time with him. Zhang had lost his position as well and was having difficulty settling his debts at year's end. After he consulted with me, I lent him the last twenty taels of silver I had remaining in my purse and told him, "I was saving this to cover the cost of bringing my deceased wife's coffin back home. You can pay me back once I hear from my family." I spent the rest of the year with Zhang, hoping and praying day and night for word from home, but none came.

~

In April of 1804 I received a letter from Qingjun telling me that my father was sick.

I wanted to go back to Suzhou and yet I was afraid that I might stir up his old resentments. I was wavering and unsure of how to proceed when I received another letter from Qingjun in which I learned the painful news that my father had passed away. Cut to the bone and pierced through the heart, I wailed to heaven but it was already too late. Without regard for anything else, I sped home through the starlit night. I wailed and struck my head before his coffin until my blood was flowing. Oh, what a life full of suffering my father had, always away from home in search of work. He sired such an unworthy son in me: I spent so little time by his side and I was not even there to tend to him on his sickbed! How can I ever escape the shame of being so unfilial?

My mother saw me crying and asked, "Why are you only back today?"

"It was only thanks to a letter from your granddaughter, Qingjun, that your son returned at all," I replied. My mother glanced at my younger brother's wife, then grew quiet.

I stayed inside, keeping watch over my father's coffin for seven weeks, and during that whole time not one person told me what was happening with our family affairs nor did anyone discuss the funeral arrangements with me. I myself felt that I had failed in my duties as a son, so I could not bear to ask questions of anyone.

~

One day there was a sudden disturbance at the gate when some men came looking for me to repay a loan.

I went out to respond to them, saying, "If we owe you money and we have not returned it, then you are certainly within your rights to demand repayment, but my father's body is not even cold yet and you take this opportunity to harass us? This is going too far!"

One of them whispered to me privately, "Someone here summoned us to come. If you would move to one side, sir, then we can seek repayment from the person who called us here."

"I am responsible for paying my own debts. All of you leave now!" I shouted. They all murmured their assent and left.

Then I shouted for my brother, Qitang, and made the following declaration to him: "While I, your older brother, may be unfilial, I have never done anything evil or dishonorable. When it comes to my being our uncle's heir, it's true I may have a reduced mourning period because of it, but I never took the least bit of inheritance from him.[20] The only reason I have rushed home for the funeral now is because it is the proper thing to do as a son. How could it be to fight with you over an inheritance? A real man's honor comes from relying on himself. I returned here with nothing and I will leave here with nothing!" After I finished speaking I went back inside and lamented uncontrollably at the coffin.

Then I kowtowed to my mother in farewell and went to tell Qingjun that I was about to retire deep into the mountains, where I would pursue a life of reclusion in pursuit of the immortal Red Pine.[21]

Qingjun was in the midst of urging me not to leave when two of my friends, the brothers Xia Nanxun—courtesy name Dan'an—and Xia Fengtai—courtesy name Yishan—came by in search of me. They both joined in dissuading me. "When your own family acts this way, it certainly makes sense that you would get angry," they said. "But your father has died, leaving your mother behind, and your wife has passed away before your son has even established himself. Could you really be at peace in your heart if you flitted away to become a recluse right now?"

---

20. Shen Fu mentions in Record One that he was made the designated heir of his eldest paternal uncle, Shen Sucun, which meant he was responsible for tending his uncle's grave and was permitted a reduced period of mourning for his own father (from three years to one).

21. Red Pine (Chisong) was a mythical immortal spirit said to be the rain master of the legendary Emperor Shennong.

"Then what can I do?" I asked them.

"Please consider staying in our humble abode for a while," said Dan'an. "I hear that Principal Graduate Shi Zhuotang has requested leave to return home. Why not wait until he gets back and then go to pay him a visit? He is bound to have a position for you."

"The full hundred days of mourning my father have not yet passed," I replied. "And the two of you still have your parents living at home with you, so I'm afraid it would be too inappropriate."

Yishan said, "Our modest invitation to you is also our father's wish. But if you still think it would be innapropriate, then there is a Buddhist temple to the west of us where I know the abbot very well. You could set up a room there. How would that be?" I agreed to this.

Then Qingjun spoke to me, "Grandfather left behind an estate worth no less than three or four thousand taels from which you took not one iota. How can you leave your bags and belongings behind too? I can go get them and bring them straight to the temple where you are staying, father." In this way, in addition to my bags, I also received several scrolls, ink stones, and brush holders left behind by my father.

~

The monks at the temple arranged for me to stay in the Hall of Great Mercy, which faced south, with a statue of the Buddha to the east.

I set up my quarters in a chamber at the western end of the hall, with a moon window that looked right out onto the niche. It was the place where the congregants would usually have their vegetarian meals together. A statue of Sage Guan stood guard at the entrance to the hall, brandishing his sword with warlike ferocity.[22] In the courtyard was a large gingko tree three arm spans in circumference, which covered the entire hall in shade; in the still of the night the wind sounded like a roar as it blew through its branches.

Yishan was always bringing by wine and fruit to have a drink with me. "You are staying here all by yourself," he said. "Don't

---

22. Sage Guan refers to Guan Yu (160–219), a famous general at the beginning of the Three Kingdoms era (220–265) who was romanticized in popular fiction and later deified as a bodhisattva who stands guard over Buddhist temples.

you get afraid in the middle of the night when you can't sleep?"

I replied, "I've been an upstanding man for my entire life and harbor no improper thoughts in my heart. What is there to fear?"

After I had been there for a while there was a heavy downpour that lasted for more than thirty days. I worried that a branch might snap off of the gingko tree and knock down the roof beams of the hall, but I trusted in the silent protection of the gods and emerged safe and sound. Outside the temple countless walls and buildings collapsed and the crops of nearby farms were completely washed away, but I spent each day painting with the monks and took no notice of it.

~

By August 1804 the weather finally cleared and Yishan's father, Chunxiang, was making a business trip to Chongming.

He took me with him and paid me twenty taels to act as his personal secretary and accountant. When I returned, it was the time of my father's burial and Qitang sent Fengsen to inform me, "Uncle is short of money for the burial expenses and wants you to help out with ten or twenty taels." I was going to empty my purse, but Yishan would not hear of it and paid for half of the expenses himself. So I took Qingjun with me and was the first to pay my respects at the grave. After the burial was over, I went back to stay at the Hall of Great Mercy.

~

In October 1804 Yishan brought me with him to collect rent from his properties on the island of Yongtaisha in the East Sea.

We stayed there for two months, and it was already nearing the end of winter when we returned. I moved into Snow Goose Cabin at his home to spend the New Year. He really did treat me as his own flesh and blood even though we had different family names.

~

In September 1805 Shi Zhuotang finally returned home from the capital.

Zhuotang's personal name was Yunyu, his courtesy name was Zhiru, and his sobriquet was Zhuotang. We had been friends since we were young children. He placed first in the imperial civil service examinations of 1790, in the fifty-fifth year of the Qianlong reign, and was assigned a post as the Prefect of Chongqing in Sichuan. He won high degrees of merit for three years of fighting to suppress the rebellion of the White Lotus Sect. When he arrived home, we were overjoyed to see one another again.[23]

~

Soon it was the time of the Double Ninth Festival on October 30, 1805; Zhuotang was taking his family with him to resume his post at Chongqing in Sichuan and he invited me to go with him.

So I kowtowed my farewells to my mother in the household of Lu Shangwu, who was married to my sworn Ninth Sister, as my deceased father's former residence already belonged to someone else.

My mother gave me the following admonition: "Your younger brother is not dependable, so you must make extra efforts in everything you do. All my hopes for restoring our family's reputation are resting on you!" Fengsen accompanied me part way on my journey, but his tears suddenly started streaming down and he could not stop crying, so I urged him not to escort me any farther and to return home instead.

When our boat left Jingkou, we made a detour to visit an old friend of Zhuotang's, Provincial Graduate Wang Tifu, who was stationed at the salt office in Yangzhou. I accompanied Zhuotang on this side trip and I was able to visit Yun's grave one more time.

We turned our boat back onto the Yangtze and headed upstream, passing many scenic spots along the way. When we arrived in Jingzhou in Hubei, Zhuotang received notice of his promotion to Intendant of the General Administration Circuit of Tong Pass, so he left me, his eldest son Dunfu and the rest of his family to stay behind for the time being in Jingzhou. Zhuotang traveled lightly and swiftly on to Chongqing, where he wrapped up his affairs over the New Year and then went from Chengdu over plank roads

---

23. Shi Zhuotang was a renowned literatus and successful official from the Suzhou region. The White Lotus Rebellion (1796–1804) was a massive uprising based in the mountainous regions of Sichuan, Hubei, and Shanxi provinces. It began as a tax protest led by a secret Buddhist sect known as the White Lotus Society that promised salvation to its followers and advocated the restoration of the Ming dynasty. After helping to quell the uprising, Shi Zhuotang was promoted to Surveillance Commissioner of Shandong. He was later removed from that office because of a mistrial and transferred to the Hanlin Academy in the capital (Beijing). After retiring from that post he returned to live out his life in his native Suzhou, where he presided over the Neo-Confucian Ziyang Academy for more than twenty years.

along cliff faces to reach his post in Tong Pass.

~

In late March 1806 the Shi family members still in Sichuan traveled by river to Fancheng, where they came ashore to continue our journey on land. The road after that was long and cost us dearly, as the heavy carts laden with people killed the horses and broke the wheels, putting us through countless hardships. We made it to Tong Pass a month later only to find that Zhuotang had been promoted yet again to Provincial Surveillance Commissioner of Shandong. Because his two sleeves were filled with only the breeze, Zhuotang could not afford to bring his family with him immediately and arranged temporary lodging for them in Tongchuan Academy.[24]

~

It was not until December 1806 that Zhuotang was finally able to draw upon his salary and living allowances to dispatch someone to escort his family to join him.

This escort also brought a letter from Qingjun for me, in which I was horrified to learn that Fengsen had died unexpectedly in May. I recalled the tears that he had shed when seeing me off on my journey, which turned out to be our final parting in this life. Oh, Yun—she only had one son and he did not even live long enough to continue the family line! When Zhuotang heard the news, he sighed heavily over it and provided me with a concubine so that I might once again enter a springtime dream. From that point on I fell into the hurly-burly of daily life; and I no longer know when I might awaken from this dream.[25]

---

24. The wide sleeves of official robes were often used as pockets, but the sleeves of an honest official such as Shi Zhuotang were empty of the ill-gotten gains that a corrupt official would enjoy.

25. Shi Zhuotang presents Shen Fu with a concubine so that he can sire another male heir to carry on his family line. The closing line of this record recalls a passage from *Zhuangzi* (Chapter 2): "When we are in a dream, we do not know that it is a dream. Within a dream we may even interpret a dream and only realize we were dreaming when we wake. One day there will be a Great Awakening and only then will we know that this has all been a Great Dream. And yet fools believe they are already awake, so sure in their knowledge that they think of themselves as lords or herdsmen. Such imbeciles!"

RECORD FOUR

Pleasures of Roaming

詩思在灞橋驢子背上

征馬望春草
行人看暮雲

After THIRTY YEARS OF TRAVELING FOR WORK AS A PRIVATE SECRETARY, the only places I have not yet been are Sichuan, Guizhou, and Yunnan.

It is unfortunate that in rushing by on hoof and wheel I have always been following others. The mountains and rivers may have been a restful sight as their clouds and mists passed before my eyes, but I only ever grasped them in their broad outlines and was not able to explore their far reaches or seek out their deep recesses on my own.

In all matters I enjoy forming my own opinion rather than blindly following what others say is good or bad. Especially in discussing poems or judging paintings I am always of a mind to reject what others treasure while choosing what others reject. So too with famous scenic sites: whether I esteem them or not is found in my own heart. There are some famous spots that I do not feel are particularly beautiful, and there are others not so famous that I personally feel are quite superb. So here I have made a record of all the places that I have visited over the course of my life.

~

When I was fifteen, my father Jiafu was stationed in the offices of District Magistrate Zhao in Shanyin as a private secretary.

There was a venerable scholar from Hangzhou known as Master Zhao Xingzhai—given name Zhuan—whom Magistrate Zhao engaged to tutor his son. My father ordered me to pay my respects to him and I became his student as well.

On my days off I would go out exploring, and once I made it to Roaring Mountain, which was almost four miles from the city and inaccessible by land. As my boat neared the mountain, I spied a cave with a stone slab above it that had split lengthwise and looked as though it might fall down at any moment. I rowed my boat right underneath the slab into the cave, where it suddenly opened out into a cavernous space surrounded on all sides by towering cliffs. This place was commonly known as the Water Garden. Overlooking the water was a pavilion built of stone, five spans in width, and across from it on the cliff face were inscribed the characters "View Fish Leaping." The pool of water was bottomless and people said that gigantic fish were hidden in its depths. I threw some crumbs into the water to see if this was true, but all I saw were little fish, less than a foot long, come up to nibble on them.

Behind the pavilion there was a path leading to the Land Garden.

It was all a rockery jutting up here and there with most rocks about a hand-span in thickness. There were also some flat-topped stone pillars with boulders resting on them, but they bore the chisel scars of carving that rendered them entirely unattractive.

After looking around I had my meal in the pavilion overlooking the water and told the attendants to set off some firecrackers. A roaring echo indeed came forth as the mountains on all sides answered with a noise that sounded like a thunderclap.

This was the first pleasurable trip of my youth. Unfortunately, I never made it to Orchid Pavilion nor Yu's Tomb, which I regret to this day.[1]

~

The year after I arrived in Shanyin, my teacher decided to set up a school in his own home, as his parents were aging and he did not want to be so far away from them. So I followed him to Hangzhou, where I was able to freely explore all the famous sites of West Lake.

I felt that Dragon Well was the most exquisite place in terms of its layout, followed by Little Bit of Heaven Garden. As for rock formations, I would choose the Flying Peak of Tianzhu Mountain and the Old Lucky Stone Cave on City God Hill. Among bodies of water, I would pick Jade Spring because its limpid waters and plentiful fish lend it such a lively charm. I suppose the least desirable place would be Agate Temple on Ge Ridge. After that, Mid-Lake Gazebo and One-of-Six Spring may each have their nice spots—more than can be enumerated really—but still they both cannot shed that look of a made-up woman. None of these places can compare to the peaceful seclusion to be found at Little Serenity Studio with its completely natural elegance.

~

---

1. Orchid Pavilion (Lanting) was southwest of Shanyin at the foot of Orchid Isle Mountain (Lanzhushan). In 353, during the Eastern Jin dynasty, a renowned calligrapher by the name of Wang Xizhi (303–361) gathered with friends and associates to enjoy the scenery, drink wine, and write poetry at the pavilion. Wang Xizhi wrote the preface for the resulting collection of poetry in his own hand and it became the most famous and widely copied piece of calligraphy in Chinese history. Yu's Tomb was the reputed burial site of Great Yu, the mythical founder of China's ancient Xia dynasty (2100–1600 BCE).

The tomb of Little Su is on one side of West Purl Bridge.[2]

The locals had to point it out to me, as it used to be barely more than half a mound of brown dirt. But in 1780, in the forty-fifth year of the Qianlong reign, the imperial cortège made its tour of the south during which the emperor asked about this site. By the spring of 1784, when the welcoming ceremonies for the emperor's next tour of the south were prepared, Little Su's tomb had been rebuilt in stone, with an octagonal monument bearing a tablet upon which a large inscription read, "The Tomb of Little Su of Qiantang." After this, people writing poems in her memory no longer needed to wander around in search of her grave.[3]

I often think of the countless ardent and loyal souls of deceased virtuous women whose names are lost to us, or the many who are remembered but briefly. And here is this Little Su, nothing more than a singing girl of some renown, who is known by all from the time of the Southern Qi dynasty until the present day. It is almost as though the strength of her reputation has embellished the very lakes and mountains.

Several yards to the north of West Purl Bridge is the Academy of Cultural Veneration, where I once signed up for the examinations with my schoolmate Zhao Jizhi.[4] It was during the long days of late summer and we arose very early that morning to go out by the Qiantang Gate, past Zhaoqing Temple, and up to Broken Bridge, where we sat upon the stone balustrade. The sun was just rising and dawn's rosy clouds shone through the branches of the weeping willows, revealing nature's beauty at its finest. Through the fragrance of white lotus blossoms a cool breeze blew gently,

---

2. Little Su (Su Xiaoxiao) was a legendary courtesan of wit, beauty, and literary talent who supposedly lived during the Southern Qi dynasty (479–502) in Hangzhou, which was known as Qiantang at the time. She was an inspiration to many later poets, including Bai Juyi and Li He.

3. Between 1751 and 1789, the Qianlong Emperor made four grand inspection tours of the southlands. It is said he made additional trips incognito to observe his subjects secretly and to spare them the expense of preparing for his visits.

4. The Academy of Cultural Veneration was established as a school for the local gentry class in Hangzhou during the Ming dynasty by wealthy merchants from Anhui province. The examination that Shen Fu attempted here at the age of sixteen was likely the initial step in the multi-stage civil service examinations that could lead to a successful career as a government official. He did not pass this examination and gave up his studies at the age of nineteen to become a private secretary alongside his father.

cooling both body and soul. We strolled to the academy and arrived before the examination essay topics were even posted.

We submitted our essays that afternoon and Jizhi and I went to cool off at Purple Cloud Cavern, which could accommodate several dozen people and had an opening at the top to let in the sunlight. Someone had set up several small tables with stools and was selling wine there. We loosened our robes, poured ourselves some wine, and ordered some snacks—including a particularly nice venison jerky accompanied by fresh water chestnuts and tender white lotus roots—and ended up leaving the cavern a little tipsy.

"Up there is Sunrise Terrace, which is quite lofty and spacious," Jizhi said. "Shall we go up and have a look around?"

My interest was piqued by this too, so we mustered up our courage and made the climb to the summit. From there West Lake looked like a mirror, while the city of Hangzhou resembled a small pellet, and the Qiantang River stretched out like a sash. The view extended for hundreds of miles as far as the eye could see. It truly was the sight of a lifetime. We sat there for a good while until the sun began to set, then we descended the mountain hand in hand to the tolling of the evening bells in the temples of South Screen Hill.

We did not go to Hidden Brightness Temple nor to Cloud Roost Temple, as they were too far away. And neither the plum blossoms of Red Gate Compound nor the sago palms of Auntie Temple were particularly extraordinary. I thought that Purple Sun Cavern must be worth seeing, but when we found it, the opening to the cavern barely admitted a finger and there was only a stream of water trickling from it. I have heard that there is a whole other world within the cave, but I regret that we were not able to find an entrance.

~

During the Clear Bright Festival my teacher went to carry out the spring offerings and the sweeping of his ancestral grave site, and he took me on the trip.[5]

The gravesite was located on Eastern Peak, which was an area thick with bamboo. The gravekeeper dug up some bamboo shoots

---

5. The Clear Bright Festival was observed fifteen days after the spring equinox (around April 5). It was a time when families would tend the graves of their ancestors.

that had not even sprouted above the soil yet; they were shaped like pointy pears. He used them to make a soup for us, which I relished so much that I went through two bowls.

"Hey!" my teacher exclaimed. "That soup may be tasty, but it can overpower the blood in your heart. You had best eat more meat to dispel its effects." But I had never been one to crave the butcher's fare, so I satiated my appetite with nothing but the bamboo shoots, and by the time I was on my way home I felt thirsty and restless and my lips and tongue were nearly cracked.

We went by Stone House Cavern, but it was not really worth seeing. The cliff faces at Water's Delight Cave were covered in wisteria vines, and when we entered it seemed like a small room with a swiftly flowing spring that made a pleasant tinkling sound. The pool of water it formed was just over three feet wide and around six inches deep and was neither overflowing nor draining away. I bent down to take a drink from the running water and my restless thirst was immediately quenched.

Just outside the cave were two small gazebos; we sat in one and could still hear the sound of the burbling water. One of the monks invited us to view the Eternal Cistern, which was located in the temple kitchen nearby. The stone cistern was very large and fed by bamboo pipes that drew water into it from the spring, which kept it full to overflowing. Over the course of years, moss had grown more than a foot thick on the sides. As it never froze during the winter, the cistern had never cracked.

~

In September of the autumn of 1781, my father fell ill from malaria and returned home.

When he had chills, he asked for fire, and when he had fevers, he asked for ice. I warned him against this, but he paid no heed and his illness ended up turning into typhoid, worsening with each passing day. I tended him with medicinal broths day and night and hardly slept a wink for an entire month. My wife, Yun, was also bedridden and weary with a serious illness. There are no words to describe what an awful state of mind I was in at that time.

One day my father called for me and gave me the following advice: "I fear that this illness may be the end of me. You have a few books-worth of learning in you, but that will not put food in your mouth at the end of the day. I will put you under the supervision of my sworn younger brother, Jiang Sizhai, so that you may carry on in my profession."

The following day Sizhai arrived and I was ordered to bow to him as my teacher before my father's bed. Before long, however, we obtained the services of a famous doctor, Master Xu Guanlian, who diagnosed and treated my father's illness. My father gradually recovered and even Yun was able to leave her sickbed thanks to Master Xu's efforts.

And so, it was from this point forward that I began to learn how to serve as a private secretary in the offices of local government. These events were certainly not pleasures, so why do I record them here? This was when I first cast aside books and began my roaming, that is why I record them.

~

Master Sizhai's personal name was Xiang. In the winter of that year, I went with him to learn how to serve in the government offices of Fengxian.

One of my fellow apprentices was surnamed Gu—personal name Jinjian, courtesy name Honggan, and sobriquet Zixia. He was also from Suzhou and was a generous, stalwart fellow of honest character, not given to toadying. I greeted him as Older Brother, as he was a year older than me, and Honggan immediately insisted on calling me Little Brother. We became extremely close friends. Actually, he was the first true friend I ever made and it was such a pity that he died when he was only twenty-two years old. Ever since, I have been utterly bereft of such friends. And now I am forty-six years old, adrift in a vast azure sea, without knowing whether I will ever meet another true friend like Honggan in this life again.

~

I remember when Honggan and I first got to know each other and the two of us harbored such grand aspirations in our hearts, often thinking that we might go off and live a life of reclusion in the mountains.

On the Double Ninth Festival of that year, both Honggan and I were in Suzhou together when our seniors, Wang Xiaoxia and my father, Jiafu, summoned actresses to put on a performance at a banquet in our home. I feared that it would be too noisy, so I made plans with Honggan the day before to go climbing in the vicinity of Cold Mountain Temple instead, ostensibly to search for a suitable site on which to build a small cottage one day.[6] Yun prepared a small basket of wine and cups to take with us.

At daybreak Honggan was already at my door asking for me. So I took up the wine basket and we left the city by Xu Gate, making our way to a noodle shop where we each ate our fill. Then we crossed Xu River and walked all the way to Date Market Bridge at Cross Levee, where we hired a skiff and made it to Cold Mountain Temple before midday.

The boatman was an amiable sort, so we asked him to buy some rice and cook it. The two of us went ashore and first made our way to Middle Peak Temple, which was south of the ancient monastery on Zhiyan Mountain. We followed the road to find the temple secluded deep within the trees. The temple's "mountain gate" was quiet and the monks had little to do in such a remote place, but when they saw that the two of us were not dressed nicely, they were not terribly welcoming. We decided not to go in, as our hearts had not been set on going there anyway.

By the time we got back to the boat, the rice was already cooked. After we finished eating, the boatman picked up the wine basket and came with us, warning his son to keep a good eye on the skiff. We made our way from Cold Mountain Temple to White Cloud Monastery in Lofty Truth Garden. The veranda there overlooked a sheer cliff, at the bottom of which a small pool of clear autumn water had been fashioned surrounded by a stone balustrade. Climbing figs hung from the cliff face and the walls of the monastery were covered with moss. We sat down on the veranda and heard nothing but the rustling sound of falling leaves in the deserted quietude.

When we left the gates, we came upon a gazebo and told the boatman to take a seat there and wait for us. Then Honggan and I went through an opening in the rocks, named A Thread of Sky, and followed the winding steps all the way up to a peak called White Cloud Ascent. There we found the ruins of an old nunnery, of which only one tower was left standing just high enough to provide us with a panoramic view. We rested a short while, then helped each other all the way down.

---

6. Cold Mountain Temple (Hanshansi) is located near Maple Bridge (Fengqiao) just beyond the western gate of Suzhou. It was first built in the sixth century but was renamed after the legendary Tang dynasty Buddhist monk and poet Hanshan who was said to have lived there and served as abbot in the seventh century.

The boatman said to us, "You climbed all the way up there and forgot to bring along your wine basket!"

"We made this trip because we want to find a place where we can retire," replied Honggan. "It wasn't just to scale heights."

"Not even a mile to the south of here is Upper Sands Village," the boatman informed us. "It's a place where quite a few people make their homes. There is some vacant land there and I have a cousin named Fan who lives in the village. Why not go take a look?"

I was delighted. "That's where Master Xu Fang lived in retirement at the end of the Ming dynasty!" I said.[7] "I have heard that he had a garden of the utmost elegance and refinement, but I have yet to visit it." And so the boatman took us there.

The village lay on a road running between two mountains; the garden was at the foot of one of these mountains but was devoid of stones, being more of the type with all sorts of gnarled old trees wound about one another. The windows and railings of all the pavilions and gazebos followed an understated, simple style, and there was a humble thatched cottage surrounded by a bamboo fence, worthy of any recluse. In the center of the garden was a honey locust arbor surrounding a tree two arm-spans in circumference. Of all the gardens I have ever visited, this one ranked first.

To the east of the garden was a mountain known locally as Birdcage Hill, with a tall vertical peak atop which sat a large boulder. It resembled the site of Old Lucky Stone Cave back in Hangzhou but did not measure up to that mountain's exquisite charm.

To one side was a large green stone that looked like a bed. Honggan stretched out on it and said, "From here we can look up to admire the peak and look down to see the garden pavilions. With such a vast and serene view before us, we can open up the wine!" So we invited the boatman over and we all drank together, singing and whistling without a care in the world.

The locals knew that we had come in search of property, but they mistakenly thought we were trying to select an auspicious

---

7. Xu Fang (1622–1694)—courtesy name Zhaofa, sobriquet Sizhai—was an accomplished poet, painter, and calligrapher from Suzhou in the late Ming who remained loyal to the dynasty by going into reclusion after its fall.

gravesite and kept telling us which plots had good feng shui.[8] "We only want a place that suits us," said Honggan. "The feng shui doesn't matter!" How could he have known then that his words would end up being a prophecy! After we polished off the wine, each of us went off to gather wild chrysanthemum blossoms and wore them at our temples. By the time we returned to the boat, the sun was sinking. It was night by the time we reached home, but my father's party had not yet broken up.

Yun told me privately, "One of the actresses, known as Lan Guan (Chief Orchid), is quite dignified and appealing." I called her in, saying that my mother wished to see her, and took a hold of her wrist to look her up and down. Indeed, she had a plump face and smooth white skin.

I looked back at Yun and said, "Well, she is beautiful, but I'm not so sure her name matches her figure."

"Plump people have lucky figures!" she said.

"If that's true," I replied, "where was Yang Guifei's luck when calamity struck her down at Mawei?"[9]

Yun said something to send the girl on her way. Then she asked me, "So, did you get completely drunk again today?" I started to tell her about all the different places I had visited and she listened, lost in wonder for a long while.

~

In the spring of 1783, I left my teacher Master Sizhai to take up a position in Yangzhou and saw the faces of Mount Jin and Mount Jiao for the first time.

Mount Jin is best viewed from a distance, while Mount Jiao is better when seen up close. I often traveled back and forth between these two mountains, but I regret that I never had the chance to climb them to see the view.

When I crossed the Yangtze River and headed north, Wang Shizhen's line, "Green willows along the city walls: this is

---

8. The Chinese practice of geomancy—or feng shui (wind and water)—is still used today to select appropriate sites for erecting structures and tombs according to how the natural features of the area accord with the auspicious circulation of *qi* energy.

9. Yang Guifei, the favorite (and reportedly plump) concubine of Tang Emperor Xuanzong (r. 712–756), was put to death at Mawei Station to pacify imperial troops who felt she and her family had provoked the An Lushan rebellion, which threatened to bring down the dynasty.

Yangzhou," came to life before my very eyes![10]

Even though Mount Ping Hall is only about a mile from the city wall, the path that leads to it is almost three miles long. Everything along the way is man-made—the product of marvelous thoughts and fantastic imaginings—yet it is touched with a sense of the natural, and I imagine it could not be surpassed even by the lofty gardens, jasper pools, nephrite towers, and jade mansions of the immortals.

The most wonderful part is that the gardens of over ten households have been combined into one park that stretches all the way to the mountains with a unified sense of wholeness. The difficulty of its positioning is that the scenery begins just outside the city gate, with the path holding close to the city wall for a third of a mile or so. Towns appear most picturesque set alone against a vast backdrop of towering mountains. Placing the park right there was the utmost in ineptitude. And yet, when viewing the gazebos and terraces, the walls and rocks, the bamboo and the trees—half hidden and half revealed—they do not seem too obvious to the traveler's eye. It takes someone with hills and ravines in his heart to accomplish something like this.

At the end of the city wall, Rainbow Garden is the first section, and a turn to the north brings you to a stone bridge called Rainbow Bridge. I am not sure whether the garden got its name from the bridge or the bridge from the garden. The people rowing their boats past this spot call it Longbank Spring Willows. That this scenery is placed here and not attached to the foot of the city wall is further evidence of the marvelous layout and design of this park.

Another turn to the west brings you to a temple built upon an earthen mound known as Little Golden Hill. With this obstruction of your line of vision, you start to sense a concentration of energy, which really is a master stroke of the design. I heard that repeated attempts to build here failed on account of the sandy soil, so they used countless wooden posts to build a frame to hold the soil in place, spending tens of thousands of taels before they

---

10. Wang Shizhen (1634–1711)—sobriquet Yuyang shanren—was a Qing dynasty official, poet, and literary theorist who published twenty collections of poetry during his lifetime. This is a line from the "Red Bridge" (Hong qiao) lyrics to the melody "Washing Creek Sands" (Huan xi sha) describing the beautiful scenery of Yangzhou, where Wang Shizhen began his illustrious official career. Much of the scenery Shen Fu describes in the following passages is in the Slender West Lake (Souxihu) district.

finished. Who but the merchants of this city could afford to carry out something like this?

Just past this place is Scenic Tower, from which people watch the dragon boat races every year. At this point the surface of the river is fairly broad and is spanned from north to south by Lotus Blossom Bridge, which has eight underpasses beneath it and five towers on top that the natives of Yangzhou call the Four Plates and a Pot. This bridge seems overwrought to me with too much thought and effort and I do not find it terribly appealing.

South of the bridge is Lotus Seed Temple. A white Tibetan-style pagoda springs up from the center of the temple. Its golden finial and fringes thrust up into the clouds while the red walls and cornice at its base are covered by the shade of pines and cypress. You can hear the bells and chime stones ring now and then. There truly is no other garden like this in the world.

After crossing the bridge, you see a three-story building with painted ridgepoles and upturned flying eaves in all sorts of brilliant colors. There are mounds of decorative rocks from Lake Tai and the whole place is ringed by a balustrade of white stone. It is named the Abode of Many Splendid Clouds and it is positioned in the park like the climax at the height of a literary composition. Just past it is a spot called Sunny Slope of Shu Ridge, a flat place of no particular interest that has been stuck on as a kind of forced addendum to the main work.

As you approach Mount Ping the surface of the river gradually narrows and forms four or five bends that are filled with earth and planted with bamboo and trees. It seems as though the hills and waters are coming to an end when suddenly a bright panorama reveals itself as the myriad pine trees of Mount Ping's forest are arrayed before you. The sign reading "Mount Ping Hall" was written by the hand of Ouyang Xiu himself.[11]

As for what is called the fifth spring east of the Huai River, the genuine one is actually housed in a grotto inside an artificial mountain; even though it is nothing more than an ordinary well, the water tastes like fresh rainwater. In the Lotus Pavilion there is a spring surrounded by an iron railing with six openings, but it is artificial and the water is not even worth drinking.

Nine Peaks Garden lies somewhat apart in a secluded and quiet

---

11. Ouyang Xiu, a powerful official, literary figure, and famous calligraphist in the Northern Song dynasty, hosted poetry parties at Mount Ping Hall while he was stationed in Yangzhou.

place by the Southern Gate and is distinguished by its abundance of natural charm. I consider it to be the crown jewel of all the gardens in Yangzhou.

I never made it to the Prosperity Hill estate, so I have no idea what it is like.

The account above is merely an overview of the main sites in Yangzhou, as I am unable to exhaust every detail of fine craftsmanship and exquisite elegance in my description. Overall, it is best to view the city as one might a beautiful woman made up sumptuously, rather than view her as an unadorned rustic beauty washing silk in a stream.

By luck, I happened to arrive in Yangzhou to reverently witness the grand ceremonies for the emperor's tour of the south. All the public works were finished and the pomp to respectfully welcome the Emperor's cortège was on display. I was thus able to delight in a great spectacle, the likes of which few people get to encounter in their lifetime.

~

In the spring of 1784, I followed my father to serve in the offices of District Magistrate He in Wujiang, where we worked with Zhang Pinjiang of Shanyin, Zhang Yingmu of Hangzhou, and Gu Aiquan of Tiaoxi.

We reverently arranged a temporary palace at Southern Dipper Levee for the Emperor's tour and so I was able to raise my eyes and look up to His Celestial Visage for a second time.

One day, when the sky was drawing toward evening, I was struck with a sudden impulse to return home. I availed myself of one of those small swift-boats used by our bailiffs that can fly across Lake Tai in no time with double sculls at the stern and oars at either side. People in Suzhou call them Spouting Steeds. In the blink of an eye I had already reached Wumen Bridge. Had I been astride a crane soaring through the sky, my journey could not have been swifter and I made it home before dinner was even ready.

The people of my hometown have always been fond of putting on a big show, but they had never been so extravagant in their pursuit of the marvelous and superb before this day. The colorful lanterns dazzled the eyes and the sound of piping filled the ears. It surpassed even the painted ridgepoles, carved roofs, pearl-sewn curtains, embroidered drapes, jade banisters, and brocade screens mentioned by the ancients. My friends dragged me to and fro to help them arrange flowers and hang garlands.

When we could finally relax, we called all our friends together to revel in drink and boisterous song as we roamed about to take everything in without a care in the world. Such was the keen spirit of our youth that we grew neither tired nor weary. If I had been born into such a prosperous time but was stuck in a backwater somewhere, how would I ever have been able to see such sights?

~

That year, District Magistrate He was dismissed for his involvement in some matter, so my father took up an offer to serve District Magistrate Wang in Haining instead.

In Jiaxing, there was a man named Liu Huijie, a strict vegetarian and devout Buddhist, who came to pay his respects to my father. He called his home Water Moon Abode and it was a pavilion overlooking the river adjacent to Misty Rain Tower. This was the place where he recited passages from the sutras, and he kept it as spotless as a monk's chamber.

Misty Rain Tower stood on an island in the middle of Mirror Lake, with green willows on every bank but, unfortunately, little bamboo. There was a terrace from which we could gaze afar at the panorama of fishing boats dotting the misty waves, like stars in the sky, which looked best on a moonlit night. The local monks prepared delectable vegetarian meals.

~

Back in Haining, my father worked with Shi Xinyue of Baimen and Yu Wuqiao of Shanyin.

Xinyue had a son named Zhuheng who was calm and quiet, with an air of scholarly refinement. We were never at odds and he became the second true friend I have made in my lifetime. It is too bad that we only met like duckweed drifting together on the water and did not have many days with one another.

~

I once visited the Garden of Unruffled Waters belonging to the Chen clan, which measured over sixteen acres in extent and had multiple towers, a profusion of pavilions, narrow lanes, and winding verandas.[12]

---

12. The Chen clan of Haining was an illustrious family of officials whose members had served in top posts during the reigns of no less than three Qing emperors.

There was a very large pond, spanned by a bridge with six bends in it. The decorative rocks were fully covered in wisteria vines that completely concealed the chisel marks. There were a thousand ancient trees, all stretching upward to the sky. Amid the calls of birds and falling flower petals, it seemed as though you had entered deep into the mountains. This was truly a case of being man-made and yet ending up seeming completely natural. Of all the decorative rock gardens on flat ground that I have visited, this one ranked first.

Once, we put on a dinner banquet in Sweet Osmanthus Hall at the garden and all the food's flavors were overpowered by the scent of the sweet osmanthus blossoms. Only the pickled ginger remained unaffected; but then it is the nature of both ginger and sweet osmanthus that they become stronger as they age, which is why it is no idle comparison to use them as figures for loyal old officials.

~

When you leave the South Gate of Haining, you are at the sea, where the tidal bore occurs twice a day, bursting forth like a mile-long silver wall of water.[13]

Some boatmen meet the tidal bore, using their oars to turn their boats into the wave as it arrives. They fasten a wooden "greeter" to the prow of their crafts in the shape of a long-handled broadsword that thrusts downward into the wave as it breaks across the bow and brings the boat along with it. As soon as the boat emerges from the wave, the boatman swiftly turns the prow around and rides the wave as it surges on, covering miles in a brief time.

There is a pagoda on the embankment where I once went with my father on the night of the Mid-Autumn Festival to observe the tidal bore. Almost ten miles farther east along the embankment is Razor Hill, with a peak that thrusts straight upward, looming over the sea. On top of that hill is a pavilion with a plaque bearing the words "The sea is vast, the sky is boundless."[14] From there

---

13. Twice daily a tidal bore moves as a large wave from the East China Sea into the mouth of the Qiantang River, gaining speed and height as Hangzhou Bay narrows. The phenomenon is the largest of its kind in the world, with the tallest waves topping thirty feet and moving at twenty-five miles per hour.

14. "The sea is vast, the sky is boundless" is an allusion to a couplet by Tang dynasty poet Liushi Yao in the poem "Parting in Darkness" (An

we had a limitless view and all we could see were raging billows stretching to the edge of the sky.

~

When I was five years past my twentieth birthday, I received an invitation to serve in the offices of District Magistrate Ke at Jixi in Anhui.

I took the River-Mountain Boat from Hangzhou past Fuchun Mountain and went ashore at Ziling's Angling Terrace. The terrace rests halfway up a mountain that shoots up over one hundred feet above the water. Could it really be possible that the water level was as high as the terrace back in the time of the Han dynasty?[15]

Under a moonlit night, we moored the boat at Jiekou, where there was a police station. The scenery was true to the lines, "Mountains high, moon small / waters recede, rocks emerge."[16] I could only see the foot of Mount Huang, however, and regret that I was not able to view its entire face.

~

Nestled among myriad mountains, Jixi was just a speck of a town inhabited by simple-hearted folk.

Nearby was Stone Mirror Mountain, which I reached by following about a third of a mile of winding mountain paths until I came to an overhanging cliff with water coursing down its face through wet greenery dripping with moisture. I gradually moved higher to the midpoint of the mountain, where there was a square-shaped pavilion made of four steep walls of stone. The left and right walls of the pavilion were honed as smooth as screens with a blue-green glossy sheen. They could reflect a person's image and the local tradition claimed that they used to show who one was in a previous life. Huang Chao visited there once but saw himself reflected as an ape, so he set fire to the place to burn the stone

---

libie): "The splendid bird flies silently to the west, / the sea is vast, the sky is high, where will it go?"

15. Ziling's Angling Terrace is high above the Fuchun River southwest of Hangzhou and was named for an Eastern Han dynasty recluse, Yan Ziling (ca. 40 BCE to ca. 40 CE), who went to fish there after retiring from court. It became a rallying point for later literati who sought to escape political strife for a peaceful life of contemplation.

16. Shen Fu borrows his description of the scenery from Su Shi's "Second Rhapsody on Red Cliff" (Hou Chibu fu).

walls, after which the images no longer appeared.[17]

~

Just over three miles from the town was the Heavenly Cave of Fiery Clouds, where the veins intertwine and coil in rocks that recede and protrude in craggy configurations, as in the style of paintings by Wang Meng the Woodcutter of Yellow Crane Hill.[18]

But these rocks were all in jumbled disarray and the stones inside the cave were uniformly deep red in color.

Off to one side was a single Buddhist monastery, most secluded and peaceful, where the salt merchant Cheng Xugu once invited me to attend a dinner banquet. The meal included steamed dumplings stuffed with meat, and I caught a young novice monk looking at them greedily out of the corner of his eye, so I gave him four.

When we were leaving we gave the rustic monks two coins of foreign silver to show our appreciation, but they did not recognize them and refused to accept them. We told them that one coin could be exchanged for more than seven hundred green coppers, but they still refused to take them because there was nowhere nearby to exchange them. So we had to scrape together six hundred green coppers to pay them, for which they were finally happy and thankful.

On another occasion, I invited some colleagues to take along a basket of food and wine to visit the temple again and the old monk there advised me, "Last time, I had no idea what that little novice was eating and he ended up with diarrhea, so please refrain from giving him anything this time." From this we can see that a stomach used to simple vegetarian fare cannot tolerate even a taste of meat—what a pity! I turned to my colleagues and said, "To be a Buddhist monk, you must repair to a remote place such as this and live out your life without seeing or hearing anything so that you may cultivate truth and nourish tranquility. If it were Tiger Hill back in our hometown, with the sights of enchanting boys and alluring girls in your eyes; the sounds of strings, pipes,

---

17. Huang Chao (d. 884) was the rapacious leader of a massive popular rebellion near the end of the Tang dynasty that caused widespread pillaging and destruction. He sacked the capital city of Chang'an in 881 and hastened the demise of the entire dynasty.

18. Wang Meng (1308–1385)—sobriquet Huanghe shanqiao—lived in the Lake Tai region and was one of the Four Masters of Yuan dynasty painting. He used highly textured, layered brushstrokes to produce an almost tactile quality in his depictions of landscapes.

and song in your ears; and the aroma of fine food and wine in your nose all day, how could you ever hope to make your body like a withered tree and your mind like dead ashes?"

~

About ten miles from the town of Jixi is a place called Beneficence Village, where the Flower and Fruit Festival is held every twelve years, during which everyone brings out flower arrangements for a competition.

I happened to be in Jixi just at the time of this festival and was very much looking forward to attending, but was lamenting the fact that there were no sedan chairs or horses for hire. So I taught the locals how to cut bamboo into sturdy poles and fasten seats to them to make sedan chairs. Then I hired some men to hoist the poles on their shoulders, and we were off. My colleague Xu Ceting was my sole traveling companion, and everyone who saw the two of us laughed out loud in amazement.

When we arrived in Beneficence Village, we came to a temple, but I was not sure which god it was for. In a broad, open space in front of the temple the villagers had erected a high opera stage with painted beams and impressive, towering square pillars. On closer inspection, however, we found the beams were just wrapped in brightly colored paper that had been lacquered over. The sound of gongs suddenly burst forth and four villagers entered carrying a pair of huge candles the size of broken pillars. They were followed by eight people carrying a pig the size of a bull, which the village had raised together over the past twelve years expressly for butchering as a sacrificial offering to the god.

Ceting laughed and said to me, "This pig has certainly had a nice, long life, but the god's teeth will have to be sharp! If I were the god, I doubt I would relish it."

"It's enough that it serves to show their simple sincerity," I answered.

We went into the temple and saw that the potted plants set out for display in the main hall and courtyard had not been cultivated through deliberate pruning and training but derived their beauty instead from their strange and ancient natural vitality. Most of them were Mount Huang pines. Soon after, the opera performance began and people started gathering like a swelling tide, so Ceting and I left to avoid the crowds.

~

Before two years were out, I had a disagreement with my colleagues at work, shook my sleeves free of them in disgust and returned home.

During my sojourn in Jixi I had seen such despicable conduct in that fractious office that I could scarcely bear to witness it, so I switched from being a scholar to being a merchant instead. I had a paternal uncle named Yuan Wanjiu who made a living fermenting wine at Immortal Levee in Panxi, so Shi Xingeng and I went in together as partners and invested in the operation. Yuan's wine had always been shipped by sea, but before a year had even passed we were faced with Lin Shuangwen's rebellion on the island of Taiwan, which cut off all the sea routes.[19] Our inventory began to pile up and we went broke, leaving me with no choice but to go back to my old profession just like the tiger fighter, Feng Fu.[20]

~

I spent four years working in the region north of the Yangtze but did not make a single trip pleasurable enough to record here.

~

While Yun and I were staying in the Tower of Tranquility, living life as immortals amid the smoke of cooking fires, my younger cousin's husband, Xu Xiufeng, came home from eastern Guangdong.[21]

When he saw that I was without work, he very generously said, "Relying on the dew for sustenance and plowing with your brush for food cannot remain a long-term plan for you. Why not make a trip with me to Lingnan? You are bound to make more than a fly's-head worth of profit."[22]

Yun also urged me to go by saying, "You should seize this time when your parents are still in good health and you are still in your prime. It would be far better to secure our future with one bold

---

19. Lin Shuangwen (1757–1788) led an insurrection against the Qing government on Taiwan from 1786–1788.

20. *Mencius* (7B.69) tells the story of a tiger wrangler named Feng Fu who tried to leave his old job behind to become a respected scholar but had to give up his new position when he was forced to confront a cornered tiger.

21. Shen Fu is making an ironic reference to his poverty because immortals were able to subsist on wind and dew without need of food and cooking fires.

22. Lingnan (literally, south of the mountains) was the old name for Guangzhou, the capital of Guangdong province, but it could also refer to the entire Guangdong/Guangxi region in general.

move than to continue trying to find happiness by counting out every stick of firewood and grain of rice."

So I consulted with my various friends and raised enough funds to finance the trip. Yun herself also managed to obtain some embroidered goods and items not found in Lingnan, such as Suzhou wine, liquor-soaked crabs, and the like. I told my parents about the trip and on November 13, 1793, Xiufeng and I set out together from Eastern Dam and made our way to the river port of Wuhu.

It was the first time I had ever traveled on the Yangtze River and I felt wonderfully carefree. Every evening after mooring the boat we would have drinks together in the bow. Once, I spied a fisherman with a small square net about three feet on a side with openings in the mesh about five inches wide and iron rings at each corner, which must have been to help it sink more easily. I laughed at this and said to Xiufeng, "The sages may teach us that 'nets should not be finely meshed,' but how can anyone catch anything in such a small net with such large openings?"[23]

Xiufeng replied, "This net is specially designed to catch bream."[24]

As I watched, the fisherman tied a long rope to the net and rapidly raised and lowered it in the water as though he were checking to see if a fish was in it or not. Before long, he swiftly pulled the net out of the water and it came up with a bream already caught in the mesh. At this I finally sighed deeply and said, "Now I see that my own experience wasn't enough to figure out this amazing trick!"

On another day I saw a single hill rising straight out of the middle of the river, with no other land around it. Xiufeng told me it was called Little Orphan Hill. A scattering of pavilions and halls were visible through the frosty forests. We were catching a favorable wind past the island, so I regret that I was unable to visit it.

When we arrived at Prince Teng's Pavilion, I found it looked like

---

23. *Mencius* (1A.3) describes the proper management of natural resources by a wise ruler: "If he does not go against the farming seasons, then there will be more than enough grain to eat. If finely meshed nets are not permitted into the deep ponds, then there will be more than enough fish and turtles to eat."

24. Bream are freshwater fish that grow up to eighteen inches in length. They have prominent dorsal fins that get caught in wide-meshed nets that allow other fish to slip through.

nothing more special than if the Pavilion of Venerating Classics in Suzhou were to be moved from the prefectural academy over to the water by Grand Wharf at Xu Gate. Wang Bo's description of it in his famous preface was not reliable at all.[25]

We changed boats beneath the pavilion, switching to a craft with an elevated prow and stern, called a *sampan*, or "triple-planker," which we sailed from the Gan River Pass to Nan'an before heading ashore. It was my thirtieth birthday, so Xiufeng provided us with a feast of long noodles to wish me a long life.

The following day we passed over the Dayu Ridge and came upon a pavilion at the very summit, which displayed a placard bearing the words "Lift your head, the sun is nearby," alluding to the lofty height.[26] The mountaintop was split in two, with sheer cliffs on either side forming a sort of stone alleyway running between them. At the opening stood two stone stelae: one read, "Bravely retreat from the torrential flow" and the other read, "Do not proceed when you have attained your goal."[27]

The mountaintop also had an ancestral shrine dedicated to a General Mei, but I never found out in what era he lived. The ridgetop plum trees I had heard about were nowhere in sight, and I suspect that Plum Blossom Peak must have been named

25. Teng Pavilion was first built by a Tang dynasty prince in 659 on the banks of the Gan River and was refurbished in 675 by Yan Boyu, who hosted a banquet at which the assembled guests wrote a series of poems. Wang Bo (650–676)—courtesy name Zian—wrote a preface for the collection that became a paragon of the ornate parallel prose style. The pavilion was rebuilt repeatedly over the centuries and would have been completely different by Shen Fu's time.

26. "Lift your head, the sun is nearby" is a variation on a couplet by Song dynasty poet Kou Zhun (961–1023) on Mount Hua (Huashan): "Lift your head, the red sun is nearby, / turn your head, the white clouds are below."

27. "Bravely retreat from the torrential flow" is from a couplet in Su Shi's "Presented to Auspicious Cheng Jie" (Zeng shanxiang Cheng Jie) on the wisdom of retiring at the height of one's career: "Although a ruddy complexion foretells swift success, / are there not those who bravely retreat from the torrential flow?" The other line, "Do not proceed when you have attained your goal," is a more prosaic expression of the same sentiment drawn from an extremely popular Qing dynasty domestic handbook called *Maxims on Managing the Household* (Zhijia geyan) by Zhu Bolu (1627–1698).

after General Mei instead.[28] Even the potted plum trees that I had brought with me as gifts for people had already dropped their flowers and turned yellow, as it was already so late in the year by the time we reached there.

After passing through the mountain range I sensed a distinct change in the natural scenery around us. There was another mountain west of the range, with exquisite rocks and crevices, but I have already forgotten its name. My sedan chair porters told me of a rock formation there known as the Divine Divan, but we passed by in a rush, and I regret that I did not have the chance to visit it.

When we arrived in Nanxiong we hired an old dragon boat and passed through the Foshan commandery, where we saw that people had arranged potted flowers atop their garden walls. The leaves of these plants resembled winterberry, while the blossoms looked like peonies and came in red, white, and pink varieties. They were actually a kind of camellia.

~

On January 16, 1794, we finally arrived in the provincial capital of Guangdong and stayed just inside the Jinghai Gate, where we rented a suite of three rooms overlooking the street, from a man named Wang.

All Xiufeng's merchandise was for sale to powerful government officials, so I tagged along with him to write out receipts and call on the customers. People searching for suitable formal gifts came in an endless stream to buy our goods and it was not ten days before we sold out completely.

Even on New Year's Eve the mosquitoes were still thrumming like thunder and the well-wishers on New Year's Day wore only cotton gowns covered by silken voile. Not only was the climate so different, but the native people too had completely different facial expressions even though they looked like us physically.

~

On February 15 three officials in town, also from Suzhou, came to take us with them to see the singing girls on the riverboats.

Such outings are known as "paddling around," and the girls are called *"laoju"* in the local dialect. So we set out together from the Jinghai Gate and boarded a tiny skiff, which resembled half

---

28. *History of the [Western] Han* tells of a minor general named Mei Xuan (whose surname means "plum") who fought briefly in 207 BCE for Liu Bang, the founder of the Han dynasty.

an eggshell with a canopy stuck on top, to make our first stop at Shamian.[29] The singing-girl boats are called "flower boats," and they were arranged in two rows facing one another, with a water lane between them to allow skiffs to pass through. Every group of ten to twenty boats was fastened to a horizontal beam to keep them from blowing away in the ocean breeze. Sunk between each pair of boats was a wooden pile to which the vessels were tied with a rattan hoop that allowed the boats to rise and fall with the movement of the tide.

The madam on one boat was called Granny Coiffure because on her head she had a hollow arrangement of silver wire about five inches high, around which she coiled her hair. She fastened a cut flower in her hair with a long ear pick and wore a short black jacket with black trousers that extended to the tops of her feet. She had a red and green sash tied around her waist and wore slippers on her bare feet, which made her look like the lead actress in an opera.

When we boarded her flower boat, she immediately bowed to us, and she smiled in welcome as she pulled aside the curtain for us to enter the cabin. Chairs and stools were arranged along the sides and a large *kang* platform occupied the middle, with a door at the other end leading to the aft of the boat.[30]

The woman called out that guests had arrived and suddenly we heard the sounds of scurrying feet as the girls came out. Some wore their hair tied up in a bun, while others had theirs wound up in braids. They were all powdered up like whitewashed walls and wore rouge as fiery as pomegranate blossoms. Some had on red jackets with green trousers, while others had green jackets with red trousers. Some wore short stockings with embroidered butterfly slippers, while others went barefoot with silver bangles on their ankles. Some kneeled down on the *kang,* while others leaned in the doorway. All of them looked at us with sparkling eyes, but not one spoke a word.

I turned to Xiufeng and asked, "What's all this for?"

"After you've looked them over, just summon one and she will come right over to you," Xiufeng replied.

So I tried beckoning one of them and she did indeed appear

---

29. Shamian is an island in the Pearl River that runs through Guangzhou. It was the location of the key port for foreign trade with China during the Ming and Qing dynasties.

30. The *kang* is a broad platform that can be used as a bench or table during the day and as a place to sleep at night.

before me with a smile on her face. She produced a betel nut from her sleeve and handed it to me politely. I popped it into my mouth and chewed on it vigorously, but it tasted too sharp for me and I quickly spat it out. I wiped my mouth with a napkin and saw that my spit was as red as blood. The entire boat was laughing about it.

Next we went to a place called The Gunworks, where the girls were made up the same way but all of them could play the mandolin. When I tried to speak to them, they would just reply, "Hmn?" which I took to mean "What?"

I said to my companions, "There is a warning that young men should not enter Guangdong lest they become bewitched by beauties, but who could be moved by these women with their coarse appearance and barbaric speech?"

"Well, the Chaozhou women are supposed to be done up like angels," said one of my friends. "Let's go pay them a visit!"

When we got there, the boats were all lined up as they had been on the river at Shamian. There was a well-known madam by the name of Aunt Su who dressed like a female flower-drum performer. Her "powder face" girls were all dressed in high-collared jackets and wore small locks around their necks. Their hair was cut in bangs at the front, was shoulder-length at the back, and was drawn up into two tufts on top, like a servant girl's. Those with bound feet wore skirts, while the ones with unbound feet wore short stockings and butterfly slippers with long trousers. I could make out their speech, but their strange attire put me off in the end and my interest waned.

"Just across the river from the Jinghai Gate there is a group of girls from Yangzhou," said Xiufeng. "They still dress in the Wu manner, so if you go there, I'm sure you'll find someone to suit you."

Another friend mentioned, "That so-called Yangzhou crowd all belong to one madam named Widow Shao. She brought along a daughter-in-law, whom everyone calls Big Sister. They may be from Yangzhou themselves, but the rest of the girls are from places like Hunan and Hubei, Guangdong and Jiangxi." So we went off to see the Yangzhou girls.

It ended up being no more than a dozen boats lined up in two rows opposite each other. The girls onboard all wore their hair up in cloud buns, with misty wisps at their temples. They applied their makeup lightly and wore wide-sleeved jackets with long skirts. I could understand their speech clearly and the woman called Widow Shao received us with utmost cordiality.

One of my friends called a wine-boat over—the big ones are called "steady boats" and the little ones are known as "sand sister boats." He wanted to treat us, so he invited us aboard to have a drink and asked me to select a singing girl to bring with me. I chose a young one whose figure and appearance reminded me of my wife, Yun; her feet were very delicate and she went by the name Delight. Xiufeng summoned a girl called Emerald and the rest of our group each ended up with their usual favorites. We had the boat move out to the middle of the river, where we drank freely to our hearts' content.

Around midnight, I was afraid that I might not be able to control myself any longer and I resolved to return to my lodgings. But the city wall had long since been locked down, as it was the custom to shut up the gates of coastal cities at sunset, which I had not known.

When our eating and drinking was over, some people reclined to smoke opium while others held girls in their arms and joked with them. Then servants came in with quilts and pillows for everyone and prepared to spread them all out side-by-side.

I whispered to Delight, "Isn't there somewhere on your boat we could lie down?"

"There is a loft we could stay in, but I don't know whether a guest is already in it," she replied. A loft is an elevated cabin above the ship's deck.

"Let's go over to find out," I said.

I called the skiff to take us to Widow Shao's boat. All I could make out in the dark were the two rows of lantern flames forming a corridor of flickering light. The loft turned out to be empty and the madam welcomed me aboard with a smile, saying, "I knew the honored guest would be arriving this evening, so I made sure the loft was waiting for you."

"Madam, you truly are a fairy beneath a lotus leaf!" I said with a laugh. Then one of the servants brought a candle and led us from the back of the boat's cabin up a ladder into the loft. It was just like a tiny cabin, complete with a long divan to one side and a small table. I lifted up a curtain and went through to find a private room atop the main cabin with a bed against one wall opposite a square window inlaid with glass panes. Even without a candle, the room was filled with light, which turned out to be lantern light from the boats outside. The quilts, bed curtains, mirror, and vanity were all in exquisite taste.

"You can gaze at the moon from the upper deck," said Delight. We folded open the shutters of a window above the ladder hatch and wriggled through it to find ourselves atop the stern of the boat. A low railing ran around the deck. Beneath the glowing wheel of a full moon the broad waters stretched to open skies. Scattered like fallen leaves floating on the water were the wine-boats. Twinkling like a canopy of stars arrayed in the sky were the wine-boat lanterns. The skiffs weaved their way back and forth as the strains of music and song mingled with the surging tide. It was enough to move a man's heart.

"So this is the reason young men should not enter Guangdong!" I exclaimed. I felt bad that my wife, Yun, was not able to come here with me. I turned back to look at Delight, who did resemble Yun slightly in the moonlight, pulled her to me, and took her below, where we blew out the candle and went to bed.

Just as dawn was breaking the next morning, Xiufeng and the rest came aboard with a great racket. I threw on my clothes and went to greet them, only to be upbraided for leaving all of them the night before. "It was only because I feared you might pull off the quilts or open the curtains!" I replied. Then we returned to our lodgings together.

~

Several days later I went on an outing with Xiufeng to Sea Pearl Temple.

The temple stood in the middle of the river and was surrounded by a wall on all sides, in the manner of a fortified city. About five feet above the water were gun ports in the walls, with large cannons stationed at them to ward off pirates. As the tide went out and came in, the cannons seemed to float up and sink down with the movement of the water, as if the gun ports were somehow raising and lowering according to an uncanny physical principle.

The Thirteen Foreign Firms operated west of Orchid Gate, so all the buildings there looked as though they were out of a foreign painting.[31] Across the river was Flower Land, thick with all kinds of plants and blossoms, as it was Guangzhou's major flower market. I thought I knew every flower, but I was only familiar with six or seven out of every ten there. I inquired about the names

---

31. In 1757 the Qianlong emperor restricted all trade with Western countries to the port of Guangzhou and authorized thirteen firms within a designated district to do business with foreign companies, which built Western-style buildings there.

of the others and found that some were not even recorded in the *Collected Fragrances Registry*, but that may have been a matter of the difference in the local dialect.

Sea Pillar Temple had extensive grounds in which a huge banyan tree had been planted, more than ten arm-spans in circumference, which provided a canopy of deep shade and kept its leaves throughout the autumn and winter. The pillars, thresholds, window frames, and railings throughout the temple were all fashioned from iron pear wood. There was also a bodhi tree, similar to the persimmon, with leaves that when soaked in water and peeled made a delicate gossamer that could be bound into small booklets for copying the holy sutras.

On our way back from the temple that day, we stopped to visit Delight on the flower boats. It happened that neither she nor Emerald was entertaining guests at the time. After we had tea with them we wanted to be on our way, but they kept on urging us to stay. I had a mind to go to the loft, but Madam Shao's daughter-in-law, Big Sister, was already up there entertaining a guest. So I suggested to Madam Shao, "You know, if we could go back to our place with the girls, we could carry on with our chat."

"Fine," said Madam Shao, so Xiufeng went ahead to our lodgings to tell the servants to lay out some wine and snacks while I accompanied Emerald and Delight back to our place. In the midst of our chatting and laughing, by chance we met our landlord Wang Maolao from the prefectural offices and brought him along with us to drink together. But suddenly, before the wine had even touched our lips, we heard a commotion from downstairs as though someone were trying to force their way up. It turned out to be our landlord's good-for-nothing nephew who had found out that we had invited singing girls over and rounded up some people with the purpose of extorting money from us.[32]

Xiufeng blamed me by saying, "This was all on your whim, Sanbai, and I should never have gone along with it."

"Well, we're in this now," I replied. "We need to think of how to turn them away fast—it's no time to quarrel."

"I'll go down and have a word with them first," said Maolao.

I immediately called for my servant to quickly hire two sedan chairs to get the girls out first. Then I would have to think of a plan to get them past the city gates. I could hear that Maolao was

---

32. Prostitutes from the flower boats were not permitted to practice their trade in the city.

not having any success in persuading our visitors to leave, but at least he was keeping them from coming up. The sedan chairs were ready to go, so I had my servant, who was quick with his fists and feet, go before us to open up a path. Xiufeng took Emerald with him while I took Delight right behind them, and we all went down the stairs with a great shout. Xiufeng and Emerald had already made it out the door, thanks to my servant's efforts, when Delight was grabbed by a hand blocking her way. I swiftly raised my leg and kicked the arm. The hand let go and Delight got away. I got myself out of there too while my servant stayed at the door and fended off our pursuers.

"Did you see Delight?" I asked him urgently.

"Emerald has already left in a sedan chair," he replied. "I only saw Delight escape, but I didn't see her get into a sedan chair."

I hurriedly lit up a torch and saw the empty sedan chair still sitting at the side of the road. I rushed over to the Jinghai Gate, where I found Xiufeng standing with Emerald's sedan chair and asked him Delight's whereabouts.

"She was supposed to go east, but maybe she ran west instead!" he replied.

I spun back around and headed past a dozen houses in the other direction when I suddenly heard someone calling to me from the darkness. I lit up the area with my torch and saw that it was Delight. I bundled her into the sedan chair and was helping to shoulder it when Xiufeng ran up and said, "I found an aqueduct over by Orchid Gate that we can use to leave the city. I sent someone to bribe the gatekeeper, and Emerald has already left for there. Delight must go quickly!"

"You hurry back to our place and get rid of the intruders," I said. "Leave Emerald and Delight with me!"

When we arrived, we found the aqueduct unlocked and Emerald already there. I took Delight under my left arm and Emerald under my right, and we stooped over and walked like cranes until we stumbled out of the aqueduct. There was a fine drizzle coming from the sky just then, and the path was as slick as oil. When we reached the riverbank at Shamian, music and song filled the air. On one of the skiffs were some people who recognized Emerald and called us over to board their boat. It was only then that I stopped to notice that Delight's hair was a mess and that every single one of her hairpins and earrings was gone.

"Were you robbed?" I exclaimed.

Delight laughed and replied, "I heard that they are all made of pure gold. And they belong to my mistress. I took them off at your place right before we headed downstairs and hid them in my pockets. If they had been stolen, wouldn't it have been you who would end up paying for them?" When I heard these words, I felt truly grateful to her for her kindness. I asked her to put her hairpins and earrings on again and told her not to mention anything to her mistress except to say that there were too many people at our lodgings, so we were returning to the boats. Emerald also told this to their mistress, then added, "We've had our fill of wine and food, but we could do with some congee."

The guest up in the loft had already left so Madam Shao told Emerald to go up there with me and Delight. As they climbed up to the loft I noticed that their embroidered shoes were soaked through with mud. The three of us shared the congee, which filled us up for the time being. Then we chatted deep into the night by candlelight.

It was then that I found out that Emerald was from Hunan and that Delight was born in Henan and her real surname was Ouyang. She had been sold into prostitution by an evil paternal uncle after her father died and her mother remarried.

Emerald spoke of how difficult it was for them to constantly welcome new guests and see the old ones out the door, all the while forcing themselves to smile when unhappy, to drink when sick of wine, to flirt when feeling unwell, and to sing with a sore throat.

And there were guests of a perverse nature who would throw wine cups, overturn tables, and bellow insults at the slightest provocation. The madam never bothered to look into matters but would blame it on the poor service provided by the girls. There were even depraved customers who would ravage girls for the entire night until the abuse became unbearable. Delight was younger and newly arrived, however, so the madam still took some pity on her.

As Emerald told me all this tears began to run down her face without her even realizing it. Delight was weeping silently as well so I took her into my arms to console her. I told Emerald to stay on the divan in the outer room as she was sleeping with Xiufeng.

~

From that time on, every five or ten days or so, they would send someone for me.

Sometimes Delight herself would set out in a skiff and greet me personally at the riverbank. Every time I went I never failed to invite Xiufeng along, but we never invited anyone else and we never went to a different boat. One night of bliss would only cost us four coins of foreign silver. Xiufeng would be with one girl one night and a different one the next, which was known as "jumping troughs," and he sometimes even had two singing girls at once! I, however, kept to Delight and no one else.

If I happened to go on my own, we might have drinks on the upper deck or chat about nothing in the loft. I never asked her to sing for me, nor did I force her to drink too much. I was compassionate and gentle with her, and her entire boat was happy about it, although the singing girls on the neighboring boats all envied her. When the girls on her boat found themselves with some free time without guests, they would come to visit me in the loft if they knew I was there. There was not a single girl in their clan that I did not get to know, so every time I boarded the boat, they would all call out to me repeatedly and I would be looking left and right trying to keep up with the greetings. You could not buy this sort of treatment for ten thousand taels of silver!

In my four months there, I spent just over a hundred taels of silver in total and was able to taste fresh lychee fruit too. It truly was one of the greatest pleasures of my life. Later, Madam Shao tried to get five hundred taels of silver out of me by forcing me to buy Delight, but I was annoyed by her harassment, so I made plans to return to Suzhou instead. Xiufeng had fallen in love with the place, though, so I urged him to redeem one of the girls as a concubine, and then we went back to the Suzhou region the way we had come.

~

The following year Xiufeng went back there, but my father would not allow me to go with him, so I went to take up a position in the offices of District Magistrate Yang in Qingpu instead.

When Xiufeng got back, he recounted how Delight sought to cut her own life short several times because I had not gone to see her. Alas! "After half a year I awoke from this dream of Yangzhou girls / with a name for being heartless on their flower boats."[33]

---

33. Shen Fu is paraphrasing a famous couplet by the Tang dynasty poet Du Mu (803–852) who cultivated an image as a roué of the entertainment quarters. Du Mu's quatrain "Releasing My Thoughts" (Qianhuai) reads: "Knocking around the lakes and rivers with a jug of wine in hand, / Southern waists, so slender and slight, rested lightly in my palm. / After ten years I awoke from this dream of Yangzhou / with a name for being heartless in its pleasure quarters."

I was stationed in Qingpu for two years after my return from Guangdong, but there were no pleasurable trips to tell of during my stay there.

Soon after, Yun and Hanyuan met one another and all sorts of criticism about them began to boil over, which made Yun ill from her seething indignation. I set up a shop with Cheng Mo'an next to our front gate to sell paintings and calligraphy, which helped somewhat to provide medicines for Yun.

~

Two days after the Mid-Autumn Festival my friend Wu Yunke along with Mao Yixiang and Wang Xingcan all invited me to go on a trip with them to Little Serenity Studio on West Hill.[34]

I was busy bending my wrist for calligraphy without pause, so I urged them to go on ahead of me.

"If you can get out of the city," Wu said, "we will wait for you around noon tomorrow at the Alighting Cranes Temple in front of the hill just over Water Step Bridge." I agreed to this.

The next day I left Cheng in charge of the shop while I strolled out of the western city gate by myself. I arrived in front of West Hill and went over Water Step Bridge, heading west along the ridge paths between the rice paddies. I caught sight of a south-facing temple with a clear stream running by its gate. I knocked on the door and asked about the temple.

The monk who answered asked, "What way did you come?"

When I told him, he laughed and said, "This is Cloud Catcher Temple. Can't you see the plaque overhead? You've already passed Alighting Cranes Temple!"

"But from the bridge all the way here, I didn't see any other temple," I replied.

He pointed behind me and said, "Don't you see the thick bamboo forest behind the earthen wall over there? That's it."

So I went back to the wall and found a small locked door set deep within it. I peeked through a gap in the door and saw a winding path with a low fence and an abundance of flourishing, green bamboo. The entire place was silent, with not a murmur of human speech. I knocked on the door but there was no answer.

Someone passing by told me, "You will find a stone in a hole

---

34. Scholars would visit Buddhist or Daoist temples in the countryside for meditation and self-cultivation or to enjoy a quiet time with friends away from the stresses of city life. West Hill was on an island in Lake Tai.

in the wall that you can use to knock on the door." So I tried that several times and a young novice did indeed show up. I followed the path into the grounds, crossed over a small stone bridge, and turned west, where I finally saw the main gate. A large black sign was suspended from it, with two white characters that said "Alighting Cranes." There was a lengthy postscript after the characters, but I did not take the time to look at it carefully. I entered the gate and passed through the outer hall of the temple guardian, which was gleaming from top to bottom completely spotless, and I knew this place was Little Serenity Studio.

Suddenly, I noticed a young novice emerge from a hallway to my left, carrying a kettle. I called to him loudly and was asking about my friends when I heard the sound of Xingcan's laugh coming from within the studio as he said, "How about that? I told you that Sanbai would never let us down!"

I turned around to see Yunke coming out to greet me. "We've been delaying breakfast for you! Why are you so late?" he asked. There was a monk directly behind him, who raised his hand in greeting and informed me that he was called Zhuyi.

We went into the studio, which was nothing more than a small chamber spanned by three rafters with a plaque that read "Sweet Osmanthus Chamber"; outside in the courtyard a pair of sweet osmanthus trees were in full bloom. Xingcan and Yixiang both got up and called to me, "Latecomers must drink a three-cup penalty!" The meat and vegetarian dishes were impeccably prepared, and both rice and sorghum wines were on hand.

"How many spots have you visited already?" I asked them.

"It was too late when we arrived yesterday," replied Yunke, "but this morning we just went to Cloud Catcher Temple and River Pavilion so far."

We drank together happily for a good while and after our meal we set out from Cloud Catcher Temple and River Pavilion and visited eight or nine other places until we ended up at Mount Hua, where we stopped. Every one of these spots has its fine qualities, but I am not able to relate them all here.

Lotus Flower Peak is on the heights of Mount Hua, but we decided to visit it another time as it was already getting dark. The sweet osmanthus flowers were just at their height when we arrived at Mount Hua, so we enjoyed a pure cup of tea beneath the blossoms, and then rode in bamboo sedan chairs all the way back to Alighting Cranes Temple.

Just east of Sweet Osmanthus Chamber was yet another small

pavilion, called the Hall of Nearing Purity, where cups and plates had already been laid out. Zhuyi sat quietly and spoke little, but he was fond of receiving guests and was an excellent drinker. So we started a drinking game called "pass the flower" with a sprig of sweet osmanthus and continued until everyone had a turn, not stopping until an hour or two before midnight.[35]

"Tonight," I said, "the moon is so beautiful. If we just crawl into bed drunk then we will turn our backs on its pure radiance! Is there somewhere we can find a lofty vantage point to enjoy the moonlight together? How can we let such a lovely night go to waste?"

"Freed Crane Pavilion is worth climbing," suggested Zhuyi.

"Xingcan brought his zither along," said Yunke, "but we have yet to hear his peerless melodies. Why not go there and have him play for us a while?" So we all went together.

All we could see was a road stretching through a forest touched with hoarfrost and wrapped in the fragrance of sweet osmanthus. Beneath the moon the empty sky stretched into the distance and, in the stillness of nature, not a sound was to be heard. Xingcan played "Three Variations on Plum Blossoms" and it was as though we were about to drift off to the realm of the immortals.[36] Yixiang was so moved that he drew an iron fife from his sleeve and played it hauntingly.

"Who among the moon gazers on Stone Lake tonight can compare to our joy?" said Yunke. He was referring to our Suzhou custom of gathering for a grand party on Stone Lake to view the string of moon reflections on the eighteenth day of the eighth lunar month, beneath Spring Outing Bridge.[37] The pleasure boats jostle for position as music and song lasts through the night. It is all in the name of viewing the moon, but it is really just an excuse to drink boisterously with a singing girl under one's arm.

Before long the moon set, the frost grew chilly, and our mood

---

35. In the drinking game "pass the flower" players pass a sprig of blossoms to the beat of a drum until it stops; whoever was left holding the flower had to have a drink as a penalty.

36. "Three Variations on Plum Blossoms" (Meihua sannong) was a melody on the theme of the hardiness of plum blossoms persisting through the winter. The earliest references to it are in Jin dynasty sources from the fourth century.

37. On a single night each year the moon is aligned properly over Stone Lake in Suzhou to shine directly through fifty-three circular apertures on Spring Outing Bridge and produce a string of lunar reflections on the surface of the lake.

had passed, so we returned to our beds.

~

The next morning Yunke said to all of us, "Deserted Monastery is in the area and is meant to be very peaceful and secluded. Have any of you ever been there?" We all replied that we had never even heard of it, let alone visited it.

"Deserted Monastery is surrounded by mountains," said Zhuyi. "It is so remote that monks are not able to remain there for very long. I have been there once in the past and it had already fallen into disrepair. I haven't been back since it was restored by Patron Peng, but I might still be able to figure out where it is.[38] If you would like to see it, then please let me act as your guide."

"So, are we meant to leave with empty stomachs?" Yixiang asked.

Zhuyi laughed, "I already have some vegetarian noodles ready for you. And I can even have a monk bring along a wine basket."

Once the noodles were finished, we set out on foot for the temple. When we passed by Lofty Friendship Garden, Yunke wanted to go to White Cloud Temple, so we went through the gates and sat down. A monk walked up to us deliberately, then cupped his hands before his chest in salute to Yunke, and said to him, "You have been away from us for two months. What news is there in the city? Is the governor still in the saddle?"

Yixiang rose impatiently and sneered "Baldy!" at him as he flicked his sleeves and made his way out of the temple.[39] Xingcan and I followed behind him, holding back our laughter, while Yunke and Zhuyi remained to say a few words of thanks to the monk before saying good-bye.

Lofty Friendship Garden was also the location of Fan Wenzheng's tomb, right next to White Cloud Temple.[40] There was a veranda opposite a cliff draped in wisteria vines with a pool at

---

38. Peng Shaosheng (1740–1796)—courtesy name Yunchu—was a famous Qing Dynasty patron and scholar of Buddhism from Suzhou.

39. Mao Yixiang was cross that the tonsured monk would spoil their refined, leisurely outing with crass inquiries regarding local politics.

40. Fan Zhongyan (989–1052)—courtesy name Xiwen, posthumous name Wenzheng—was a native of Suzhou and a renowned scholar and high official famous for advocating sweeping reforms of the government and education system in the Song dynasty. He was admired for his sincere remonstrations to the throne and once wrote, "I would rather speak out and die than live in silence."

the bottom about ten feet in diameter. The water was a clear, deep blue with golden-scaled fish swimming about in it. It was called Alms Bowl Spring. There was even a bamboo-covered stove for boiling water to steep tea. It was a truly lovely and secluded spot. Within the lush thickets of greenery spread out behind the veranda we could survey the whole layout of Fan's Garden. It was too bad that we could not bear to sit there any longer because of that monk's coarse behavior.

By that time we had traveled from Upper Sands Village to Birdcage Hill, right to the very place where Honggan and I had once scaled its heights. The natural scenery was the same as before, but Honggan was no more, and I was overwhelmed by my memories of the past. In the midst of my melancholy, I suddenly came upon a stream of water flowing across our path, blocking the way. Several local children were digging for mushrooms in the wild grasses, and they poked up their heads and laughed, seemingly amazed that this many people would arrive there at once. We asked them the way to Deserted Monastery, and they replied, "You won't be able to get across the floodwaters ahead, so please go back a few steps and you will find a small path to the south that will take you over the mountain, and you'll soon be there."

We followed their directions, crossed the mountain to the south, and walked for a half-mile or so until we began to notice the bamboo trees were growing denser and wilder, the mountains surrounded us on all four sides, and the path was blanketed in green moss without a trace of anyone having passed by. Zhuyi paused and looked all about him. "It's supposed to be here," he said, "but I can't make out the path any longer. What should we do?"

So I squatted down to take a better look and through the thousands of stalks of bamboo, I could faintly see a pile of stones, a wall, and some kind of structure. We made our way through the bamboo, pushing it aside and penetrating deeper in search of what I saw, when we finally came upon a gate over which were written words to the effect that Deserted Monastery was restored by a certain Old Man Peng of South Garden in a certain year on a certain date. Everyone exclaimed with delight, "If not for you, this would have remained a 'Peach Blossom Spring' of Wuling!"[41]

---

41. Another allusion to the famous story by Tao Qian regarding a fisherman of Wuling who stumbles upon an idyllic hidden world but is unable

The gate to the monastery was shut tight, and we knocked on it for a good while but received no answer. Suddenly a door to one side creaked open, and there appeared a young man in tattered clothes and frayed sandals who looked as though he had not been eating well.

"What are you visitors doing here?" he asked.

Zhuyi raised his hand in greeting and said, "We have been seeking the secluded serenity of this monastery and have come especially to view it with reverence."

The youth replied, "This mountain monastery is so poor that the monks have all scattered and there is no one left to receive you properly. I would ask that you look for somewhere else to visit." And with that he began to close the door and go back inside. But Yunke moved quickly to stop him and promised that if he would just open the gate and allow us to visit, then we would certainly show our appreciation.

The young man smiled at this and said, "It's just that I am completely out of tea to serve you and I was afraid of showing my guests a lack of hospitality. Did you really think I was looking for a payment of some kind?"

Once the main gate was open, we found ourselves gazing upon the face of the Buddha, its golden light shining against a backdrop of verdant shade. The stone steps and foundations in the courtyard were covered in a fine embroidery of moss. Behind the entrance hall terraced platforms rose up like a wall surrounded by a stone balustrade. We headed west alongside the terraces and came to a huge boulder over twenty feet high and as round as a steamed bun, with slender stalks of bamboo growing at its foot.

We went further west, then turned north and followed an inclined veranda to ascend the terraces, where we came upon a reception hall with three columns directly opposite the boulder. At the foot of the boulder there was a small moon-reflecting pool fed by limpid spring water crisscrossed with fringed water lilies.

To the east of the reception hall was the main hall and to its left, facing west, were the monks' chambers and kitchen. The rear of the main hall looked out onto a sheer cliff and a profusion of trees so thick with shade that you could not even see the sky when looking up. Xingcan was growing weary and stopped by the pool for a short rest, so I accompanied him. We were about to break

---

to find it again after leaving.

out the wine for a drink when we suddenly heard Yixiang's voice come to us from the treetops.

"Sanbai, come quickly!" he shouted. "The view is wonderful up here!"

I raised my head to look at him but could not see anyone, so Xingcan and I followed the sound of Yixiang's voice in search of him. We passed through an eastern chamber of the hall and left by a small door. We turned north and found several dozen stone steps rising up like a ladder to a bank of bamboo within which we could catch a glimpse of a tower. So we went up into the tower and found eight windows opening out onto vistas with a placard that read, "Soaring Clouds Pavilion." Mountains enclosed us on all four sides, ranged like a city wall, with a single gap in the southwest corner through which we could just see in the distance innumerable sails sweeping across a stretch of water, soaking up the sky. This was Lake Tai. I leaned on a windowsill and looked down to see the wind moving across the bamboo tops like waves billowing over wheat fields.

"So, what do you think?" asked Yixiang.

"The view really is wonderful," I answered.

Suddenly we heard Yunke's voice calling to us from west of the tower, "Yixiang, come quickly! This view is even more wonderful!"

So we made our way back down from the tower and headed west up a dozen more steps when a brightly lit clearing suddenly opened up before us, as smooth and level as a veranda. We guessed this place was atop the cliff behind the main hall of the monastery. Some broken bricks and crumbling cornerstones were still there from what must have been the foundation of an older temple. We gazed all around us at the surrounding mountains, and it felt even more liberating than in the pavilion. Yixiang called out long and loud in the direction of Lake Tai and the mountain ranges all echoed in unison.

Then we sat down upon the ground and opened up the wine jug. We were struck with sudden pangs of hunger, so the young monk said he would fry up some toasted rice instead of making tea, but we told him to make congee out of it instead and invited him to join us in eating it. We asked him how the monastery had ended up falling into such a state of neglect.

"There is no one else living nearby," he replied, "and at night many bandits come to rob us of our food whenever we manage to store up any. And as for any fruits and vegetables we manage to plant, the woodcutters help themselves to half of those. We are actually affiliated with Venerate Tranquility Temple, but the head kitchen only sends us three bushels of dried rice and a jar of salted vegetables once a month.[42] I'm staying here for a time to look after things for the descendants of the Peng family, but I'm preparing to go home. Before long there won't be a trace of anyone left here at all." Yunke thanked the young man and gave him a coin of foreign silver.

When we got back to Alighting Crane Temple, we rented a boat and returned home. I painted a piece called "Deserted Monastery" and presented it to the monk Zhuyi as a record of such a pleasurable trip.

~

In the winter of that year I had a falling out with my parents on account of my involvement as a guarantor for a friend's loan, so we had to go live in the Hua household at Mount Xi.

In the spring of the following year I was set to go to Yangzhou, but I was short of funds. So I went to call on my old friend Han Chunquan, who worked as a private secretary in the regional offices at Shangyang. My clothes and shoes were in such a tattered state that I could not bear to show up at his place of work, so I sent my card instead to invite him to meet with me in the gardens of the prefectural temple.

When Chunquan came out to see me, he discovered how poorly I was faring and was generous enough to aid me with ten taels of silver. The garden we were in was constructed with donations from a comprador merchant. While it certainly was vast in scope it was unfortunate that the embellishment of each vista was a complete hodgepodge and the stones piled up into artificial mountains in the background also lacked any sense of composition in their placement.

On my way back home I suddenly thought of the wonderful sights of Mount Yu, and it happened there was a boat I could take that would pass nearby. It was already March, in spring, and the peach and plum blossoms were each vying to be more beautiful, but I felt badly that I had no companion with whom I could share the trip.

Clutching three hundred coins of copper cash, I strolled over

---

42. Venerate Tranquility Temple (Chongningsi) was established in the early sixth century on the eastern shore of Lake Yangcheng, northeast of Suzhou.

to Mount Yu Academy. I looked up at the walls surrounding it and saw a thick grove of profusely flowering trees showing forth delicate red blossoms and new green stems; the grove ran along a stream at the foot of a mountain—truly a place rich in the charms of refined seclusion. Unfortunately, I could not find the main gate into the academy, so I just asked someone where to pick up the road to Mount Yu and forged ahead.

I came upon a tea vendor who had set up shop beneath a canopy. I went in and he boiled up a cup of Green Gossamer Spring tea, which was very fine to drink. I asked which sight on Mount Yu was the most outstanding and another traveler replied, "From here, head through the Western Pass and you'll be close to Sword Gate, which is truly Mount Yu's most exquisite spot. If you want to go there, please allow me to be your guide." I was delighted to go with him.

We left through the West Gate and followed the foot of the mountain up and down for a few miles until I gradually came to see its peak towering overhead with horizontal striations in its rock formations. When we arrived, it turned out to be one mountain peak split into two cliffs, one concave and one convex, hundreds of feet high. When I stood close and looked up at them, it seemed they were on the verge of falling over. "I've heard," said my guide, "that there is a cave dwelling up there with views worthy of the immortals. It's too bad that there is no path up to it."

But my interest was stirred, so I rolled up my sleeves, hiked up my robes, and started clambering up the slope like an ape until I reached the summit. The so-called cave dwelling was no more than ten feet deep and had a fissure in the ceiling that opened up to a view of the sky. When I bent my head to look down, I felt my legs buckle and almost fell, so I kept my front pressed against the cliff face and lowered myself with vines and creepers. My guide let out a sigh and said, "Impressive! When it comes to heroic explorers, I've never seen the likes of you before!"

My throat was parched and I longed for something to drink, so I invited my companion to a rustic wine shop nearby and bought us a few rounds. The sun was already setting and I was not able to visit all of Mount Yu, but I did pick up about a dozen chunks of ochre to bring back with me. Then I slung my bag onto my back, took the night boat to Suzhou, and made my way back to Mount Xi.[43]

---

43. Ochre is a reddish brown earth pigment used to tint paintings.

This was my pleasurable trip in trying times.

~

In the spring of 1804, in the ninth year of the Jiaqing reign, I suffered through my father passing away.

I was on the verge of abandoning my family to flee far away into reclusion when my friend Xia Yishan urged me to stay in his home. That autumn in September he invited me to go with him to Yongtaisha in the East Sea to help him collect rent from his land there.

Yongtaisha was an island in Chongming county, over thirty miles by boat from the mouth of the Liu River. It had recently emerged from the waters and was just being opened up for cultivation. There were still no streets or markets, and everything was covered with reeds and silver grass as far as the eye could see. There were virtually no signs of human habitation aside from a grain storehouse spanning several dozen rafters, operated by one of Yishan's colleagues named Ding. A moat had been excavated around the granary, with willow trees planted all along the outer embankments.

Ding—courtesy name Shichu—was a native of Chongming and the chief settler on Yongtaisha. He had an accountant named Wang and the two of them were very forthright, hospitable, and unconstrained by niceties of etiquette, treating me as an old friend moments after meeting me. Ding would butcher a pig for our feast and empty the jug for our drink. Our drinking games were played with our fingers because he knew nothing of poetry and prose and when he sang it was all hooting and hollering because he could not carry a tune. When we got drunk together, he would command his workers to box and wrestle for our amusement.

Ding kept more than a hundred head of cattle, which slept out in the open atop the embankments. He also raised geese, as their honking could warn of approaching pirates. Each day he would head out with his hound and falcon to hunt amid the thick stands of reeds between the sandy islets, bringing down many birds. I would sometimes accompany him on his hunting excursions, but if I grew weary I would just lie down to rest.

Ding took me once to the fields in his farmland where the crops were ripening; each field was marked with a written character and surrounded by a high embankment to keep out the tidewaters. The embankments had sluiceways in them that could be opened and shut with a sluice gate. When the fields were dry, he would open the sluice gates at high tide to irrigate them. When the fields were sodden, he would open the gates at low tide to drain them.

The tenant farmers lived scattered between the fields like a constellation of stars, but Ding could gather all of them with a single shout. They all addressed the owner of their property as "Landlord" and were very compliant in listening to his orders with a charming unaffected sincerity. Yet if they were stirred by an injustice, they could be wilder than any wolf or tiger. Fortunately, one word of fair treatment would quickly return them to a proper attitude of respect. They lived by the wind and rain, in the darkness and the light, as the ancients used to do.

I would lie in my bed at night and look out my window to watch the billowing waves. From my pillow the sound of the surging tide sounded like singing gongs and booming drums. One night I caught sight of a red light as big as a wicker basket, floating in the ocean about ten miles offshore. Then I saw red rays of light illuminating the sky so brightly it seemed to catch fire. Shichu told me, "When divine lights and fires appear in this region, it means that a new sandbar will soon emerge from the waters."

Yishan always had a bold and carefree spirit about him, but when he came to this place he was even more liberated. I too was more unbridled in my behavior and took to singing out wildly from atop an ox and dancing drunkenly on the beach. I just followed my impulses wherever they might lead, and it truly was the most unrestrained, delightful trip that I have made in my entire life. It was already November by the time we wrapped up our affairs and returned home.

~

When it comes to the memorable sights of Tiger Hill in my hometown of Suzhou, I would rank a place behind the hill called Thousand Acre Clouds first and put Sword Pond second.[44]

The rest of the places are all too artificial and ruined by cosmetic additions, which has made them lose their original natural appearance. The newly erected ancestral temple for Bai Juyi and the Pagoda Reflection Bridge do no more than perpetuate pretty sounding names. And Smelting Works Shore, which I playfully renamed "Wild Scent Shore," is really nothing more than a mass of rustic ornamentation that makes it look like a seductress.

---

44. Sword Pond is said to be the location of the tomb of the founder of Suzhou, King Helü of Wu (r. 514–496 BCE), who was was reputedly buried with thousands of swords. Tiger Hill is also said to get its name from a white tiger that guarded King Helü's tomb for three days after his burial.

The most famous garden in the city of Suzhou, Lion Grove Garden, is said to be laid out in the style of paintings by Ni Zan.[45] While its stonework is delicately wrought and it has many ancient trees in it, its overall layout really looks like nothing more than random piles of coal cinders covered with moss and pierced with ant holes. It has none of the authentic natural feel of a forest in the mountains. I may be too narrow in my view, but I do not understand what is so marvelous about it.

On Lingyan Mountain, which is the ancient site of King Fuchai of Wu's Beauty Abode Palace, there are sights such as Xi Shi's Cave, Sounding Clogs Hall, and Gathering Fragrances Path, but their positioning is careless, as they are spread too far apart without a sense of cohesion. They are no match for the exceptionally rich charms of refined seclusion to be found in the Tianping and Zhixing Mountains.[46]

Dengwei Mountain is also called Yuan's Tomb. Lake Tai is behind it to the west and it faces Brocade Summit to the east. Its vermilion cliffs and emerald pavilions make it look like a painting when viewed from afar. The people who live there raise plum trees for a living, and when the flowers are in bloom, for miles and miles the whole vista looks as though it is covered in snow—so it is also known as the Ocean of Scented Snow.

On the east slope of the mountain there are four old cypress trees nicknamed Pure, Marvelous, Ancient, and Weird. The Pure one has a perfectly straight trunk and leaves as dense as an emerald green canopy. The Marvelous one runs along the ground and has three bends in its trunk in a zigzag formation. The Ancient one has balding branches on top and is flat and spread out and half rotted; it looks a bit like the palm of a hand. The Weird one is twisted into a spiral shape, branches and trunk and all. It is said that these four trees survive from before the Han dynasty.

~

---

45. Lion Grove Garden was attached to Lion Grove Temple, founded in 1342 by Chan Buddhist Master Tianru, and housed an unusual rock that resembled a lion.

46. Legend has it that King Fuchai of Wu (r. 495–473 BCE), the son of King Helü, built Beauty Abode Palace for his favorite concubine Xi Shi, who caused his downfall by distracting him from battling his enemies. She is credited with inventing a style of tap dancing called "sounding clogs," which employed wooden-soled shoes affixed with tiny bells.

In February 1805, Yishan's venerable father, Master Chunxiang, and Yishan's uncle, Jieshi, took four of their sons and nephews to visit Kerchief Hill to carry out the spring sacrifices at their ancestral temple and to sweep the family graves.

They invited me to go with them and our road led first to Lingyan Mountain, then over Tiger Hill Bridge, after which we followed the Fei Family River into the Ocean of Scented Snow to view the plum blossoms. Their family shrine on Kerchief Hill was actually ensconced right in the midst of the Ocean of Scented Snow. Just at that time the flowers were at their height and every cough or sputter on our part was scented with their fragrance. I once painted for Jieshi an album with twelve leaves called "The Wind and Trees of Kerchief Hill."[47]

~

In October of that same year I went with Principal Graduate Shi Zhuotang when he left to take up his post as Prefect of Chongqing in Sichuan Province.

We traveled upriver on the Yangtze until our boat arrived at Wancheng. At the foot of Mount Wan was the tomb of Yu Que, a loyal minister of the late Yuan dynasty.[48] Beside this tomb was a hall with three rooms called Prospect Pavilion, which looked over South Lake and backed up against Mount Qian. The pavilion was perched on one of the mountain ridges and commanded an expansive view into the distance. A deep veranda ran along one side, with north facing windows opened wide. It happened to be the season of first frost, when the leaves begin to turn red, and they were as brilliant as peach or plum blossoms. Jiang Shoupeng and Cai Ziqin were traveling with me at the time.

There was also the Wang Clan Garden just outside the southern wall of the city, which was quite long from east to west but rather narrow from south to north, as it was restricted on the north by backing onto the city wall and on the south by overlooking the lake. Being so narrow in terms of land, it must have been rather difficult to lay out properly, but I observed that in its construction

---

47. "Wind and Trees" alludes to lines from a Han dynasty handbook of poetry usage, *Unofficial Account of Han School Poems* (*Hanshi waizhuan*): "Just as a tree longs to be still, but the wind does not stop, so too does a child long to care for his parents even though they have left him behind."

48. Yu Que (1303–1358)—courtesy names Tingxin and Tianxin—fought on behalf of the Yuan dynasty against the Red Turban rebels for many years.

the methods of layered terraces and storied buildings had been used to compensate.

The layered terraces were platforms on top of the buildings that were turned into courtyard gardens piled with stones and planted with flowers so that visitors were unaware of the buildings beneath their feet. The piles of stone on top were over the solid parts of the buildings, while the courtyard gardens were over hollow parts, where the flowers and trees could thrive on soil below.

The storied buildings were two-floor structures that had a sort of loft on top with a terrace on top of that, resulting in four stacked levels from top to bottom. There were even small pools from which water could not escape and the whole effect made it impossible to determine what was an illusion and what was real.

The buildings all rested on brick footings, with the load-bearing pillars fashioned after the European style.[49] Happily, they all faced South Lake, so there was nothing to obstruct the eye. I wandered around that garden to my heart's content and found it to be superior to a garden built on level ground. It truly was a marvel of human ingenuity.

~

The Yellow Crane Tower of Wuchang is on Yellow Swan Point, which extends back to Yellow Swan Hill, commonly called Snake Hill.[50]

The tower has three stories, with painted ridgepoles and upturned flying eaves, and rises prominently next to the city wall,

---

49. European style refers to the square shape of the base and capital of the pillars used to support weight across a greater surface area than a traditional Chinese column with round ends.

50. Yellow Crane Tower is one of the most famous landmarks in China and was reportedly first built in 223 CE to commemorate the site where an immortal named Wang Zi'an ascended to the heavens astride a yellow crane. The Tang dynasty poet Cui Hao (?704–754) composed a widely imitated poem on the view called "Yellow Crane Tower" (Huanghe lou) that reads: "The ancient one has departed on a yellow crane; / this place is now empty save for Yellow Crane Tower. / The yellow crane is gone and will never return; / white clouds drift in the sky for a thousand years. / Along the sunny river run the trees of Hanyang; / sweet grass grows thickly on Parrot Isle. / As the sun sets I wonder where is my hometown? / These misty waves on the river make a man sad."

overlooking the Han River just across from the Sunny River Pavilion in Hanyang.[51]

Zhuotang and I braved the snow to ascend the tower and looked down at the never-ending sky filled with snowflakes dancing like flower petals; we pointed out silvered mountains and jade-frosted trees in the distance, and it seemed as though I found myself on a terrace of the immortals made of the whitest nephrite. In the river below, the tiny boats traveled to and fro, pitching and yawing back and forth like so many fallen leaves caught in the roiling waves. A heart yearning for fame and fortune was cooled in such a place.

So many poems were written on the walls that I cannot remember them all, but I do recall one pair of columns that had the following parallel couplet written on them:

> When will the yellow crane ever come again,
> so that we may tip our golden flagons together
> to water the ancient sweet grass on the river isle?

> I only see the white clouds scudding away,
> so who will play the jade flute now
> to fell the June plum blossoms in river town?[52]

Huangzhou's Red Cliffs stand just outside the Han River Gate of the prefectural capital. They tower over the riverbanks, cut from the rock like vast walls. The stone is a uniform deep red color, which is the reason for their name. The *Classic of Waterways* refers to them as the Red Nose Mountains.[53] Su Shi once traveled here and composed two rhapsodies referring to them as the site where the forces of the Wu and Wei kingdoms clashed, but he was

---

51. The Sunny River Pavilion was built in the Ming dynasty and named for the third couplet in Cui Hao's poem quoted above.

52. This unattributed poem echoes Cui Hao's poem above and the following lines from a poem by Li Bai, "With Director Shi I Admire the Flute Playing from Atop Yellow Crane Tower" (Yu Shi langzhong qinting Huangheloushang chuidi): "From atop Yellow Crane Tower the piping of a jade flute: / river town in June and 'Falling Plum Blossoms.'" The old flute melody "Falling Plum Blossoms" (Luo meihua) is being used in this couplet to evoke ephemerality as plum blossoms fall in late winter or early spring and would be long gone by June.

53. The *Classic of Waterways* (*Shui jing*) is an early record of the bodies of water in China, compiled in various versions between the first and third centuries CE.

mistaken about the location. There is dry land at the foot of the cliffs now, but there is still a Two Rhapsodies Pavilion on top.[54]

~

In December of that winter we arrived at Jingzhou.

Here Zhuotang received notice of his promotion to Intendant of the General Administration Circuit of Tong Pass, so he left me behind to stay in Jingzhou and I was upset that I was not going to have a chance to see the rivers and mountains of Sichuan.

While Zhuotang went on to Sichuan by himself, his son Dunfu and his family, including Cai Ziqin and Xi Zhitang, all stayed with me in Jingzhou, where we lived in the remnants of the Liu Clan Garden. I recall that there was a plaque over the main hall that read, "Wisteria and Mangrove Studio." The courtyard steps had stone balustrades running around them and there was a square pond almost thirty yards per side in which a pavilion had been erected with a stone bridge crossing over to it. The area behind the pavilion had been built up with mounds of earth and piles of rock and planted with all kinds of trees, but everywhere else was a lot of barren land and the towers and buildings had all collapsed into ruin.

We had nothing to do away from home like this, so we chanted poems or whistled tunes, went out for walks, or got together to chat. As the year drew to a close our travel funds ran out, but we were all getting along well. We pawned our clothing to buy wine and even set up a gong and drum to strike for music. We drank every night and every time we drank we played drinking games. We were so hard up that even a single cup of cheap sorghum spirits would necessitate a grand game of Ruler of the Wine Vessel.

We happened to meet someone from our hometown with the surname of Cai, and when Cai Ziqin related his lineage to him it turned out that they were cousins, so we asked him to show us around some of the famous sights. We went to Serpentine River

---

54. Su Shi wrote his pair of "Rhapsodies on Red Cliff" (Chibu fu) (already cited several times by Shen Fu) to celebrate outings made with friends to the Red Cliffs at Huangzhou. The pieces are largely philosophical reflections on the ephemerality of life and happiness but they do evoke the famous Battle of Red Cliff on the Yangtze River near the end of the Eastern Han dynasty in 208 CE, which ushered in the era of the Three Kingdoms. Even though the actual site of the battle was farther upstream, Su Shi's rhapsodies made the red cliffs at Huangzhou equally famous.

Tower, in front of the prefectural school, atop which Zhang Jiuling of old had written a poem when he was serving as an administrator.[55] Zhu Xi also has a poem about it that says, "When I feel like looking back in longing for you, / I need only climb Serpentine River Tower."[56]

On the city wall there is also the Grand Chu Tower, which was built by King Gao during the Five Dynasties. It really is of grand, imposing dimensions, and you can see for over a hundred miles from up there.[57] All around the city the riverbanks are planted with weeping willows and the small boats ply their way to and fro beneath them, lending the whole scene the quality of a painting.

The prefectural offices of Jingzhou were actually once the military headquarters of Guan Yu the Brave and True. Inside the gate to his residence there is a broken granite manger that people say was the very trough used to feed his renowned steed Red Hare.[58]

We asked about Luo Han's house, located on a small lake west of the city, but we did not come across it. So then we asked about Song Yu's former residence north of the city. Yu Xin of old once stayed there when he was fleeing back home to Jiangling to escape Hou Jing's rebellion. The house was supposedly turned into a tavern at some point, but no one could recognize it any longer.[59]

~

55. Zhang Jiuling (673–740) was a Tang dynasty poet from Qujiang (Serpentine River) in Guangdong Province.

56. Zhu Xi (1130–1200) was the leading philosopher and educational reformer of the Song dynasty and a founding father of Neo-Confucian philosophy. These lines are from his "Short Verses Welcoming the Secretariat of Jingnan" (Duanju fengying Jingnan mufu).

57. The Grand Chu tower was first built in 912 by King Gao Jixing (r. 907–928), who established Jingnan, one of the Ten Kingdoms during the Five Dynasties and Ten Kingdoms period of disunion (907–960).

58. Guan Yu (160–220 CE) was a brilliant general at the beginning of the Three Kingdoms era. After he helped Liu Bei (161–223 CE) to secure victory at Red Cliff against the forces of Cao Cao (155–220 CE), he governed Jingzhou. His life and military exploits became the stuff of legend in the novel *Romance of the Three Kingdoms* (*Sanguozhi yanyi*). Guan Yu received Red Hare, the renowned steed of a fierce defeated warrior named Lü Bu (d. 199), because he was the only man who was able to ride it.

59. Luo Han (292–372) was a powerful Western Jin official from the Hunan region who went to live as a recluse in Jingzhou. Song Yu (third

At the end of that year it turned bitterly cold after a snowfall.

With the arriving year and the blooming of spring, we found ourselves without the bother of having to pay calls on friends and relatives, so to amuse ourselves we spent the day setting off firecrackers, flying kites, and making paper lanterns. Before long the warm breezes brought us word of blooming flowers, and rains washed away the dust from spring. Zhuotang's concubines brought his young daughter and son downriver to us from Sichuan. His eldest son Dunfu had our baggage repacked and our party set out together. We went ashore at Fancheng and from there made our way straight to Tong Pass.

From west of Wenxiang County in Henan Province we went through Hangu Pass. The words "Violet Vapors Arrive from the East" were inscribed there, as it was the place where Laozi rode through astride a black ox. The mountains on either side pressed in on the path, which was only wide enough to admit two horses traveling abreast.[60]

After about three miles we arrived at Tong Pass, which backed onto a sheer cliff on the left and looked over the Yellow River on the right. The pass was between the mountains and the river and was choked off by a formidable phalanx of towers and battlements that rose up there. And yet in the stillness there was no sound of horse and cart and virtually no trace of cooking fires. As one of Han Yu's poems says, "The sun shines down on Tong Pass, its four gates stand open"—does that not almost capture its feeling of desolation?[61]

The General Surveillance Circuit in the city only had one

---

century BCE) was a legendary composer of rhapsodies said to have lived in the Chu kingdom during the Warring States era. Yu Xin (513–581) was an ambassador for the Liang Dynasty who was famous for his poems and rhapsodies. Hou Jing usurped the throne of the Liang Dynasty from 548 until his death in 552. It is highly unlikely that any structure over one thousand years old would have survived until Shen Fu's time.

60. Legends about the Daoist sage Laozi say that an auspicious violet-colored vapor preceded him as he traveled westward through Hangu Pass astride a black ox, pausing only to write down the book known as the *Laozi* or *The Way and Its Power* (*Dao de jing*).

61. This line is from "Sent Ahead to Elder Official Zhang Twelfth Upon My Arrival at Tong Pass" (Ci Tongguan xianji Zhang Shier gelao) by Han Yu. Tong Pass was the most important strategic point in Northern China and was pivotal in the battles that led to the establishment of both the Tang and Ming dynasties.

assistant department magistrate under it. The offices of the circuit intendant were right up against the north wall, with a garden in the back that extended for about half an acre. Two ponds had been excavated at the eastern and western ends; a stream entered from outside the southwest corner of the walls and flowed eastward to a spot between the two pools, where it split up into three channels: one flowed southward into the main kitchen, where it supplied water for daily use; another flowed eastward into the east pond; and the last flowed north, then turned west where it ended up spouting forth from the mouth of a hornless stone dragon into the west pond. After that the stream bent back to the northwest corner, where a sluiceway had been installed to drain the water along the foot of the city wall until it turned north and flowed out through an opening in the wall directly down to the Yellow River. Day and night the water flowed around us with a sound that penetrated the ears with great clarity. The bamboo and trees provided such thick shade that you could not see the sky when you looked up.

In the middle of the west pond there was a pavilion encircled with lotus blossoms. To the east of that there was a three-room library that faced south; it had a grape arbor in its courtyard with a square stone table underneath, perfect for playing *weiqi* or drinking. The rest of the courtyard was planted with chrysanthemum beds. On the west side of the pavilion was an east-facing veranda with three partitions where you could sit and listen to the sound of the flowing water. At the south end of the veranda was a small door leading to the living quarters. Beneath a window at the north end of the veranda was yet another small pond, which had a tiny temple on its north side dedicated to the Flower Goddess.

In the very center of the whole garden was a three-story tower built against the north city wall; it was the same height as the wall and from there one could look down to see the Yellow River. On the northern bank of the river the mountains stretched out like a screen over in Shanxi Province. It truly was a spectacular sight!

I lived in the south part of the garden in a small boat-shaped building with an earthen mound in its courtyard. Atop the mound was a small gazebo I could climb to take in the whole layout of the garden. It was enclosed by cool green shade on all sides and provided respite from the summer heat. Zhuotang wrote the words "Unmoored Boat" on the lintel for me.[62] In all my travels in search of employment this

---

62. From a well-known passage in *Zhuangzi* (Chapter 32): "A skillful man toils, a wise man worries, but a man without ability seeks nothing

was the most pleasant place to live. Several dozen varieties of chrysanthemum had been planted on the earthen mound, but sadly they did not even have a chance to bud before Zhuotang was transferred to the post of Provincial Surveillance Commissioner in Shandong Province. His family moved to live at Tongchuan Academy and I went with them to take up residence there.

~

Zhuotang went ahead to take up his post in Shandong, while I, Ziqin, Zhitang, and the rest were left with nothing to do, so we went on outings.

Once we rode horses to Huayin Temple, passing through Huafeng Village on the way, the site of the Three Prayers in the time of Yao.[63] Within the temple grounds there were numerous pagoda trees from the Qin dynasty and cypress trees from the Han dynasty, as big as three or four arm-spans around. There were even cypress trees growing in the midst of pagoda trees and pagoda trees growing in the midst of cypress trees. The halls housed many ancient stelae, including one bearing the characters "Blessings" and "Longevity" in the hand of Chen Xiyi.[64]

At the foot of Mount Hua was Jade Spring Courtyard, where Master Xiyi shed his mortal body and was transformed into an immortal. Inside a cave no larger than a small chamber was a statue of the master reclining on a stone bed. The area had pure water and bright sandy soil with plants that were mainly deep red in color. The spring flowed very swiftly and was surrounded by tall, thin bamboo. Just outside the cave was a square gazebo with a tablet reading, "Untroubled Pavilion." Beside it there were three ancient trees with lines on their bark resembling cracked charcoal and leaves that looked like those of the pagoda tree but deeper in color. I did not know the proper name, but the local people just called them "untroubled trees."

I have no idea how many thousands of feet high the peaks of

---

and is happy to roam about with a full belly; adrift as an unmoored boat, he roams without purpose."

63. *Zhuangzi* (Chapter 12) relates the story of Sage-King Yao at Huafeng Village refusing prayers for long life, riches, and many sons because they only bring worries. That did not keep people from praying for those very things at this site in Shaanxi Province.

64. Chen Xiyi (d. 989) was a Daoist diviner and practitioner of meditation who lived in the Five Dynasties to early Song eras. He retired to the sacred Daoist mountain, Mount Hua, near the Huayin temple.

the great Mount Hua are, but I regret that I was unable to pack up some provisions and climb them.

On my way back, I saw persimmons in the forest that were just turning ripe, so I plucked them from atop my horse to eat them on the spot. The local people shouted for me to stop, but I did not listen to them. Instead I munched on one, only to find that it was exceedingly bitter! I spat it out quickly and then had to jump down from my horse and find some spring water to wash out my mouth before I could even speak. The locals all had a great laugh at this. In fact, a persimmon has to be boiled after it is picked to get rid of its bitterness, something I did not know.

~

In November 1806 Zhuotang sent someone from Shandong to retrieve his family members, so we finally left Tong Pass and went through Henan into Shandong.

In the western part of Shandong's prefectural capital city of Ji'nan there is a Greater Brightness Lake on which you will find the famous sights of Lixia Pavilion and Water's Fragrance Pavilion. In the summer months, in the places where the willow shade gathers thickly and the fragrance of lotus blossoms arrives, to drift in a boat with a jug of wine must be full of the charms of refined seclusion. But I went to see it during the days of winter and was met only with drooping willows and chilly mists stretching endlessly over the water.

Geyser Spring is the champion of Ji'nan's seventy-two springs. It is split into three fountains through which the water angrily gushes forth from underground as though it were boiling fiercely. Most springs flow down from above, but this one is distinctive in flowing up from below, which makes it singularly rare. By the pool there is a building for making offerings to a statue of Ancestor Lü, where many visitors savor a cup of tea made with the spring water.[65]

~

In March of the following year I took up my assignment at Laiyang in Shandong.

In the autumn of 1807 Zhuotang was demoted to the Hanlin Academy and I also went to the capital.[66]

---

65. Lü Dongbin was a Tang dynasty literatus who cultivated the Dao and was later deified as one of the Eight Immortals of the Daoist pantheon.

66. The Hanlin Academy was located at the imperial court in Beijing and

As for what is known as the Ocean Mirage of Dengzhou, I never did find a way to see it in the end.[67]

---

was staffed by scholars in charge of drafting and editing imperial documents. The posts were prestigious but had no administrative power.

67. Atmospheric conditions over the ocean off the coast of Shandong occasionally create a mirage of an entire city floating over the water. Su Shi wrote a poem on the phenomenon called "Ocean Mirage" (Haishi): "Swirling and tossing, this world adrift gives rise to myriad forms, / could those palaces of pearl, behind cowry gates, really be there?"

Chronology

To aid the reader in keeping track of the non-linear narrative in *Six Records of a Life Adrift*, this table lists the events in the lives of Shen Fu (SF) and his wife Yun (Y) chronologically by year, and cross-references them with SF's location, age, and the record (R) in which they are narrated. (For location, Yangzhou includes Hanjiang.) Ages are approximate, as Chinese custom dictates that people are one year old at birth and then turn a year older with each passing of the Lunar New Year. The table following this one charts the span of time that is covered by each of the four records.

Year	Event	Location	Age	R
1763	Y is born (Feb.). SF is born (Dec. 26).	Suzhou	1	1
1766	Y's father dies.	"	4	1
1770s	SF observes nature in the garden as a child.	"	8–12	2
1775	SF meets Y at her home and his mother arranges their engagement (Aug. 11).	"	13	1
	The "congee incident" occurs in the winter.	"		
1777	SF begins studies with Master Zhao in Shanyin.	Shanyin	15	4
1778	SF follows his teacher to Hangzhou and explores the sights.	Hangzhou	16	4
	SF takes examinations with classmate Zhao Jizhi.	"		
	SF visits his teacher's ancestral grave.	"		

1780	SF and Y are married (Feb. 26). SF's sister is also married (Feb. 28).	Suzhou	18	1
	SF leaves to study again with Master Zhao in Hangzhou.	Hangzhou		1
	SF returns to spend the summer with Y at My Choice Hall, where they celebrate various festivals.	Suzhou		1
	SF and Y raise flowers and make bonsai arrangements together.	"		2
1781	SF's brother, Qitang, is married. Family moves to Granary Lane. Opera performance for birthday of SF's mother.	" "	19	1
	SF and Y rent a house for the summer by Golden Mother Bridge.	"		
	SF's father and Y fall ill (Sep.).	"		4
	SF gives up his studies to become a private secretary like his father.	"		
	SF goes to Fengxian to apprentice with Jiang Sizhai in the winter, befriends Gu Honggan, and explores the local mountains with him.	Fengxian		4
1783	SF takes up his first independent post in Yangzhou in the spring. (Yangzhou is also called Hanjiang in the text.)	Yangzhou	21	4
1784	SF goes to work with his father in Wujiang.	Wujiang	22	4
	SF makes a brief trip via Lake Tai to visit home.	Suzhou		4
	SF follows his father who is transferred to Haining.	Haining		4
1785	Y has a falling out with SF's father over her handling of letters.	"	23	3
1787	SF takes a post in Jixi and sees the local sights and festivals.	Jixi	25	4
1788	Y gives birth to daughter Qingjun.	Suzhou	26	3

1788	SF leaves in disgust at the corruption in Jixi and returns home to try his hand at the wine trade without success.	Suzhou	26	4
1790	Y gives birth to son, Fengsen.	"	28	3
	SF goes to work with his father in Hanjiang (Yangzhou) in the spring. Y has a falling out with SF's mother over Y arranging to procure a concubine for SF's father.	Yangzhou		3
1792	SF transfers to Zhenzhou (and returns briefly to Hanjiang).	Zhenzhou	30	3
	SF's father intercepts a letter to SF from Y discussing a loan Qitang has failed to repay, which causes his father to banish SF and Y from the family.	"		3
	SF and Y are invited by Lu Banfang to live in the Tower of Tranquility.	Suzhou		3
1793	SF and Y socialize and go on outings with friends during their stay in the Tower of Tranquility.	"	31	2
	SF and Y take a trip together on Lake Tai to Wujiang.	Wujiang		1
	SF makes his first journey up the Yangtze River and south to Lingnan (Guangzhou) on his lengthy trade trip with his cousin-in-law Xu Xiufeng. (Arrives Jan. 1794.)	Lingnan		4
1794	SF spends a hundred taels on the flower boats with a prostitute named Delight.	"	32	4
	SF returns from Lingnan (Aug.).	Suzhou		1
	SF takes up a post in Qingpu (near Suzhou).	Qingpu		4
	SF and Y are forgiven by his father and allowed to return home.	Suzhou		3

1795	SF and Y meet Hanyuan, the courtesan in training. Y convinces her to become her sworn sister (Sep. 30).	Suzhou	33	1
	Hanyuan is purchased by another man. Y falls ill.	"		3
1795– 1800	Y gets sicker, the family slips into poverty, SF guarantees a bad debt, and his father becomes enraged at the Hanyuan affair.	"	33–38	3
	SF and his friends take trips to visit Buddhist monasteries around Suzhou.	"		4
1801	SF and Y are expelled by his father and stay with her friend Madam Hua in Xishan. They part from their children (Fengsen, 12, and Qingjun, 14) on Feb. 9.	Xishan	39	3
	Y decorates Mrs. Hua's courtyard with flower screens.	"		2
	SF goes to Jingjiang to get funds from his brother-in-law (Feb. 28).	Jingjiang		3
	SF goes to Shangyang to borrow money from his friend Han Chunquan.	Shangyang		4
1802	SF gets a post in the salt office in Yangzhou (Mar.).	Yangzhou	40	3
	Y is well enough to join SF in Yangzhou (Nov.).	"		3
	SF and Y arrange their house in Yangzhou in the Taiping boat style.	"		2
	SF loses his job.	"		3
1803	Y falls seriously ill	"	41	3
	SF makes another trip to Jingjiang to borrow money from his brother-in-law (Mar.).	Jingjiang		3

1803	SF returns to find that they have been robbed by their servant boy Shuang.	Yangzhou	41	3
	Y dies at the age of 41 (May 20). SF waits for her ghost to return.	"		3
	SF buries Y in Yangzhou, returns to Suzhou, but is told to leave by his younger brother, Qitang.	"		3
1804	SF learns that his father has died (Apr.) and returns home to mourn him.	Suzhou	42	3
	SF fights with his younger brother over the inheritance, disowns the family, and goes to stay in the Hall of Great Mercy.	"		3
	SF makes trips with his friend Xia Yishan and his father to collect rent from their lands in Yongtaisha, Chongming (Aug.–Nov.).	Chongming		4
1805	SF visits Kerchief Hill with Xia Yishan's father and uncle.	Suzhou	43	4
	SF is invited to join the staff of his childhood friend Shi Zhuotang, a prefect in Sichuan. SF bids farewell to his mother and son (Oct. 30).	Journey to Sichuan		3
	Shi receives a new post, so SF stays with Shi's family in Jingzhou (Dec.).	Jingzhou		4
1806	Shi is transferred again, so SF stays with the family in Tong Pass (Mar.).	Tong Pass	44	4
	SF learns by letter from his daughter in Dec. that his son Fengsen died in May.	"		3
1807	SF works as Shi's secretary in Laiyang, Shandong (Mar.).	Laiyang		4
	SF moves to Beijing in the autumn, when Shi is appointed to the Hanlin Academy.	Beijing	45	4

1807	SF does not mention it in his book, but historical records indicate that he visited the Ryuku Islands on a diplomatic mission in this year.	Ryukyu	45	-
1808	SF mentions that he is forty-six.	-	46	4
1811	SF mentions that he worked as a private secretary for thirty years (starting in 1781), but this number could be approximate.	-	49	4

Years Covered by Records

Year	Age	R1	R2	R3	R4
1765	3	x			
1770	8	x	x		
1775	13	x	x		
1780	18	x	x		x
1785	23	x	x	x	x
1790	28	x	x	x	x
1795	33	x	x	x	x
1800	38		x	x	x
1805	43			x	x
1810	48				x

R1: *Delights of Marriage*
R2: *Charms of Idleness*
R3: *Sorrows of Hardship*
R4: *Pleasures of Roaming*

Shen Fu's Associates and Family Tree

Colleagues

Cheng Mo'an	Ke (Magist.)	Wang (Magist.)	Yu Futing	Zhao (Magist.)
Gu Aiquan	Qian Shizhu	Wang Tifu	Yu Wuqiao	Zhao Xingzhai
Han Chunquan	Shi Xin'geng	Wang Xiaoxia	Zhang Pinjiang	
He (Magistrate)	Shi Xinyue	Xu Ceting	Zhang Yingmu	
Hu Kentang	Shi Zhuotang	Yang (Magist.)	Zhang Yuan	

Friends

Cai Ziqin	Jing Yunxiang	Qi Liudi	Xia Fengtain	Zhang Xianhan
Ding Shichu	Liu Huijie	Shi Zhuheng	Xia Jieshi	Zhang Yumen
Gu Honggan	Lu Banfang	Wan Caizhang	Xia Nanxun	Zhao Jizhi
Guo Xiaoyu	Lu Juxiang	Wang Xingcan	Xia Yishan	Zhou Chunxu
Hua Dacheng	Mao Yixiang	Wu Yunke	Yang Bufan	Zhou Xiaoxia
Hua Xingfan	Miao Shanyin	Xi Zhitang	Yuan Shaoyu	
Jiang Shoupeng	Miao Zhibo	Xia Chunxiang	Zhang Lanbo	

Sworn Relatives

Mrs. Hua *Yun's sworn sister*
Hanyuan *Yun's sworn sister*
Jiang Sizhai *SF's sworn uncle*
Sister Wang *sworn daughter of SF's mother*
Sister Yu *sworn daughter of SF's mother*
Ninth Sister *sworn daughter of SF's mother*
Lu Shangwu *husband of Ninth Sister*

Other Cousins

Xu Xiufeng (male paternal cousin-in-law)
Chen Yuheng (male maternal cousin)

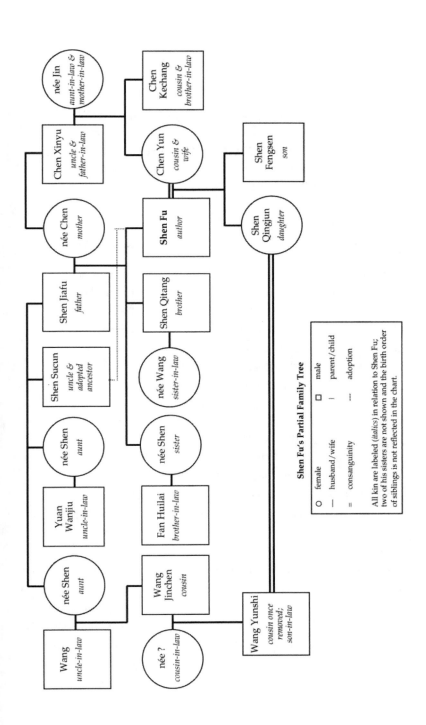

Shen Fu's Partial Family Tree

○ female	□ male
— husband/wife	| parent/child
= consanguinity	--- adoption

All kin are labeled (*italics*) in relation to Shen Fu; two of his sisters are not shown and the birth order of siblings is not reflected in the chart.

née Jin
aunt-in-law & mother-in-law

Chen Kechang
cousin & brother-in-law

Chen Xinyu
uncle & father-in-law

Chen Yun
cousin & wife

Shen Fengsen
son

née Chen
mother

Shen Fu
author

Shen Qingjun
daughter

Shen Jiafu
father

Shen Sucun
uncle & adopted ancestor

Shen Qitang
brother

née Shen
aunt

née Wang
sister-in-law

Yuan Wanjiu
uncle-in-law

née Shen
sister

née Shen
aunt

Fan Huilai
brother-in-law

Wang Jinchen
cousin

Wang
uncle-in-law

née ?
cousin-in-law

Wang Yunshi
cousin once removed; son-in-law

Historical Figures
Mentioned by Shen Fu

Listed Chronologically by Dynasty

Dynasty	Person	Reason for mention
E. Zhou	Mencius (371–289 BCE)	Philosopher
(770–256 BCE)	Zhuangzi (fourth century BCE)	Philosopher
	Song Yu (third century BCE)	Poet
W. Han	Mei Xuan (fl. 207 BCE)	General
(206 BCE–9 CE)	Jia Yi (201–169 BCE)	Poet
	Sima Qian (?145–?86 BCE)	Historian
	Sima Xiangru (179–117 BCE)	Poet
	Dong Zhongshu (179–?104 BCE)	Essayist
	Kuang Heng (first century BCE)	Official
	Liu Xiang (79–8 BCE)	Bibliographer
E. Han	Yan Ziling (?40 BCE to ?40 CE)	Recluse
(25–220 CE)	Ban Gu (32–92 CE)	Historian
	Guan Yu (160–220 CE)	General
W. Jin (265–316)	Luo Han (292–372)	Recluse
E. Jin (317–420)	Tao Qian (365–427)	Poet
S. Dynasties	Su Xiaoxiao (d. ca. 501)	Courtesan
(420–588)	Hou Jing (d. 552)	Rebel
	Xu Ling (507–583)	Parallel prose writer
	Yu Xin (513–581)	Parallel prose writer
Tang	Wang Bo (650–676)	Parallel prose writer
(618–907)	Zhang Jiuling (673–740)	Poet
	Li Bai (701–762)	Poet

	Du Fu (712–770)	Poet
	Yang Guifei (719–756)	Concubine
	Lu Zhi (754–805)	Official
	Han Yu (768–824)	"Old-style" prose writer
	Bai Juyi (772–846)	Poet
	Liu Zongyuan (773–819)	"Old-style" prose writer
	Yuan Zhen (779–831)	Poet
	Li He (791–817)	Poet
	Lü Dongbin (b. ca. 796)	Daoist immortal
	Du Mu (803–852)	Poet
	Li Shangyin (ca. 813–858)	Poet
	Cui Jue (fl. 859)	Poet
	Huang Chao (d. 884)	Rebel
N. Song	Kou Zhun (961–1023)	Poet
(960–1127)	Lin Bu (967–1028)	Recluse
	Fan Wenzheng (989–1052)	Official
	Ouyang Xiu (1007–1072)	Prose writer / Calligraphist
	Su Shi (1037–1101)	Poet
S. Song (1127–1279)	Zhu Xi (1130–1200)	Poet
Yuan (1279–1368)	Wang Shifu (ca. 1260–1336)	Playwright
	Ni Zan (1301–1374)	Painter
	Yu Que (1303–1358)	Official
	Wang Meng (1308–1385)	Painter
	Zhang Shicheng (1321–1367)	Rebel
Ming (1368–1644)	Xu Fang (1622–1694)	Recluse
Qing (1644–1911)	Li Yu (1610–1680)	Playwright
	Wang Shizhen (1634–1711)	Poet
	Peng Shaosheng (1740–1796)	Buddhist
	Shi Zhuotang (1757–1837)	Official

Index

academies, 15, 81, 87, 103, 121, 132, 134
accountant, 79, 123

betrothal, 1, 2, 20, 66, 67
bonsai, 36, 39–40, 101
books, 1, 2, 3, 5, 8, 20, 36, 47, 73, 89, 90, 109
bridges, 16, 22–23, 27, 29, 31, 87, 91, 94, 96, 114, 116, 124, 125
Buddhism, 43–44, 60, 78, 97, 100, 119

calligrapher/painter, 46, 59, 60, 75, 113, 114
calligraphy, 20, 22, 45, 46, 59, 95, 104, 113, 114, 118, 119, 128, 130, 132, 133
caves, 85, 86, 88, 89, 92, 99, 100, 122, 124, 133
ceramics, 37, 38, 42, 50
children, 55, 59–64, 66, 67, 71, 72, 75–78, 79–81
class difference, 30, 61, 62, 70, 80
clerk, 68
clothing, 3, 13, 25, 45, 49, 50–51, 59, 61, 65, 66, 73, 75, 91, 105–7, 111, 118, 121
concubines, 29, 31, 56–57, 81, 113
courtesans. See prostitutes
cousins, 3, 4, 62, 67

Daoism, 73, 81, 130, 132, 133, 134

death, 71–72, 76
decorating, 23, 41–42, 51, 108
deities, 12, 21–22, 43, 60, 69, 71, 119, 132
Delight (singing girl), 107–13
drama (opera), 5, 16–17, 25, 32, 63, 90, 93, 101, 106
dreams, 1, 71, 81, 113
drinking wine, 5, 8, 13, 14, 24, 27–29, 30–31, 45–50, 65–66, 78, 88, 92–93, 96, 100, 107–8, 110, 112, 115, 120, 122, 123, 129, 134

embroidery. See needlework
etiquette, 11–12, 55, 57, 61, 123, 124
examinations, 46–48, 79, 87–88
excursions, 15, 26–27, 30–31, 48–50, 85–134

fate. See omens
feng shui, 75, 92–93
Fengsen (son), 59, 62–64, 67, 71, 75, 77, 79–81
festivals, 12–13, 15–16, 25–26, 64, 75, 80, 88, 90, 96, 101, 105, 129, 130
fishing, 7, 23, 24, 27, 55, 99, 103
flowers (flower arranging), 18, 24, 25, 35–40, 42–44, 48–51, 93, 100–101, 105, 109, 125, 132, 134
food, 3–4, 13, 18–19, 23, 24, 26,

27, 45, 49–50, 63, 66, 69, 78,
  88–89, 91, 98, 100, 102, 104,
  111, 113, 115, 120, 123, 133
fragrance, 14, 22, 28, 43, 45, 74,
  88, 98, 116, 125, 134
funerals (mourning), 26–27, 72,
  73, 75, 76, 77–78, 79

garden design, 40–41
gardens, 15–16, 17–18, 22, 23,
  24, 35, 37, 40–41, 45, 48–49,
  85–86, 91, 92, 94–96, 97–98,
  117, 121, 124, 126–27, 128,
  131–32
gender roles, 21, 25–27, 73
ghosts, 13, 14, 73–74
gossip, 29, 55, 113
grave tending, 17, 42, 75, 80, 88

Haining, 97–98
hairstyles, 14, 25, 105–7
Hangzhou, 86–89
Hanyuan (courtesan), 30–32,
  58–59, 61, 70, 113
hills, 17, 21, 30–31, 75, 86, 88, 92,
  95, 98, 100, 103, 113–14, 117,
  124, 125, 127
Honggan (friend), 90–93, 117–18
Hua, Mrs. (friend), 44, 61–62,
  64, 67–68, 70, 121

illness, 14–15, 56–63, 68, 70–73,
  76, 89–90, 113
immortals, 43, 71, 77, 94, 102,
  116, 122, 127, 133
incense, 22, 25, 43, 47, 69
in-laws, 5, 6, 56–58, 62–63, 65,
  66, 67, 69–70, 71, 102

Ji'nan, 133–34
Jingjiang, 66–67
Jingzhou, 128–30
Jixi, 98–101

lakes, 21, 24, 26–27, 32, 86, 88,
  95, 96, 97, 116, 120, 125, 126,
  133
legal matters, 57, 61, 66, 70
letters, 7, 13, 55–58, 67, 68, 75, 76
Lingnan (Guangzhou), 105–13
love (passion), 6, 7, 12, 31, 32,
  59, 63, 71–74, 113

magistrate, 85, 96, 97, 98, 113,
  131
marriage, 1–3, 6, 11–13, 16, 21,
  62, 71–73
merchants, 39, 62, 67, 94, 100,
  101–2, 105, 109, 121
monasteries. *See* temples
money, 23, 30, 31, 32, 45–49, 55,
  58, 65–67, 70, 73, 76, 79, 81,
  94, 100, 102, 111–13, 119–21,
  129; foreign coins, 67, 100,
  112, 120; income, 23–24,
  45–47, 59, 65, 69, 73, 81, 102,
  122; inheritance, 62, 77–78;
  loans (debt), 57, 59–62, 65,
  67, 68, 70, 76, 77, 102, 121;
  pawning, 46, 55, 59, 65, 129;
  property, 79, 80, 90, 92, 123
monks, 78–79, 89, 91, 97, 100,
  114–17, 118–20
moon gazing, 8, 13–15, 24,
  27–28, 97, 99, 108, 115–16
mountains, 21, 41, 42–43, 44,
  61, 62, 64, 65, 68, 72, 85–86,
  90–91, 92, 93, 94, 95, 99, 101,
  104, 115, 118, 121–22, 124,
  125, 126, 128, 130, 133
mourning. *See* funerals
music, 11, 25, 29, 100, 101, 106,
  108, 111, 116, 123, 129

needlework (embroidery), 2, 3,
  8, 24, 45, 51, 60, 61, 102, 106,
  111

ocean. *See* sea
offerings, 12, 21–22, 44, 73, 88, 101
omens (fate), 2, 3, 10, 14–15, 60, 71, 93, 123–24
opera. *See* drama
opium, 108

painting, 20, 21–22, 24, 44, 45, 46, 48, 59, 60, 75, 79, 85, 100, 113, 120, 122, 125
parents, 2, 6, 23, 25, 26, 55–59, 61–62, 71–72, 75–78, 80, 85, 86, 89
poetry, 1, 2, 3, 7, 8, 10–11, 13–14, 22, 24, 29–30, 31, 46, 47–48, 72, 75, 85, 87, 93, 99, 104, 113, 123, 127–28, 129, 131
prose, 7, 8–9, 64, 95, 103, 118
prostitutes (courtesans, singing girls), 29–32, 58–59, 61, 105–13, 116

qi (life force), 75
Qingjun (daughter), 59–63, 67, 75–79, 81
Qitang (brother), 16, 20, 56, 57, 75, 77, 79–80

reading, 2, 5, 44, 59
rivers, 27, 42, 70, 80, 88, 91, 93, 95, 99, 102–3, 104, 122, 125, 126, 127, 128, 129, 131, 132
rocks. *See* stones

sea (ocean), 67, 79, 90, 98, 102, 105, 109, 122, 123, 125, 134
seal carving, 13, 45, 46
secretary, 6, 46, 65, 68, 75–76, 79, 85, 90, 93, 96, 98, 101, 113, 121
servants, 5, 15, 24, 27, 35–36, 45, 49, 57, 64, 68, 70, 101, 110
sex, 5–6, 13, 16, 28, 35, 108, 112
Shanyin (Kuaiji), 85–86

Shi Zhuotang (patron), 22, 78–81, 126, 127, 128, 132, 133, 134
siblings, 2, 4, 15, 56–57, 75, 77, 79, 80
singing girls. *See* prostitutes
souls (spirits), 6, 7, 71–75, 87, 88
springs, 64, 86, 88, 89, 95, 117, 118, 119, 121, 133, 134
stones (rocks), 17–18, 40, 42, 86, 94, 95, 97, 99, 104, 119
storytelling, 24
Suzhou, 1, 48, 96, 124–25
sworn relations, 16–18, 31–32, 58–59, 61, 80, 89

tea, 15, 18, 26, 40, 46, 49, 51, 115, 117, 119, 121, 134
temples (monasteries), 24–26, 78–79, 86, 87, 88, 89, 90–91, 94, 95, 100, 101, 109, 114–20, 121, 124, 125, 132–33
Tong Pass, 131–33

uncles, 1, 17, 62, 77, 101, 112, 125

views (vistas), 23, 31, 45, 88, 91, 92, 93–95, 97, 98, 108, 119–20, 121, 122, 125, 126, 127, 129, 132

weddings, 3, 4–5, 20, 71
Wujiang, 26–27

Yangzhou (Hanjiang), 93–96
yin/yang, 20, 74
Yongtaisha, 122–24
Yun (spouse), 1–32, 36, 42–51, 55–75, 81, 89–90, 93, 102, 107–8, 113